I0692112

Impending Love and War

by

Laura Freeman

Impending Love Series

This is a work of fiction. Names, characters, places, and incidents are either the product of the author's imagination or are used fictitiously, and any resemblance to actual persons living or dead, business establishments, events, or locales, is entirely coincidental.

Impending Love and War

COPYRIGHT © 2014 by Laura Freeman

All rights reserved. No part of this book may be used or reproduced in any manner whatsoever without written permission of the author or The Wild Rose Press, Inc. except in the case of brief quotations embodied in critical articles or reviews.
Contact Information: info@thewildrosepress.com

Cover Art by *Debbie Taylor*

The Wild Rose Press, Inc.
PO Box 708
Adams Basin, NY 14410-0708
Visit us at www.thewildrosepress.com

Publishing History
First American Rose Edition, 2014
Print ISBN 978-1-62830-508-1
Digital ISBN 978-1-62830-509-8

Impending Love Series

Both turned at the sound of a thud against Nell's wooden wall.

"It's Nell kicking the wall," Cory excused.

"I better check." Tyler grabbed the burning lantern from her hand.

Cory followed behind him. She needed to prevent him from discovering the slave's hiding place. She couldn't overpower him. What could she do?

Tyler's body blocked the lantern's light, and Cory bumped into him when he stopped at the stall wall. Her instinct was to back away, but instead, she reached out with her hands to locate him. She ran her fingertips upward to his shoulders as she pressed herself against him. Cory rested her cheek against the bare skin of his wide back. "Your skin is so cool."

He froze.

Now what? She remembered something her mother did when her father had an exhausting day. She caressed his shoulders with her hands, shocked by the hardness beneath smooth flesh. Her fingertips danced downward along the damp skin of his back and circled beneath the strip of white bandage to hold him in a gentle grip. "I'm so hot." Her lips brushed against his back. "Let's get out of here."

The lantern shook in Tyler's hand. He placed it on the stall wall, turned, and captured her in his arms. "Let's see what I can do about the heat." His deep, throaty tone sent a shiver through her body.

Cory had started something she had no way of stopping. She recalled her parents always retired to bed after one of her mother's massages. Why hadn't she remembered that earlier? She panicked as Tyler drew her close against his body.

Dedication

To my mother, Rosemary, who loved books

Chapter One

Tyler Montgomery paused at the stone pillar marking the entrance to the drive from the dusty road to the house. A wooden sign hanging on a shepherd's hook at the top of the pillar was carved to spell Glen Knolls. The young man removed a folded paper from his coat pocket and looked at the words. "*Mr. Glen knows the way*." This must be the place. The cryptic message led nowhere else.

Two parallel paths worn in the grass wound their way along the side of a yellow two-story framed farmhouse with Greek fluted pillars and a triangular portico common in Northeast Ohio architect. The driveway ended in front of a gray weathered bi-level bank barn. Midway, pieces of slate created a path from a hitching post to the entrance door. Small fluted pillars and sectioned windows framed the doorway.

Tyler debated what story to tell the owners of Glen Knolls in order to gain their trust. The sound of hoof beats of a lone rider approaching from the north interrupted his thoughts. He ducked into the thick woods on the opposite side of the farm.

Unfortunately, the rider turned into Glen Knolls and tied his horse to the hitching post beneath a shady elm. The stranger wore a black suit even though it was summer. He removed a bouquet of flowers from the stovetop hat he'd tied to the saddle and headed for the door. Since he didn't appear to live at the farm, Tyler remained in the shadows of the trees and waited for the caller to leave.

The time dragged. Two dairy cows and a calf grazed in the pasture on the other side of the road where a split rail fence kept them from wandering into the yard. Chickens rooted for worms and grubs in the heat of the first day of July. When the long shadows of evening fell across the field, the chickens retired to their coop, and the bovines headed for the back of the barn.

The sound of a window opening focused his attention on the house. Maybe the visitor was finally leaving.

****

Inside the brightly colored farmhouse, Cory Beecher propped open the window with a notched board. She had kept the tall sectioned windows closed during the day but hoped the evening air would offer some reprieve from the heat. She took her seat across from Douglas Raymond at a small table in front of the unused fireplace in the front parlor. Although his initial visit three weeks before had been to show his concern for the recently widowed Adelaide Thomas, his subsequent visits had been to court her.

Cory was flattered such an eligible bachelor was paying attention to her. She'd never had a shortage of male callers, but she had turned twenty in May. Time was running out to choose a husband. The pool of desirable suitors was shrinking, and younger, more aggressive ladies snatched up the coveted prospects.

Most of her friends were married, and they said it was time she did the same. She could do worse than Douglas. He was an instructor at the Western Reserve

College in a town northeast of Darrow Falls. He had to travel more than ten miles to call upon her. A good sign.

She had hoped someone college educated like Douglas would prove interesting, but her thoughts drifted as the evening wore on. If only Douglas didn't consider himself an authority on nearly every subject and monopolize the conversation.

Although Douglas appeared arrogant, a wife could teach him tact. She studied his face. He wasn't handsome, but he wasn't repulsive either. Douglas had a high forehead, thin face, and a narrow angular nose. Cory debated the merits of his features and missed Adelaide's last remark. She looked at the elderly woman rocking beside her. "Excuse me."

"We were talking about slavery," Adelaide said. "Mr. Raymond is of the opinion race defines a man."

Cory frowned. "In what way?"

"There are three races of men in this world, each with distinct characteristics." Douglas stood, bumping the table and rattling the floral tea cups. "But more than physical differences, are their thoughts and mental abilities." He paced in front of the two women. "The black race lacks the intelligence other races exhibit to become superior."

Cory was tired of mindlessly smiling, and his words lit a fuse to her tongue. "I have children in my classroom who can't read or write until someone teaches them. It doesn't mean they aren't intelligent. It means they haven't been taught, and slaves aren't allowed to be educated."

"A person doesn't need to attend school to be wise," Douglas replied.

"But a person can be scholarly and still be a fool." Adelaide turned her head to look at the clock on the mantel.

Cory regained her composure. She smiled, hoping to repair any damage her outburst may have caused. She could be more outspoken after she was married. "Politicians prove they're fools every day."

"It is difficult to discern between a wise man and a fool, especially in politics," Douglas said. "That is why I disagreed when they changed the law ten years ago to let any man vote."

"Every white man," Adelaide corrected.

Douglas raised his voice. "Even though eliminating the land ownership requirement permitted me to vote, how can a man who can't even write his own name make a decision as important as choosing the next President of the United States? These uneducated men will probably choose someone like Abraham Lincoln. The man has barely a year of proper schooling, and yet he thinks he's qualified to become the next President of the United States." Douglas pointed his index finger upward. "I will not vote for him."

"Neither will I," Cory agreed, forgetting to keep her thoughts on women's rights a secret. Her crusade to change a woman's status had cooled the ardor of too many admirers, and she had decided to keep her ambitions a secret. Maybe her daughters would change the world instead.

Douglas frowned. "Women can't vote."

"They can't?" Cory prayed Douglas didn't recognize the sarcasm in her voice. She tried reason. "Maybe now that white men can vote, they'll let their mothers, sisters, wives, and daughters vote, too."

Douglas laughed. "Women are too emotional to make such an important decision. They would base their vote on a man's appearance or his eloquence of speech and not on his real qualifications to lead the country."

Cory seethed, but she schooled her face to remain calm. How could a man like Douglas understand how it felt to be treated like a second-class citizen? A woman couldn't vote, own property, or sign a legal document. She was barely better than a slave, which made her completely sympathetic to their cause.

Douglas continued his lecture. "It takes an educated, intuitive man to discern an honest man from a liar. Why earlier this day I met a Southerner at the college looking for a runaway slave."

Adelaide stopped rocking. Cory looked at the old woman to see if something was wrong. Adelaide leaned forward, fixed on Douglas. Cory turned to her suitor. What was he saying that was so interesting?

"And not the usual bounty hunter." He lowered his voice. "He was too well dressed for a chaser. I suspect he was the owner of the runaway."

"A slave owner?" Cory studied Adelaide. "Must be an important slave to come for him in person."

Adelaide's hands had paled to a bloodless white from gripping the arms of her rocker. "Must be." She resumed her rhythmic rocking.

Cory glanced at the clock behind her. Douglas had stayed too long, but politics and slavery were his favorite topics.

He pounded his fist into the palm of his hand. "I've always made my thoughts on slavery quite clear. Colonization is the answer. Send the Africans back to

Africa where they came from."

"But this is 1860. None of the slaves in the United States were born in Africa," Adelaide corrected. "Why most of their ancestors were here long before yours or mine."

"Makes no difference," he argued. "They're African. It's in their blood."

"Why stop at Africans?" Adelaide demanded. "Why not ship the Irish back to Ireland? Or the Germans back to Germany?"

"The Germans are hard workers, but no one would miss the Irish." He laughed, but the women remained silent.

Cory focused on the empty teacups as she placed them on the tray with the teapot and dirty cake plates. Her grandfather was Irish, and her grandmother was German. Douglas had unwittingly insulted her ancestry, but Cory was equally upset with Adelaide. She'd posed the question to make Douglas look bad. From the first visit, Adelaide had voiced her unfavorable opinion about Douglas. Cory wanted him to approve of her, especially since there were rumors he was shopping for a wife. She frowned. Why was Adelaide meddling in her affairs?

When no one joined in his merriment, Douglas reddened. "The Beecher's aren't Irish, are they?"

"No, but my Grandpa Donovan is."

"I do apologize." He withdrew his pocket watch and studied the timepiece. "I can't believe the late hour. I must return to the college. Even instructors have a curfew."

He was leaving. Cory stood and fluffed her skirt, allowing the crinoline beneath to regain its bell shape.

"Thank you for visiting."

"I want to thank you ladies for the dessert and excellent conversation."

"The time certainly went by quickly." Cory wanted to end the night on a happy note. "Stop by any time."

"Are you attending the Independence Day activities?"

Cory looked to Adelaide for permission.

"I can spare you for one day. After all, it's a holiday, and your family will want to spend time with you."

Cory followed him into the hallway. She had placed the flowers he had brought in a vase on the sideboard. "The flowers are lovely. Thank you." She handed him his hat. "I'll see you at the celebration on the square on Wednesday." She stepped outside onto the porch and led the way toward his horse, swishing her wide skirt side to side. For a few minutes, they would be alone.

She had worn her best-looking frock, an emerald and blue plaid made with a gathered skirt, wide shoulder straps and a tightly cinched waist to create an hour-glass figure. The bodice was altered for evening wear and cut perilously low in the front. Adelaide had threatened to tell her mother if she didn't sew some modest lace inserts above the bodice, but she had postponed the work until after Douglas called. Now it appeared to have been a futile attempt to attract his attention.

She stood by his horse, anticipating a declaration of love or a gesture of affection, but after securing his hat, he awkwardly mounted the horse he had borrowed from the college stable.

Cory leaned against the elm tree as he rode off. Her ingénue attempts of seduction had failed. Most men spoke words of admiration when they called. Some held her hand. A few had the nerve to kiss her. And those advances were at home with her mother, father, and her pesky younger sisters all gathered around them. Here, she was practically alone, and Douglas hadn't even given her a warm smile. He was all prim and proper. Perhaps his position as an instructor required it. As a school teacher, she was expected to adhere to higher standards, but they were alone. Couldn't he have let his guard down a little?

She waved when he turned onto the road in case he looked back. Not even a glance. A sigh escaped her as the wooden heels of her leather shoes clicked against the slate. The visit should have been more successful with a delicious dessert, a daring outfit, and flattering conversation. What did a girl have to do to get married?

She entered the house serving as her temporary home. A long hallway ran from the front to the back of the house and allowed a strong breeze to flow through the house when both doors were opened. But it was getting late, and she reluctantly closed the front door. A steep staircase to the right of the hallway led upstairs. Cory entered the front parlor on the left where she had entertained Douglas. She kept the windows open in the event a breeze stirred and removed some of the humidity that left her dress damp and clingy. She paused at the roll-top desk between the windows and noticed an unfinished letter to Adelaide's daughter. She would leave Glen Knolls next month. Hiram had built the house thirty-six years ago, and Adelaide had meticulously furnished it. But his untimely death left her no choice but to sell. Cory admired the workmanship in the curtains, pillows, and other small touches making the home inviting. The tray of dishes was missing.

She walked through a doorway to the formal dining room overlooking the backyard. A stenciled tulip pattern decorated the walls. As she passed the mahogany Hepplewhite table, she pushed in a shield-back chair. She heard Adelaide in the adjoining kitchen singing a hymn.

Adelaide had told her Hiram built the kitchen first with its own fireplace and door to the backyard. They had lived in it for three years until he finished the rest of the house. Adelaide stood at the dry sink below the window overlooking the elm and drive to the road. She washed one of the ornate cups in a basin of soapy water and rinsed it in another bowl of clean water.

"Let me help." Cory grabbed a towel from a hook on the wall and dried the cup.

Adelaide handed her a saucer. "Did he propose?"

"He's only called a few times."

"How long does it take a man to decide whether or not he wants a woman to be his wife?" Adelaide demanded. "Hiram took one look at me and knew I was the girl for him. And you're not the first girl he's considered."

Cory almost dropped the saucer in her hand. "What do you mean?"

"I heard he asked Beth Davis to marry him, and she said no. Now he's calling here. Maybe he's more cautious this time, but he'll marry the first girl to say yes."

Cory frowned at this bit of news. She was second

choice? How humiliating. Beth Davis was the daughter of the Reverend Lawrence Davis and well-known by members of the Community Congregational Church.

Beth had been helpful during Hiram's funeral and offered to stay with Adelaide. But Beth had no farming experience, and the role of caregiver fell to Cory. "Do you know why she said no?"

Adelaide snorted. "She has more sense than you."

Cory carried the clean dishes to the dining room and placed them in the hutch. "I love my family, but I don't want to live at home forever," she defended. "I don't want to become a burden to them."

"You earn your keep, or don't I pay you enough?"

"You're very generous."

Adelaide was paying her three dollars a week. A fair wage for a man, let alone a woman, even if it did include caring for the livestock and canning the vegetables and fruit the farm produced.

"Why rush into marriage?" Adelaide asked. "I thought you considered yourself a suffragette?"

A suffragette wasn't an occupation. It was a state of mind, and ideals tended to falter in the face of reality. Most men, including Douglas, were traditional, conservative, and authoritative. They wanted a wife who was submissive.

"Some men don't like independent women."

"Men don't know what they want in a woman so why pretend to be something you aren't?" Adelaide closed the back door at the end of the central hallway. "Did you close the front door?"

"Yes," Cory answered. "I don't know why we can't keep the doors open. At least until it cools down."

"The last time you left the door open, raccoons

made a mess of my pantry. No telling what kind of vermin will wander in."

Cory had cleaned the mess the masked marauders had created and didn't want to repeat the arduous task. The doors would remain closed.

Adelaide climbed the stairs, and Cory hurried to assist her. It would never do if Adelaide followed her husband to the grave so soon.

Chapter Two

Hiram and Adelaide had raised four children at Glen Knolls. Adelaide planned to sell the farm and move in with her youngest daughter. Cory would return to teaching in the fall unless she received a better offer. She imagined what it would be like to become Douglas Raymond's wife, but her future slate remained blank.

Most Ohioans looked forward to summer after months of snow and ice, but temperatures were above normal, teasing the nineties by the afternoon. The bedrooms on the second floor had been closed all day to keep out the sweltering heat that had meandered from the south like an unwelcomed visitor, unwilling to depart. Cory pushed the window open in Adelaide's bedroom and leaned out on the sill for a puff of a breeze. None.

Adelaide struggled to remove her black mourning dress, and Cory assisted. Adelaide refused to wear the corsets and crinolines of the latest fashion, and her simple undergarments of a single petticoat and cotton chemise were easy to discard. Cory grabbed a cotton nightgown and placed the opening over Adelaide's head. She pulled it down over sagging breasts and a bony butt and helped her crawl into bed.

Cory masked any repulsion at the sight of Adelaide's wrinkled flesh. Beauty was fleeting. She would look like Adelaide someday.

Time was another reason she had become serious about choosing a husband. She loved teaching, but she wanted a home and children. Without a fortune, she would have to rely on what nature had given her to attract a man. Cory looked down at her low-cut bodice and ample display of bosom. It brought her back to the nagging question of why Douglas hadn't proposed. But more importantly, why had Beth turned down his proposal. What was wrong with Douglas?

Maybe she should encourage another suitor, but none of the local men sprang to mind. If men weren't intimidated by her status as a teacher, they were intimidated by her status as midwife. She'd helped her father with doctoring since she was twelve, stitching cuts, wrapping bandages, and all the other mundane tasks necessary for the practice of medicine. She'd delivered her first baby when she was fourteen, and her father said it was in her blood.

John Beecher was the first ancestor to come to America, and he promptly died in the winter of 1637, when he and six other men set out to settle New Haven, Connecticut. Luckily, he had a son, Isaac, and John's wife, Hannah, was a midwife. They needed her to stay and gave her John's share of the land. She was a land owner. Men broke the rules for women who were important.

She had saved nearly two hundred dollars from teaching and midwife duties for a tempting dowry, but why did a wife have to pay a man to marry her? Grandpa Donovan said a dowry put a wife on equal footing with her husband. She would bring something of importance to the marriage, and he had to respect her. It seemed archaic. Shouldn't a man marry for love?

Did she love Douglas? And why didn't she know?

Cory tucked a pillow behind Adelaide's head. An oil lamp cast a yellow glow over the pale pallor of her skin. She settled back into the feathered softness of the mattress and pulled a well-used quilt to her waist. Her gnarled hands caressed the familiar fabric, hand stitched when her fingers had been straight and nimble. Adelaide was in her fifties and still strong, but the loss of her beloved husband had left her without direction.

Hiram Thomas had gone out to cut hay with a scythe and had dropped dead from a heart attack.

Adelaide stuck out her bottom lip, which quivered, threatening to catch a few fallen tears. "I told him specifically I was to go first."

Although stoic most of the time, Cory had witnessed Adelaide's angry rants at her departed husband for leaving her behind. She needed to calm her.

Adelaide stared at the empty side of the bed. "I can't sleep alone in bed."

Cory wasn't about to climb in next to Adelaide. It was one thing to share a bed with one of her five younger sisters, but none of them was bony, wrinkled, or smelled funny. She turned away and snatched a book from a table near the window. "Would you like me to read to you?"

"Won't help." Adelaide moved around to find a comfortable spot. "I didn't mind getting old with Hiram getting old with me. Now all I want is to die."

"Don't say that."

Adelaide was sometimes bossy and set in her ways, but Cory had taken a liking to her straight-forward talk and wealth of knowledge about life.

Cory wondered if she would ever love someone so much she would want to die rather than live without him. It was romantic but unrealistic. Douglas would scoff at such nonsense. As an instructor in mathematics, he didn't believe in anything unless it could be added, subtracted, multiplied, or divided.

Cory accepted the fact men ran the world. They owned all the property. They controlled the money. They made the decisions. But Cory had been raised to believe in her abilities and possibilities. She would butt heads with any man who became her husband, and she would be the one ultimately to compromise. How much depended on the man. A sigh escaped her lips.

"What has your brow so wrinkled, missy?" Adelaide demanded.

"I was thinking of Douglas."

"That explains the worry lines."

Cory ignored the jab. Douglas had attended Hiram's funeral. He had disapproved of Cory's plans to stay alone with an elderly widow, and Adelaide had disapproved of him sticking his nose into business that didn't pertain to him. Cory had settled the war by inviting him to call and check on them. He still seemed ill at ease no matter what she did. Douglas was a nervous type. It had been endearing at first.

"Why don't you go ahead and read a couple chapters to me," Adelaide suggested. "Some of the book your cousin wrote."

Cory didn't even know Harriet Beecher Stowe. They were distant cousins, both descended from the ill-fated John Beecher. Her book, *Uncle Tom's Cabin*, had made their relationship, if only by name, a social bonus, at least with abolitionists.

She had finished reading the part about Mr. Shelby selling the slave Tom to trader Haley when a knock on the front door interrupted the story. It echoed up the steep staircase and the overlooking hallway to the master bedroom. Cory marked her place. "Are you expecting someone?"

"I don't know who it could be, especially at this hour."

Cory turned toward the open bedroom door. "I'll go see who it is."

"Better take the gun."

Cory froze and allowed the words to register before swiveling to face the woman in the bed. "What gun?" And why did she need a gun to answer the door?

"In the drawer on Hiram's side." Adelaide pointed to a four drawer high-back chest along the far wall. "Can't be too careful. A lot of sordid characters travel on Darrow Falls Road."

This was news to Cory. Her mother had reassured her she'd be fine alone with Adelaide. Now she was telling her the farm was the target of reprobates and murderers. Cory opened the drawer. Inside was a muzzle-loading pistol of polished oak with brass fittings. Some family ancestor had probably used it in the Revolutionary War. "Is it loaded?"

"The roundball and patch are packed with the powder, and there's a percussion cap to ignite the powder instead of a frizzen. Hiram had it updated from a flintlock to a caplock after too many misfires."

Wonderful! A defective gun. Cory gingerly lifted the weapon by its gracefully curved stock.

"Keep your hand off the trigger, girl," Adelaide snapped. "You have fired a pistol before, haven't you?"

Her father had a modern Colt revolver not an antique like this. "I doubt if I'll need it." She kept her fingers away from the curved trigger and made her way along the hallway to the staircase. It was dusk, but evening light filtered through the side windows along the door to guide her down the steps. The visitor knocked louder.

"I'm coming!"

The pounding ceased.

Was the caller Douglas? Had he forgotten something? Like a proposal. The steps ended at a small foyer before the door. She glanced around for anything Douglas might have left behind. The sideboard in the hallway was empty except for a couple of unlit candles and the vase of flowers. The mirror above it reflected her image. Her German, Irish, and English ancestors had waged a war over her features, but most people complimented her on the resulting combination. She had her father's dark brown hair with red highlights from her mother. Her green eyes, silky skin, and ample figure were maternal gifts as well. Maureen Rose Donovan Beecher had generously passed her beauty onto her daughters. Now, if only Cory could translate the gift into a ring on her finger.

Cory studied the pistol in her hand and considered it impolite to answer the door with it aimed at whomever was on the other side. She placed it on the edge of the sideboard and lit one of the candles with a wooden match stored in a tin on the wall. The warm light softened the harsh shadows. She carried the brass candleholder to the door and turned the knob.

Because Cory had often accompanied her father on his medical visits, she knew many of the people in

Summit County, but she had never seen this man before.

He was tall, and the breadth of his shoulders filled the doorway. He removed his broad-brimmed hat and silently stared at her. He had the palest blue eyes she had ever seen in a face that made her recall a Bible verse about angels walking among men. Her stomach fluttered, and her body responded in a confusing arousal of senses.

"Tyler Montgomery at your service, ma'am." He hesitated. "Does Glen Knolls live here?"

Cory normally would have laughed at his mistake but hadn't decided whether or not this stranger was friend or foe. "That's the name of the farm. It belongs to Mrs. Hiram Thomas."

"You're not Mrs. Thomas?"

"No, I'm Miss Courtney Beecher." She gave him a small curtsey. "May I inquire what business you have with Mrs. Thomas?"

He stepped forward, and Cory retreated in the face of the power and size natural to him. Tyler had long, dark hair that curled over his shirt collar and framed a strong jaw. His handsome face was clean shaven. Barely shaven. She calculated he was in his twenties by the youthfulness of his face. He wore a light-weight crème-colored linen jacket and brown trousers.

"I'm sorry to bother you, Miss Courtney, but I'm looking for someone."

His voice had a hint of a lazy drawl that put Cory on alert. Southerners rarely came to Darrow Falls. Douglas had said something about a stranger at the college looking for a runaway slave.

Adelaide made no pretense she was opposed to

slavery. She was quite outspoken about abolishing it, but talk didn't result in a fine or someone thrown into prison. Aiding a slave could. Cory wondered if Adelaide's farm was part of the Underground Railroad aiding runaway slaves through Ohio to Cleveland and the freedom of Canada on the other side of Lake Erie. She'd been here nearly a month. She would know, wouldn't she? She was letting her imagination run wild. Adelaide was too old and too smart to become involved in anything as dangerous as hiding a runaway. "I'm sorry, sir, but there's no one here."

"How do you know? I haven't even said who I'm looking for."

"Whom," Cory corrected.

He raised an eyebrow, and Cory looked away. This man wasn't one of her pupils in the one-room school house where she taught eight grade levels. She tried to remain calm, but something about this man was making her heart race. Was it panic and fear or something else? What was wrong with her? "Whom are you looking for?"

"I have a description of him." Tyler unbuttoned his jacket.

Cory saw a fancy embroidered vest beneath. How could the man wear so many layers of clothing and appear so cool and calm? He removed a folded paper from an inside pocket and showed her a drawing of a black man. She quickly scanned the words describing a six-foot black male named Noah, heavily muscled, trained as a blacksmith, and traveling as a free man with falsified papers.

A hundred and fifty dollar reward was offered for information leading to his capture. Information could be given to the sheriff in Akron.

He *was* looking for a runaway slave. "He's not here."

"May I look around?" Tyler stepped into the parlor.

Cory realized too late that Tyler was a formidable man against two women. If he wanted to poke around, he'd do it. And even though she had nothing to hide, she didn't want a stranger in the house. She bumped against the sideboard. She felt behind her and grasped the pistol on the table. "I told you he wasn't here." She waved the gun at him as the candle in her other hand flickered with the movement. "You better leave." Cory cocked the hammer with her thumb.

Tyler turned and stared at the barrel pointed at his chest.

She struggled to hold the heavy pistol steady.

"Are you here by yourself?"

"No." She waved the pistol to move him toward the front door, but he backed into the parlor instead. She followed and circled the parlor, trying to force him to leave. A big, strong husband would be welcomed right now. She had to smile. Douglas was rather slight in build and not known for bravery or confrontations.

"A beautiful woman shouldn't play with guns." Tyler held his hands out. "I only wanted to look around."

The compliment wouldn't gain him access. "You've seen enough." She stopped near the table in front of the fireplace where she had entertained Douglas. "Now go!"

He nodded toward the gun. "I'd feel a lot better if you lowered the pistol."

She waved it in his direction. "I'll put it down

when you leave."

Tyler placed the flier on the desk behind him but kept his gaze on Cory. "If you see this man, I'm staying at the Darrow Falls Inn. I'd appreciate any information."

"What do you want with him?" Cory glanced at the flier. "Are you a chaser?"

"No, he's a friend of mine."

"I doubt that. More likely, you own him."

Tyler moved to the center of the parlor. "He's not a slave."

"He pretends to be a slave?" Cory stepped toward the desk. "The flier says he's a runaway."

Tyler inched closer to Cory. "The flier is wrong."

"Then why are you looking for him?"

"He's in trouble."

Cory gripped the gun tighter. "Looks like you're the one in trouble."

Chapter Three

Cory had her back to the corner and realized too late Tyler had maneuvered his way to block her escape in either direction. She was trapped. As she debated her next move, Tyler reached for the pistol. She backed away, and her finger jerked against the metal trigger. The hammer slammed against the cap, which sparked and ignited the powder packed in the barrel. The lead ball discharged in a loud blast. Tyler collapsed backwards and lay sprawled out on the parlor floor rug.

"Julius Caesar!" Cory screamed her father's favorite oath. She studied the weapon and dropped the pistol on the table. She moved toward Tyler, a dark shadow on the floor and waved the candle over him. Cory fell to her knees beside his motionless body. "Tyler!" She didn't question how she remembered his name but repeated it several times before he responded.

His long, dark lashes fluttered open. "You shot me."

Cory laid the candlestick on the floor and watched the crème-colored linen of his jacket change to red beneath his left armpit. She tore open his coat and stared at the puddle of blood seeping through the embroidered vest.

"It was an accident. How did I know the gun would go off?"

She needed to control her growing hysterics. What

had her father done the last time she helped him take care of a gunshot victim? Unfortunately, whatever he had done, hadn't worked. The man had died.

"Didn't you know it was loaded?" Tyler tried to sit, but Cory shoved him down.

"Lie still!" She leaned over him to view the damage.

Tyler froze.

"Of course it was loaded. Adelaide said it was loaded." She moved the candle closer to illuminate her view.

Tyler groaned.

"Don't die on me!"

Tyler swallowed. "I've never felt more alive."

Cory puzzled over his words. "You must be delirious."

Her fingers nimbly unbuttoned his vest and undid his shirt. Tyler wore no second shirt under his white cotton one. That's how he managed the heat. Cory pushed away his clothing. He had no hair on his sculptured chest, and she only had a minute to marvel at the firm musculature before peeling the ruined fabric from the wound on his side.

Tyler stared at her chest. "You have luscious breasts."

Cory examined her décolletage. She was spilling out of her gown. She'd worn this dress for Douglas. "They're not yours."

"I'm only looking."

Cory tugged on her gown to assure her nipples were covered. She lifted her skirt and tore a strip of material from her petticoat. She folded it into a pad.

"What are you doing?"

"I'm making a bandage. You're bleeding."

"I am?" He raised his head to see.

She pointed her finger in his face. "Don't move." She shoved his clothing aside and applied the folded cloth. It soaked up the blood. She lifted her skirt and tore more strips from her petticoat.

"I'm getting seasick."

Cory paused. "Are you dizzy?"

"I'm mesmerized. It's like watching waves ebb and flow. How do you keep from spilling out?"

The man was obsessed with her breasts. *Idiot*. "I'm trying to save your life."

He gazed into her eyes. "Do you know what you're doing?"

"My father is a doctor. I've often helped him with patients."

He cocked an eyebrow. "You shoot them so he can charge to doctor them?"

Cory gasped. "I find your tone insulting. I've never shot anyone in my life."

He grinned. "So this was beginner's luck."

Cory disregarded his remark and folded another cloth strip into a pad. She pressed it on top of the soiled bandage. She had no way to secure it unless she wrapped another strip around his chest. "I have to undress you."

Tyler grinned wider. "I don't mind."

Cory tugged on the sleeve of his coat, but it didn't budge. She straddled his body, cursing the starched crinoline beneath her skirt as it flew up behind her like a bell tolling the hour.

"Can you sit?" She leaned forward and put her right hand beneath the wound and the other on his opposite side. No force on her part would have raised him, but he suddenly sat upright. He caught her with his right arm when she collapsed against his chest and rested on his lap.

"Cozy."

"Be still." Cory brushed back a loose curl shaken loose from her chignon. She rolled forward to her knees and pulled his coat sleeve off his right arm. She reached around his neck with her other arm to move it to the opposite side and tugged it off his left arm. Her face was inches from his as she repeated the motion with his vest. Tyler hadn't budged. "You could help."

Beads of perspiration glistened on his brow, and his voice was husky. "You said to be still."

So she had. Less gently she yanked his suspender straps down and undid his tie before she tugged his shirt free from his trousers and moved it around his massive back and around to the left side. His shirt stuck to the bandage and both came off. The wound burst into a fresh flow down his side.

Cory shrieked and pressed the saturated bandage against the wound. "I hope this isn't a new shirt." She wadded it over the wound to help squelch the flow. "Hold this here." She placed his right hand over the makeshift bandage. She shoved off his rock-hard body and stood.

"Where are you going?"

"I need to fetch some alcohol."

"I don't imbibe," he confessed, "but I could start."

She paused in the dining room opening. "It's not to drink. It's to clean the wound."

Cory returned with a bottle of corn liquor one of the neighbors had brewed. Adelaide said Hiram had bought it for his rheumatism and other medicinal purposes. Cory uncorked it and knew from the smell it would do the job. Her father was always reading about new medical discoveries and insisted upon cleanliness. Soap and water, alcohol, and even fire could prevent a wound from turning poisonous or gangrene. She had to help with the amputation of a foot once. The memory made her shudder.

Cory put the jug on the table in front of the fireplace, took some wooden matches from the mantel, and lit two candles on the table. "Stay there," Cory ordered when Tyler moved. She carried a candle and the jug to him. "Roll over on your good side."

Cory fetched the other candle and arranged them so she could see the wound clearly.

Tyler had his back to her, but she turned away to raise her skirt. She untied the annoying crinoline that kept popping up and exposing her drawers and stockings. She removed what remained of her torn petticoat and tore a few more strips. She arranged the folded pads of fabric near one of the candles.

Tyler looked almost comfortable stretched out on the braided rug. His right arm was cocked under his head, and his left held the bandage in place.

"Move your hand." Cory touched his shoulder. "So I can examine the wound."

"You're not going to hurt me, are you?"

Cory didn't know whether to take him seriously. He had such a boyish charm about him that she wanted to give him a reassuring hug. Then she saw the wide grin on his face and knew he was teasing. She lifted the wadded shirt and bandage, expecting a gush of blood, but the flow had slowed. She carefully cleaned the wound. Tyler cried out.

"I'm sorry."

"It's cold." Tyler unclenched his teeth. "How bad is it?"

Luckily, the ball had gone through the muscle on the edge of his ribs below his armpit and was lodged in the parlor wall. "It went clean through."

She placed a thick square of cotton on the long slice the ball had cut in his otherwise flawless flesh. "I think I did more damage to Miss Adelaide's plaster than you."

She positioned a longer strip over the bandage to keep it in place. "I need you to sit and hold this until I tie it off."

He pushed into a sitting position, his muscles rippling with the movement in the flickering candlelight. Cory forgot what she was doing. Tyler raised his arms, his muscles bulging with the flex. "Can you get around?"

Cory stared at his arms, amazed by the size and strength.

His deep masculine voice startled her. "My chest," he reminded her. "Aren't you going to wrap the bandage around my chest?"

She did a mental slap to break whatever spell left her unfocused and stretched the bandage around his body, tying off the ends near the wound.

"I heard a shot," Adelaide called from the top of the staircase. "What happened, Cory?"

"I accidentally shot a man!" Cory checked the knot she had tied.

"Are you sure it was an accident?" Tyler asked.

Cory, who was on her knees, leaned back to get a

clear view of the man who had accused her. "Of course it was an accident. If you hadn't reached for my arm, the gun wouldn't have gone off." She corked the jug and returned it to the pantry.

When she returned, Tyler stood near the wall with a letter opener in his hand and a candle in the other.

"What are you doing?" She blew out the other candles and returned them to the table before the fireplace. She gathered the clothing from the floor and joined him by the wall.

"I found the lead slug." He pried it from the wall. "Evidence if I choose to press charges." He had pulled his suspenders up, and the vertical lines only emphasized the width of his shoulders and chest.

Cory chewed on her bottom lip, wondering what the penalty was for shooting a man. She held out her hand. "Let me have it."

"It's my souvenir." He shoved the ball into his trouser pocket. "I'll think of you whenever I look at it."

"It belongs to me."

He looked at his pocket and then her. "Then take it."

Cory reached for the opening of his pocket and hesitated. Her mother had warned her never to touch a man below the waist and above the knees, and she didn't take her mother's warnings lightly. Her face grew warm, and she withdrew her hand.

He chuckled softly.

"Do you think he's going to die?" Adelaide was slowly descending the staircase.

Cory scowled at Tyler. "I don't think we're going to be that lucky."

He looked shocked. "That's not a very nice thing to

say about a guest."

"You are not a guest!"

"I am now." He examined the bandage around his chest. "You don't expect me to walk all the way to the inn in my condition. Do you want my death on your conscience?"

"You won't die," she reassured him and herself. "The ball barely grazed you."

"I've lost a great deal of blood." He staggered a few steps and reached for her with his right hand.

Cory stepped away, but his arm wrapped around her shoulders like a massive yoke.

"I feel faint. I think I should lie down." The candle in his other hand shook.

Cory adjusted her load of clothing and took the candle as they headed for the foyer.

Adelaide, wearing a robe and knitted slippers, had reached the bottom of the stairs. "What are you going to do with him?"

Cory debated. She wanted to throw out the slave owner, but she had wounded the man. She had an obligation to ensure he didn't suffer any ill effects from her carelessness. She sighed. "I guess we'll have to take care of him until he's healed."

"That is kind of you." Tyler took an unsteady step toward the staircase.

"You can stay in the barn." Cory turned him toward the hallway.

"No, he cannot," Adelaide said. "He can stay in the bedroom at the head of the stairs next to yours."

Cory couldn't have heard correctly. A man did not sleep under the same roof as an unmarried woman unless unavoidable. "That's highly improper." She lowered her voice. "We don't even know him."

"There's a lock on the door." Adelaide turned and headed upstairs.

Cory was not appeased. "On the inside."

"That is reassuring," he said. "I wouldn't want to worry about you coming into my room in the middle of the night and trying to do me harm. After all, you did shoot me."

Cory looked at the steep incline. Her voice was thick with false concern. "Do you think you can make it all the way upstairs?"

"With your help, I think I can manage."

****

Tyler's hand brushed perilously close to Cory's breast as she climbed the steps with him saddled to her slim frame.

Each movement caused an equal and opposite reaction above the barrier of her gown. Tyler was mesmerized by the firmness and suppleness of her anatomy. Nothing else existed. The only thing that mattered was the rhythm of two mounds of flesh playing a seductive dance before his spellbound eyes.

Tyler regretted wasting all his time attending school and studying law. If he could get past the girl's prickly nature, he might enjoy his temporary stay. He'd always imagined his life as a confident womanizer, a man of the world, but his Quaker upbringing and strict school masters had held a tight rein on any worldly experiences. He was hoping to change his Puritan lifestyle.

Adelaide had opened the door to the spare bedroom on the back southeast side of the house. A nightstand with a pitcher and washbowl was near the door. A chest of drawers stood opposite the bed, and a secretary was nestled in the corner along with a small storage chest. Adelaide turned down the coverlet and moved out of the way. Tyler plopped down on the edge of the bed, dragging Cory with him. She scrambled out from under his hold and joined Adelaide by the door.

Tyler wasn't ready to part company. "I need some help with my boots and trousers."

Cory turned to Adelaide.

"Don't look at me." Adelaide hurried out the door. "I've only seen one man naked in my entire life, and I have no intention of making it two. Besides, you've probably seen plenty of naked men helping your father."

"Miss Adelaide!"

Tyler heard a door close down the hall. How convenient for Adelaide to leave him alone with his prey.

Cory stomped across the room. "How dare she!"

"What has she done?"

Cory dropped the pile of clothing on the end of the bed. "Left me alone with you."

"Does that cause a problem?"

"Are you married, Mr. Montgomery?"

He was amused by her switch to formally addressing him. "No, are you, Cory dear?"

She bristled. "No. That's why we need a chaperone."

He winked. "I won't tell anyone we were alone if you don't."

Cory shook her head. "It does seem rather silly. After all, you're wounded. You couldn't do anything improper even if you wanted to."

31

She couldn't be more wrong. The wound throbbed no more than a headache. The rest of his anatomy was functioning in full force.

When Cory lit the oil lamp on the secretary, he could see her more clearly. She was young but had a woman's figure. Without the crinoline and petticoat, he could see her natural shape. His hand itched to explore the curves that flowed gracefully in seductive lines. He admired a comely woman, but Cory had ignited a hot desire he'd never experienced. He wanted her like food, water, and sleep. But he was disciplined. He could wait for her to come to him.

Chapter Four

Cory studied Tyler in the lamplight. He was heavily muscled, which is why the bullet had missed bone and simply torn a slash along the side of his chest. Cory had seen naked men. At least arms, legs, and partial areas of the torso when her father worked on patients, but nothing like this man. Tyler's body lacked any soft fat, and the muscles were clearly defined by the taut smooth skin emphasizing every bulk and shallow of his body. Cory fought the urge to stroke his tempting flesh.

Cory sorted the clothing and examined his damaged wardrobe. She poked her finger through the hole in the vest. The embroidery work was intricate and skilled. "Did someone make this for you?"

"A woman I know."

Cory felt a quick jab of jealousy. Logical reasoning replaced her sudden fit of fury. She barely knew the man. What did she care if a woman had taken the time to make the embroidered vest for him? "It's beautiful. I hope I can repair it."

"What about the hole in me?" Tyler examined the bandage under his armpit.

"It will heal. All you need is rest."

"I could use some help with these." He lifted a boot.

Cory didn't trust Tyler. In her panic to tend to his

wound, she had forgotten he was a slave owner, a stranger, and a man. What if he was dangerous? But Grandpa Donovan had taught her not to show fear in the face of an enemy. She reached for the boot and tugged. After she removed one boot and sock, she repeated the task with the other foot and placed them on the floor side by side. "I think you're ready for bed."

"What about my trousers?"

"You can drop those after I'm gone."

"I may need help getting into bed." He grimaced as he stood.

Cory turned away and heard his pants drop to the floor. Tyler hadn't worn anything under his shirt. What if he had nothing under his trousers? "You do have pants on, don't you? Men's undergarments," she clarified.

"I hope you won't peek," he said. "I'm a rather modest man."

Cory heard the ropes of the bed groan and cautiously turned.

Tyler was safely under the blanket, which he had tucked around his waist. He leaned against the pillows propped on the headboard, his right arm raised and cocked behind his head as if he was expecting company. His left arm remained by his wounded side.

"Do you need anything else?"

His brow furrowed. "I feel a bit warm."

The man was taxing her patience. "It's July."

"I may have a fever."

Cory pressed her hand against his forehead, and he snatched it into his own. "You have a gentle touch for someone so bloodthirsty."

She tugged her hand free. "Do all Southern men

talk so boldly to women they barely know?"

"Only to those who shoot them."

Cory stared him in the eye. "I'm beginning to think I should have taken better aim."

He stuck out his bottom lip. "Our children would be disappointed."

"*We're* never going to have any children." She stepped to the window beside the bed and pushed it upward. She propped a board against it to hold it open. "There's not much of a breeze, but this should help cool your ardor."

He chuckled. "Miss Adelaide called you Cory. It suits you better than Courtney."

"My sisters call me Cory. You can call me Miss Beecher."

"How many sisters do you have, Cory?"

"Five."

"Five?" He studied her. "Are they all like you?"

It sounded like an unintentional compliment, and Cory smiled. If he ever met her sisters, he'd think she was an angel by comparison. "We bear a family resemblance, but we're all different."

"Any of them married?"

"Not yet. I'm the oldest." She recalled her responsibilities. "That means I'm the first to marry."

"You're a woman looking for a husband."

"Wipe that look of panic off your face." Cory laughed. "You are off my list of suitable husbands."

"Already?"

She counted off on her fingers. "I won't marry a drunkard, a cheat, a liar, an abuser, or a slave owner."

"I'm hardly all of those."

"It only takes one," she said. "You are the worst, a

35

slave owner."

"What if I wasn't a slave owner?"

Cory dismissed him with a wave of her hand. "Then you would be a liar."

"Who else is in the house besides you and Adelaide?" he demanded. "Be careful, Cory dear, or I might call you a liar."

Cory backed away from him. "I hope you don't plan on paying back our hospitality by robbing or murdering us."

He shook his head. "No, but why are you and Adelaide alone in such a big house?"

Hiram's death was common knowledge. "Hiram Thomas died from a heart attack four weeks ago."

Tyler frowned. "How well do you know Adelaide?"

"She's an old family friend. She's having a hard time adjusting to life without Hiram. I help with the chores, make sure she eats, and keep her company."

"It's difficult being alone."

"Especially when you've been married for so many years like Adelaide."

Tyler frowned. "Family is important."

"Do you have any family?"

"I didn't see much of them while I was away at school." He grinned. "I'm a lawyer."

"Like Mr. Lincoln?"

Tyler looked like he was going to be sick. "Lincoln didn't go to law school. He's a country con man who can spin a good yarn and win over a jury with his humor and charm. I graduated from Harvard."

Why were college educated men so arrogant? She had spent all night listening to Douglas brag about his

Yale College education, and now Tyler was repeating the performance. "I am not impressed." She plucked his trousers from the floor and placed them at the bottom of the bed. She gathered his damaged clothing, her crinoline, and what remained of her petticoat. "I'll wash the blood out."

"Are you leaving?"

She had her hand on the doorknob but turned. "Is there something else you needed?"

His stare was intense, but he remained silent.

Cory recognized the unspoken invitation. Usually it preceded an attempt at a kiss. He was waiting for a sign of acquiesce from her. She turned the knob and hurried out of the room. She leaned against the door jamb to steady her racing heart. She'd almost answered his call.

She passed the top of the staircase and paused at her bedroom door. She should check on Adelaide. As she walked toward Adelaide's room, she heard familiar snoring. She was asleep.

Cory's room had belonged to Adelaide's daughters. She dropped the clothing on a cedar chest at the end of the bed and sat on a stool in front of the dressing table. She stared at her reflection in the mirror and scolded the wide-eyed innocent. "The man is a rake. The handsome ones always are. He'll steal more than a kiss. If you're not careful, you'll end up like Deborah Jackson with a baby to remind her of a handsome stranger and an old husband to give him a name."

She swung around on the stool and kicked off her shoes. Lifting her skirt, she slid down the garters, followed by her stockings. She took the scissors from her sewing basket and snipped the threads holding the bodice to the matching skirt and removed them. The corset cover came off next, but the corset took more effort. Inhaling, she pinched the hooks together to release them. Her chest rose with a deep exhale. It felt good to be free of the stiff support garment fashion dictated she wear when entertaining guests or in public. Cory discarded her chemise and drawers.

Even naked, the heat was unbearable. She soaked a large sponge in the round porcelain wash basin and gave herself a bath. The cool water caressed her flesh, and she indulged herself longer than usual. She chose her lightest nightgown of sheer cotton with a band of lace across her breast and two straps that tied at her shoulders.

Sitting at the dressing table, she removed the combs from her reddish-brown hair. After brushing it, she braided three large strands a few times to keep the hair away from her face. The remaining length cascaded down her back in a wave of thick curls.

Taking Tyler's clothing, she scrubbed the blood stains from his vest and jacket and put them aside to mend. The shirt would have to soak overnight. She piled it into the same porcelain bowl she had washed from and added the remaining water from the pitcher to cover it.

"The ball!" She had placed Tyler's trousers on the end of his bed and hadn't even thought about stealing the lead slug from his pocket. She didn't dare sneak back into his room for it. Maybe he was only bluffing about using it for evidence against her. But he said he was a lawyer. "Oh no!" She punched her pillow. She'd have to be nicer to Tyler. Not an easy task.

Unlike Douglas, Tyler had no respect for the social niceties strictly adhered to between men and women. In less than an hour, he had put his arm around her shoulders, blatantly ogled her breasts, and mutely invited her to share his bed. And all she had done was shoot him, strip him nearly naked, and put him in the bedroom next to hers. News of her actions tonight would leave her a spinster for the rest of her life or an invitation to work at the Unfortunate Maiden, a popular whorehouse in downtown Akron.

****

Cory tossed the blanket off and rolled out of bed. The ropes supporting her feather-filled mattress creaked with the movement. She paused and wondered if anyone had heard. The cold bath no longer cooled her body, but it wasn't the July heat causing her fever. Images of a nearly naked man kept invading her dreams. In the past, the man had been faceless, an image of perfection, an ideal for her to fantasize about without hope of fulfillment. But now he had a face and a name—Tyler Montgomery.

Her father had been careful not to allow her to see too much of the male anatomy when she helped set a broken arm or stitch a gash, but she'd caught enough glances to know Tyler wasn't an ordinary specimen. Hard labor had toned muscles and vanquished fat. She wondered how a lawyer could be so finely honed. Something didn't add up.

She had kept an ear cocked for any noise, half expecting Tyler to crash through her locked bedroom door, but the house remained silent. Was she disappointed? Was she so desperate for a moment of excitement in her life, she would welcome a stranger to her bed? Not that she knew what to do once he joined her. The thought of sharing a bed with Douglas gave her an involuntary shudder. How did women tolerate the touch of a man they barely knew? Could a woman accept intimacies with a man if passion was lacking?

She stood in front of the open window, wishing for a faint breeze. Nothing. She leaned out the window sill on her elbows for a hint of coolness on her face. Her neck felt damp beneath her thick hair, and her gown clung to her moist skin. She wondered how Tyler was sleeping and wondered why she cared.

As Cory was about to turn away from the window and return to bed, she heard a barn door squeak open. She focused on the large building located off the northeast corner of the house. From her window, she could see the dirt ramp to the upper level of the barn. The wide sliding doors remained unmoved. The noise had come from one of the smaller doors on each side of the lower level where the livestock spent the night. For a brief moment, a light was visible inside the window facing her. Someone was in the barn.

From a peg on the wall, Cory grabbed a light robe with a deep V-neckline and a sash at the waist. She searched the dressing table for a box of matches. She struck one to light a candle in a tin holder and cupped her hand around the flame in case a rare breeze blew into the room. She opened the door and tiptoed along the hallway. She listened for Adelaide's snoring. Her hand was on the newel post when she heard a creaking noise.

Tyler poked his head through his opened doorway. "What's wrong?" he whispered in a deep hoarse voice. A thick wave of black curls fell across his forehead, framing his pale eyes.

Cory was surprised to see him. If he wasn't out in

the barn, who was? "Go back to bed."

Tyler stepped into the hall, illuminated by the candle in her hand. He had his trousers and boots on. "Where are you going?"

Cory stared at his bare chest with a strip of her petticoat tied around the widest part. His body tapered from broad shoulders to a narrow waist. Long, lean legs crossed the short distance between them in a few strides.

"Where are you going at this time of night?" he repeated.

She hadn't meant to tell him, but the words escaped of their own volition. "I saw a light in the barn."

Tyler pulled on his suspenders, struggling with the left side because of his wound. Cory reached out and straightened the twisted strap. Her fingertips brushed against his bare skin. Her nipples, for reasons unknown, stiffened into hard peaks. She jerked her hand away and tried not to draw attention to her jutting breasts.

Tyler glanced down at her attire. "Southern women don't go out in public in their nighties."

She raised her candle to his face. "And you know this because…"

Tyler grinned. "I've never seen any out gallivanting in their nighties. Of course, I heard rumors Northern women sleep fully clothed. I'm glad they were wrong."

"It's July."

"You keep telling me that."

Cory ignored Tyler and headed down the stairs. She had expected him to return to his room and comfortable bed, but he followed her. She wondered how much he truly knew about women. If he was like the young men she had grown up with, he knew next to nothing about the female gender. He was probably full of bluff, and she was going to call him on it. "We only sleep fully clothed in February."

"It must get cold sleeping alone."

"I normally don't sleep alone."

Tyler stopped on the step behind her. "You don't?" His voice was high-pitched.

"I have five sisters. We share three beds. Two per bed. It's simple math."

"That's all Northerners learn in their public school system."

Cory stopped mid-step and turned her head. "What is wrong with a public education?"

Tyler stopped with her. "Where do I begin? I have yet to meet someone who attended public school who can spell, let alone add and subtract accurately. The only thing worse than the students are the educators. Anyone with the basic knowledge of the alphabet and crude math skills qualifies for the job of instructor and can receive a teaching certificate."

"I am a school teacher." Cory waited for an apology.

"I thought so. You corrected my grammar earlier, and you're bossy."

He was intentionally trying to insult and anger her. She measured her response. "There's a normal school for training teachers in Cleveland, but it was too far to travel. Besides, they don't require two years of extra schooling to teach in Darrow Falls. It'll probably change soon."

"You don't agree with the higher standards?"

"Sometimes talent is as important as a diploma. Do you think you're a better lawyer than Mr. Lincoln because you went to Harvard?"

He didn't hesitate. "Yes."

"You certainly have a high opinion of yourself."

"I didn't go to Harvard to be a worse lawyer."

She challenged him. "Don't you have to be a man of high moral character to be a lawyer?"

"I'm only twenty-five. I haven't had time to do anything immoral, yet." He added the last word with a glint in his eye.

"I hope you don't have anything immoral in mind when it comes to me." She had reached the foyer and turned, the flame in her hand passing close to Tyler's face.

He grabbed her hand holding the candle. "Careful, you've already maimed me once."

Cory trembled. What was wrong with her? She was too sensible to be swept off her feet by a mere touch, but her body betrayed her, longing for fulfillment of an unknown need.

Tyler released her hand and ran his fingers through his thick hair. "I shouldn't be here."

"Why not?"

"My presence in the house may have put you in danger. I have enemies."

"The only enemies I'm worried about are the gossipers in town. Are you planning to tell others you spent the night?"

"No."

He'd said it without hesitation, but she still worried. "I hope you're an honorable man and keep your word."

Chapter Five

Cory headed to the back door off the kitchen. She grabbed a pair of well-worn leather boots she wore for mucking the stalls in the barn. Tyler watched as she lifted the hem of her nightgown to step into the high boots. He was looking at her bare legs, but she hoped the dim light kept him from seeing clearly. A cloak for chilly mornings hung on a peg, but the light broadcloth was too warm for tonight. The thin robe was a better choice and certainly modest in the dark. She stared at Tyler's bare chest.

"Do you need the cloak?"

Tyler looked up. "No, I'm warm enough."

"You could have a fever." She didn't dare touch him to check. "You should stay here. Don't forget your injury."

"The exercise will do me good."

"You don't have a shirt on."

"It doesn't bother me if it doesn't bother you."

She shrugged. "Why should it bother me?" The sight of Tyler's nakedness had stirred an erotic response she'd never experienced. But how did a scholar acquire sculptured muscles that rippled with power at every movement? She wouldn't obtain the answer through silent pondering. "How did a Harvard lawyer become so strong? Carrying books around?" She hoped her witty remark camouflaged her embarrassment. How could she ask such a personal question? She turned away and lit a lantern on a peg by the door with her candle.

Tyler grabbed the lamp and whispered in her ear. "They were very big books."

Cory opened her mouth to argue but had a feeling she wouldn't uncover the truth. She looked around. "Do you think I should take Hiram's gun?" It was in the parlor but needed to be reloaded.

"Haven't you shot enough men tonight?"

"What if there's an intruder? He could be dangerous."

"I think I can handle him."

"Are you going to quote him the law?" She followed him into the dark yard.

****

Tyler chuckled. He liked her. It had been a long time since he'd met a woman he genuinely enjoyed being with for any length of time. Too many young ladies had a singular objective toward matrimony with ambitions of marrying a rich man. He had not yet acquired enough wealth to tempt anyone. The less greedy women he had met lacked any personality or depth of character to occupy his interest. Yet, Cory was not only a teacher and nurse; she had a sense of adventure. Had she seen a light in the barn? It didn't matter. He was more than willing to play along if it gave him an opportunity to take advantage of the dark.

When they reached the barn, Tyler opened the door. Rusty hinges sang in the quiet night air. Tyler waved the light to dispel some of the darkness inside. The pungent smell of earth, manure, and animals assaulted his nostrils as the more subtle scents of leather, hay, and wood tempered the stronger odors. The lower level of the barn was separated in three long sections with the stalls for the horses behind a half wall in front of them. Harnesses hung from a rack on the center section of the near wall. A wooden wheelbarrow and pitchfork rested beneath. A few remnants of hay and manure lingered on the tines of the pitchfork.

The cows mooed in their pen beyond a steep staircase next to the horse stalls. On the opposite side of the barn were two large empty pens and a cold storage bin for milk built with cut stone. The middle section was empty except for a tack box for the horses and a hay bin underneath a chute from the upper level.

A brown mare with a white blaze across her nose poked her head over the first stall. "Have you seen anyone, Nell?" Cory asked.

Two draft horses were in the neighboring stalls. Tyler paused at the bottom of the staircase. "What's upstairs?"

"Hay, oats, and straw along with the buggy and wagon. And Hiram's workbench and tools."

He lit another lantern hanging on a wooden peg on one of the thick support beams and handed it to Cory. Tyler walked up the steps to the storage level of the barn. Cory followed. Tyler glanced around for any sign of an intruder. Hiram's workbench was located at the top of the stairs along the back wall of the barn. His tools hung on the side wall near the grain storage room. The sharp metal edges of the sickle, saw, rake, hoe, and shovels reflected in his light. A pile of fresh hay was stored on the near side of the barn with straw on the other side. In the middle was a wagon and single-seat buggy.

Tyler searched the long wooden wagon used for hauling. He waved the lantern over the buggy. "Nothing here."

****

Cory couldn't see past the small circle of light into the darkness. If someone was hiding in the barn, she no longer wanted to know. Tyler was methodical in his search and taking too long. The upper level of the barn was stifling, and Cory could feel a ball of sweat roll down her back. Her nightgown clung.

"I must have been mistaken." Cory hastened to the stairs but took each step cautiously, feeling her way to the dirt floor. She waved her lantern around but saw nothing out of the ordinary. She stood in the center of the barn and listened to Tyler's footsteps above her. Should she wait for him or go to the house? A barn cat jumped on the wall of the nearby empty pen and startled her. She screamed. He had a mangled mouse in his mouth and dropped it down on a storage box in front of her like a sacrificial offering.

Cory gagged and swung around from the gruesome sight. Her lantern caught a movement in Nell's stall. She froze as she stared harder into the darkness, trying to decipher the shadows in the dim light. It was too big to be another cat. She stepped toward the stall, and the light from the lantern illuminated the man briefly before he ducked down into the stall. He was a black man. It could be the man from Tyler's flier, or it could be any runaway slave. What should she do?

If the slave belonged to Tyler, she had an obligation under the law to turn him over to his master. If she didn't, and Tyler found the man hiding in the barn, he could accuse her of aiding him. Even if a judge

47

didn't send her to jail, she'd have to pay a fine. All her money would be gone, her family would be embarrassed, and the scandal would ruin her plans for marriage.

She needed time to talk to Adelaide. Did she know about the slave? Maybe it was the reason she had insisted Tyler not sleep in the barn. Why hadn't she confided in her about the runaway? Cory heard Tyler's footsteps on the stairs. She needed to get him out of the barn before he discovered the man's hiding place.

"I heard you scream."

"A cat!" She waved at the feline batting the dead mouse back and forth between its sheathed claws. "He startled me."

"I didn't find anything." Tyler hung his lantern back on its peg and blew it out. "So what do you propose we do next?"

Cory recognized the husky change in his voice and dismissed it. "I propose we go back inside, Mr. Montgomery."

Both turned at the sound of a thud against Nell's wooden wall. "It's Nell kicking the wall," Cory excused.

"I better check." Tyler grabbed the burning lantern from her hand.

Cory followed behind him. She needed to prevent him from discovering the slave's hiding place. She couldn't overpower him. What could she do?

Tyler's body blocked the lantern's light, and Cory bumped into him when he stopped at the stall wall. Her instinct was to back away, but instead, she reached out with her hands to locate him. She ran her fingertips upward to his shoulders as she pressed herself against him. Cory rested her cheek against the bare skin of his wide back. "Your skin is so cool."

He froze.

Now what? She remembered something her mother did when her father had an exhausting day. She caressed his shoulders with her hands, shocked by the hardness beneath smooth flesh. Her fingertips danced downward along the damp skin of his back and circled beneath the strip of white bandage to hold him in a gentle grip. "I'm so hot." Her lips brushed against his back. "Let's get out of here."

The lantern shook in Tyler's hand. He placed it on the stall wall, turned, and captured her in his arms. "Let's see what I can do about the heat." His deep, throaty tone sent a shiver through her body.

Cory had started something she had no way of stopping. She recalled her parents always retired to bed after one of her mother's massages. Why hadn't she remembered that earlier? She panicked as Tyler drew her close against his body.

She gasped as his mouth found hers, plundering her lips with a savage hunger. This was no chaste peck or quick pluck she had experienced from other men. Even those who had kissed her more fervently had failed to ignite this unfamiliar heat building within her. Her body reacted against her common sense.

She should have been insulted by his actions. She should have pulled away. She should have slapped his face. Instead, she encircled his neck with her arms and kissed him in fevered abandonment.

Cory surrendered control to desire, passion, and lust. A mere kiss had never caused such wanton seduction. Her traitorous body responded with a sinful will of its own, and she rubbed against the hard, unyielding form that defined manhood in all its magnificence.

She had never touched a man, and her hands moved freely as she explored the size and hardness of his body. His bare skin flowed smooth and cool beneath her fingertips. She caressed his arms, shoulders, neck, and tangled her fingers in his hair. Cory refused to let him escape as she tasted the saltiness of his skin, felt the rough bristle of his cheek, and plundered the soft moistness of his mouth.

She gasped for breath. This strange fever clouded any clear judgment or thought of consequence.

He kissed her face and neck, blazing a trail lower and lower as her breath caught in her throat. Her pulse beat at a shattering pace beneath his mouth. A groan escaped her parted lips.

His hands explored the curves beneath her flimsy robe and lowered the fabric to reach naked flesh. He kissed her bare shoulder and caught the strap of her gown with his teeth until it came undone and fell away. His hand cupped the heavy fullness of her breast and gently squeezed. His thumb skimmed over her smooth nipple, teasing it to a throbbing peak. He lowered his mouth and suckled the swollen fruit.

Cory's eyes widened at this new and surprising sensation. She had seen the look on a new mother's face when a baby was placed on the breast to nurse. Was it like this? A wave of contractions traveled through her body and nestled between her legs. The place babies came from. He was exploring forbidden territory. She shoved against his chest. "Stop! Stop! Stop!"

Tyler raised his head, his mouth moist from feasting. She backed away, stealing the bruised fruit from his lips. Her trembling hands snatched the fallen corner of her nightgown, and her fingers fumbled at the ties as she knotted the strap.

"Where are you going?" He followed toward the door.

Cory grabbed the pitchfork in the wheelbarrow and raised it in defense.

Tyler stopped short and raised his hands. "What did I do?"

"You were taking liberties!" A sob escaped her throat. She stabbed the pitchfork in his direction.

"You were hot. I may have started the kissing, but you certainly didn't resist."

He spoke the truth, but pride dictated she protest. "I lost my head."

He stepped closer.

"For a moment." She pointed the sharp tines at his chest. "I'm a virgin and have every intention of remaining one until my wedding night."

He stopped in his tracks. A silent pause separated them. "Are you sure you want to save yourself for one man?"

Cory's arms shook. "How many holes do I need to put in you?"

"One is quite enough." He backed away and grabbed the lantern he had left near the stall. "I think it's time to go in."

Cory returned the pitchfork to the wheelbarrow and opened the barn door. Tyler reached to hold the door, but she bolted at his nearness and raced to the house. She didn't want to be with Tyler a minute longer. She didn't trust herself. She needed to erect a barrier preventing any repeat of her wanton behavior. She had kissed a man she barely knew. And more! The shame of it. If anyone found out, she'd be ruined. And a slave owner, too. What had happened to her standards? Her self-control? Her future plans?

Tyler entered the kitchen after her. "So, now what?"

Cory raised her hand as she struggled out of her work boots. "Let's promise never to talk about it again."

She stumbled, and he offered his hand. She jerked away.

"I was only going to help you."

"I know, but touching leads to kissing, and kissing leads to…babies."

"Are you that fertile?"

She put her hand on her hip. "My mother had six children in less than twelve years. Even a Harvard lawyer should be able to figure out the probability."

"So, we should plan on a large family."

"You're a slave owner. I don't want to marry you."

"Honey, you should work harder to discourage me."

She grabbed the edges of her robe and made sure her breasts were covered. "I know I behaved shamelessly." She couldn't tell him about the slave. "I have no explanation. Please, forget it ever happened."

Tyler removed the disfigured slug of lead from his pocket. "This trophy won't let me forget."

She recognized the bullet. "Give it to me!"

He raised it above her reach. "The memories tied to it are too valuable now."

"You'd ruin my life to brag about your conquest?"

"Your villainous opinion of me isn't flattering." He thrust the bullet into his pocket. "Don't worry. No one will ever know about your slip from society's Puritan principles." He raised his hand as if in court. "I swear it."

Cory lit her candle and blew out the lantern. She hurried to the foyer. She paused on the bottom step. Tyler joined her. "Do you promise never to kiss me again?"

Tyler chuckled.

"Hush." Cory glanced upstairs to Adelaide's bedroom. She cautiously climbed the steps, pausing when one creaked beneath her weight.

"That, my sweet, is one promise I won't make." Tyler patted her bottom.

Cory elbowed his side. Unfortunately, it was the one with the wound, and he nearly buckled, crying out in pain.

"I'm sorry." She put her arm around him and helped him climb the remaining steps.

They paused by his door. "I can tell you're not accustomed to having a man around, but I'll grow on you."

"Go to bed." She slipped out from under his weight and dashed to her room. She tore off her robe, jumped into bed, and snatched the blanket over her head. She had let a man touch her in an inappropriate manner, and not any man, but a Southern slave owner too handsome for mortality, who made her forget all the teachings of restraint. "Marriage first. Marriage to a respectable man like Douglas." She poked her head out from under the thin cover. She needed to think rationally, but doubts persisted. What if Douglas didn't make her weak in the knees like Tyler? She had tasted the forbidden fruit and doubted she would ever be satisfied with basic bread and butter. She groaned as she closed her eyes and wished for the answers.

Chapter Six

Cory was in a dreamy half-sleep when she heard the heavy footsteps of a man descend the staircase. At first, she thought nothing of it. It was her father responding to an early morning call. Then she realized she was alone in bed without her youngest sister, Juliet, curled against her back. Her mind focused as she stretched, opened her eyes, and looked around. The bed wasn't hers, and the footsteps she had heard belonged to Tyler. Any remnant of slumber vanished as she bolted from the bed. She flung open her bedroom door. His footsteps faded down the main hallway and toward the back door.

The barn! She ran to her window and saw him approach the door they had used the night before. He'd find the runaway slave if she didn't stop him. She tossed off her nightgown and slapped on an old dress she wore for chores. She didn't have time for undergarments. She didn't even run a brush through her hair. She hurried down the steps, hopped into the old boots parked by the back door, and barely missed a beat as she dashed across the yard.

The barn door was open, and morning light filtered inside. The barn appeared friendlier than last night. Nell munched on oats while Cory searched for any signs of the slave in her stall. Where was he? Had Tyler already found him? She heard a low baritone voice singing the pro-slavery minstrel song "Dixie." She followed the music to the cow pen. "What are you doing?"

Tyler sat on a three-legged milking stool with his hands beneath a black and white cow. He tugged on her teats and squirted milk into a wooden bucket beneath her udders. He was still bare to the waist except for the strip of Cory's petticoat. It was twisted and darkly stained near the wound. He turned his head and looked at her, his head resting against the bovine's side. "Cory?"

She carefully stepped around the piles of cow dung decorating the hard packed ground and put her hand on the cow's hindquarters. She attempted a less hysterical pitch. "What are you doing?"

He grinned. "I have my hands on a couple of teats."

She recalled last night's shameful actions. She had to put a stop to his innuendos. "I don't know what the girls are like in Virginia, but the only udders you're going to touch on this farm are the cows'."

"Bessie doesn't seem to mind."

"Her name is Gertie."

Tyler had an easy rhythm as he squeezed and squirted milk into the bucket.

"Where did you learn to milk a cow? Harvard dairy?"

Tyler laughed. "A Quaker couple raised me on a farm in Vandalia, Virginia."

"A Quaker couple?" The Quakers were peace loving, simple folk who dressed plainly and practiced restraint. Tyler hardly fit the mold. "You're joking."

"Sarah and James Yoder tolerated my shortcomings."

"Too bad you didn't learn modesty from them."

"I would dress if I could."

"Your clothes," she recalled. "I left them in my room."

"I thought it might be rude to come in uninvited."

Cory blushed. In her dreams he had entered uninvited but welcomed. All the stirring emotions of last night returned with a wet rush. She needed to put an end to this nonsense. "I need to mend the holes and put your shirt out on the line to dry. It shouldn't take long. You can probably find a ride into town."

He stood and lifted the milk bucket safely out of Gertie's way. "You can't take me?"

"I have chores to do." She realized he was doing one of them. "You shouldn't be working." She studied his soiled bandage. "You might open your wound."

He looked around the barn and focused on her. "You do all the work around this farm without any help?"

"You must be used to genteel ladies who can barely lift a pen to write a letter. I take care of the livestock, garden, and help with the cooking, cleaning, and baking," she rattled off on her fingers.

Tyler untied Gertie and smacked her on the hindquarters. She swatted a few flies with her tail and waited for Cory to open the gate to the pasture.

Cory stepped into the light streaming from the east to let Gertie pass.

Tyler stared at her standing in the morning sun.

She looked down at her attire. The dress was hemmed shorter to keep the material out of the dirt, but the only thing revealed were the old leather boots on her feet. She looked around. "What?"

He touched the ribbon of fabric across his chest. "Did you use your only petticoat for this bandage?"

"No."

"Then you must have dressed in a hurry."

"This is an old work dress. You don't expect me to muck the stalls in silk?"

Tyler put the bucket of milk down on the milking stool, passed the other cow and calf, and grabbed her skirt. He lifted it.

Cory shoved his hands. "What are you doing?" They struggled until he released the fabric.

"I'm no expert on what women wear under their dresses, but I'll wager you forgot a few things."

Cory stiffened. How did he know she had nothing underneath her dress? She felt naked under his scrutiny. "I'm covered."

"In the South, a woman, even on the hottest day, wears at least one petticoat."

"It's July, and I normally don't have a man criticizing my appearance while I'm working in the barn."

He leaned in close. "I'm surprised you don't have a dozen men helping you with your chores."

"What would I do with a dozen men?" She turned her attention to the cow. "Are you going to milk her or should I do it?"

Tyler blocked her path.

"What do you want?"

"I want to know why you kissed me last night."

"You kissed me." She needed to correct any misconceptions about her lack of outrage at his actions. "And I didn't give you permission."

He stepped closer, inches from her. "You said you

were hot." He brushed back a loose curl from her cheek.

"The barn was stifling." Cory's heartbeat raced beneath the thin fabric, and her body responded to his presence in spite of her resolve. Her nipples throbbed and breasts swelled from the memory of his touch. Cory checked her buttons. One twisted off in her hand.

"Fresh hay in the loft," Tyler whispered. "Wouldn't take much effort to shed what clothes we're wearing."

Cory fought the desire to lift her skirt and accept his offer to show their nakedness. She was no better than an animal in heat. What was this strange base urge to mate? "I have no intention of rolling around in the hay with you."

He turned and moved the milking stool under the other cow. "Then I might as well milk Bessie."

Cory was stunned. No outrageous propositions? No pursuit? Wasn't he equally affected? She followed him to the cow. "That's Lulu."

"Aren't any of your cows named Bessie?"

"No, and the calf is a bull."

"Well, I had a cow named Bessie, and she gave milk without even squeezing. Never once kicked me or smacked me with her tail."

"Are you comparing me to a cow?"

"I loved that cow." Tyler milked Lulu. "I cried all the way home when I had to take her to the butcher."

He sounded sincere in his affection. "I'm sorry. My sisters and I are always becoming attached to the animals on the farm, but I didn't think men did."

"She was sweet." He looked at her. "Unlike some females."

Did he think she was naïve to fall for this new tactic to seduce her? She patted his shoulder while restraining a slap to the back of his head. "Didn't you have any human friends, Tyler?"

"You may scoff, but I had plenty of friends in my younger days." He winked. "Even had a girlfriend."

"Bessie?"

He frowned. "Funny. Her name was Reggie Johnston, and she was a skinny little girl with dirty blonde hair and big owl-like eyes. Mrs. Yoder tutored her along with me and a few other children. They were miners' brats and lived in tiny shacks no bigger than your chicken coop."

"How old were you when this torrid romance began?"

"I was nearly nine when she started coming to the house for schooling. Reggie was three years younger and was missing her front teeth." Tyler made a face. "Kind of a homely child. She was horribly shy and traumatized from working in the coal mines."

Cory gasped. "A six-year-old girl worked in the mines?"

"Younger," he corrected. "They used small children to fit into the tight spaces in that hole of black gold. I only went down once on a dare and never complained again about helping Mr. Yoder in his sweat box of a blacksmith's workroom. Hell's heat was a lot easier to take than hell's darkness. A candle never quite dispels the thick shadows. Reggie was five when the other miners lost her."

"Lost?" Cory tried to fathom what he meant. "In the dark? In the mine?"

"It took nearly two days before they found her. I

remember Mrs. Yoder talking about her and how concerned she was for the little, lost girl. When they finally carried her out of the hole, she was hoarse from screaming. She never worked in the mines again. Couldn't. She was terrified of the dark. Mrs. Yoder offered to school her. She barely talked at first. I made friends with her by giving her candles. She was afraid she'd run out. She'd take a candle over candy any day of the week."

"That was sweet of you," Cory gushed. "What happened to her?"

"I left for boarding school when I was fourteen. She was crying about missing me, and I worked up the nerve to kiss her. First time I kissed a girl. It startled her so much, she stopped crying." He paused. "I was too young to appreciate the moment. I came home summers and watched her grow older and prettier each year. She helped Mrs. Yoder with the chores around the house to pay for schooling and shadowed me everywhere. Then she grew into a young lady and stopped following me."

"And you fell in love with her." Cory took his silence as affirmation. "Why didn't you marry her?"

Tyler finished milking Lulu. She trotted to the pasture with her calf chasing her. He placed the bucket on top of the stool. "She married another man."

"Why?"

"She said she was in love with him."

"But what about you?"

He rested his hand on his chest. "Broken heart."

"And I thought your feelings ran more toward passion than sentiment," she countered.

"I wouldn't have described my feelings for anything or anyone as passionate until last night." He stepped toward her. "And my desire hasn't diminished in the daylight." His deep voice was husky.

Cory turned her back on him before he saw confirmation of her own desire. "I don't think Mr. Douglas Raymond would approve of your words."

"Douglas Raymond? Was he the man who called last night?"

Cory faced him. "You saw him?"

"You're not going to waste your charms on that Ichabod?"

Cory prickled at his insult. "He's a mathematics instructor at Western Reserve College in Hudson. He graduated from Yale."

"Figures."

"You didn't hesitate to brag about graduating from Harvard." She stuck a ladle in the bucket of milk and poured it into a small bowl on the floor. Several cats emerged from the barn's nooks and crevices to drink the milk. She hung the ladle on a nail.

"Do you plan to marry him?"

Cory turned to face him, surprised he was only a deep breath away. She attempted an escape, but the barn steps were in the way. "He's a good catch." She ducked underneath the staircase and paused in the narrow alley next to the horse stalls.

He continued to advance. "I'd tell you to throw him back in, but I'm a man. I guess women know what they want." He spread his arms across the hallway and leaned into her. "But explain to me what makes Douglas such a good husband?"

She ducked under his arm and moved to a safe distance in the cow pen. "He comes from a good family. He's well educated, and he has a promising future as a professor."

"Those are impressive traits." He shook his head. "I doubt if I could compete against such a man."

Cory rolled her eyes. "This is where you tell me you're a lawyer."

"You're forgetting the part about a good family."

"You said the Yoders were Quakers. There can't be any scandal there." She paused as she recalled part of his confession. "You said something about a blacksmith."

"Mr. Yoder is a blacksmith. I worked summers in his shop."

Cory shook her head in disbelief. "That's how you ended up so big and strong." She also recalled something else. The runaway slave was trained as a blacksmith. His slave, Noah.

Tyler grinned. "You think I'm big and strong?"

He was a slave owner. The heat of his proximity turned cold. "It doesn't matter. The only man I'm interested in is Mr. Raymond."

"Are you going to tell him about our lovemaking in the barn?"

Cory gasped. "We didn't make love! It was a kiss."

Tyler leaned in close. "When Douglas kisses you, do you respond the way you did last night?"

"No!" Cory automatically answered. "I mean, he hasn't kissed me."

"What?"

She squared her shoulders. "He's a gentleman."

"A fool," he said. "A man doesn't go through all the tea sipping and hand holding for nothing."

She scowled. "Is a woman's companionship so boring there must be some physical reward at the end of the evening?"

"It helps."

Cory's temper took off like an angry hornet. "Well, if you think I'm going to bare my breast and wiggle my hips to keep your attention, you're wrong, Mr. Montgomery. There will be no repeat of last night's mistake. You can find some other innocent girl and seduce her into a kiss."

"Innocent girl?" He ran his finger along her jawline and lifted her chin so her gaze met his. "Honey, I could take lessons from you in seduction."

She jerked away. "I may have given you the wrong impression, but let me make this clear. I won't compromise my principles for any man, especially a slave owner."

"But if I wasn't a slave owner, you'd consider me for a beau?"

"I'd want to know you better, and that would involve silly tea parties and boring walks in each other's company."

"Oh, I think we know each other well enough." He winked. "And if I did marry you, I could steal as many kisses as I wanted and more."

Cory blushed.

"Don't be embarrassed, my love. Douglas won't hesitate to toss your skirts over your head once he has a ring on your finger."

She stomped her foot. "That's not true."

Tyler studied her from head to toe. His gaze lingered on the gap her missing button exposed on her bodice. "A husband has rights, and a man doesn't marry without an intention to enforce those rights. And you won't be able to do anything about it."

Chapter Seven

No one had ever stated Cory's fears so concisely. She could never imagine any man touching her intimately—until now. She looked at Tyler and knew he was different from all the other men who had courted her. She was drawn to him in a way that defied reason. She wanted to be with him even though she knew he was all wrong for her. And he didn't seem too eager to marry her even if she did change her mind about wanting him as a husband. She would have to settle for someone else. "I guess a woman has to make sacrifices."

"My mother made sacrifices." His voice was bitter. "One of them was me."

Cory heard the pain in his voice even though she didn't understand what he was implying. "You don't mean Sarah Yoder, do you?"

"No." He ran his hands down his thighs. "Forget me. No decent woman would marry an outsider like me. Run to Mr. Raymond or some other respectable man and never look back."

Cory reached out and stroked his arm. "She must have hurt you very much to make you believe no woman could love you."

Tyler stared at her hand on his arm. "Why do you say that?"

"You're sweet and tender one moment and a

complete rogue the next," she determined. "Do you treat every woman so cavalier? Do you believe our feelings so shallow, they cannot be crushed by a callous word or deed?"

"I do not take a lady's affections for granted. I can count the number of women I've kissed on one hand."

No man as handsome as Tyler could be so inexperienced. "Liar!"

"Honest." He crossed his heart and counted on his fingers. "Reggie Johnston, Bill Bradley's sister when I was at the academy, and two women when I was at Harvard. The last one was an heiress to a whaling fortune. After half a year of courting rituals, she let me hold her hand. And when I kissed her, it was like kissing a fish."

Cory giggled. "You kiss a lot of fish?"

Tyler retrieved the milk bucket. "In Boston, it's the preferred kissing partner." He joined her in the narrow path by the stairs. "So 'fess. How many boys' hearts have you broken?"

She smiled. "I have you beat. Seven. No, eight if I count you."

"And you call me a rogue. You'd be branded a hussy in Boston's stiff-necked society!"

"I am not!" She dipped her finger in the bucket of milk and tasted the warm liquid. "They were chaste kisses. Nothing like yours."

Some of the milk spilled over the edge of the bucket as Tyler pinned her against the stairway support. "So you felt it, too."

Before she could protest, he kissed her. This time slowly, tenderly, and with a sensuality that left them breathless. She fought to keep her head above the drowning waters luring her to immoral destruction.

"Has Douglas Raymond or any man made you feel this way? Throw caution to the wind, my dear Cory, and see where our passions lead us."

"I know where our foolhardiness will lead us." Cory shoved against his chest. "Pregnancy and ruin. Do you think any decent man would marry me or any of my sisters if word spread about how easily I succumbed to your charms? I have a responsibility to maintain the family honor with a rigid line of decorum. My sisters deserve a chance to find worthwhile husbands. I won't shirk my duty." She walked toward the horse stalls, determined to put some distance between them.

Why did she enjoy being kissed by Tyler? She should discourage him, but when he touched her, all resolve vanished. What if Douglas was a dud? Once married, she would be stuck with him. She had to encourage Douglas to kiss her. Then she'd know. If he stirred even half the excitement Tyler did, she could live with that, couldn't she?

Cory paused near the door. "Miss Adelaide is awake by now, and I have eggs to gather from the hens. You better carry the milk inside before you spill it all."

****

Cory laid the basket of eggs on the table, and Tyler dropped the bucket of milk beside it. Adelaide was heating a cast iron skillet coated with lard. "What have you two been doing?"

Cory glanced at Tyler. "Chores."

"Humpf," Adelaide replied. "You're as transparent as that dress you're wearing. And why is it missing a button?"

"It came off." Cory retrieved the button from the

egg basket. "It's an old dress."

Adelaide looked from Tyler to Cory. "A man doesn't buy the cow if he can get the milk for free."

Cory scrunched her face. "Why is everyone comparing me to a cow?"

Adelaide pointed her wooden spoon at Tyler. "Why are you half naked? Where are your clothes?"

"His shirt is soaking in my room," Cory defended. "And I have to mend the holes in his other clothes."

"Hang the shirt on the line so it can dry, and you probably have time to darn a couple of holes before breakfast is ready." Adelaide looked at Tyler as she waved her spoon toward the back window. "Are you well enough to put the horses out in the east pasture and muck their stalls?"

"Yes, ma'am."

"Might as well do it before you put on your clothes. How's your wound?"

Tyler raised his arm. "A little itchy."

"That's good," Cory said. "I'll clean it when you're done in the barn."

"I know it's going to be hot, but I suggest you add a petticoat under that dress." Adelaide said. "He's having trouble enough keeping his eyes off of you. I don't want to worry about his hands and other appendages."

"Miss Adelaide!" Cory gasped.

"I haven't been a widow long enough not to remember what a man wants or how to tell."

Tyler reddened. "I'll take care of the horses."

After he left, Cory turned to Adelaide. "How can you tell?"

"If I leave you alone with him long enough, I won't

have to tell you. He'll show you. Dress for town," she added. "I want you to run some errands."

Cory puzzled over Adelaide's words. Why did everything have to be so mysterious? No one talked about men and women coupling, but there were plenty of babies to prove it was happening. She thought of her parents and the noises echoing from their bedroom at night. Shouldn't she know what was going to happen on her wedding night before she crawled into bed with her husband?

When she opened her bedroom door, she stared at her reflection in the mirror above the dressing table. She looked wild and untamed. Maybe it was the unruly curls cascading around her shoulders or the beads of sweat forming on her skin as the sun warmed the air.

But as she stepped forward, she realized a transformation had occurred in the way she carried herself. She appeared older, more confident, but why? The only difference in her life was Tyler. How could he change her so dramatically?

She grabbed the basin with Tyler's shirt and carried it downstairs and out the front door to avoid any more scolding from Adelaide. She scrubbed it under the pump water, wrung it out, and hung it on the clothes line extending from the barn to a post in the yard. Most of the blood had come out except a brown spot around the hole. She rinsed the basin and hurried inside.

The darning didn't take long, and Cory admired the workmanship of the embroidery on the vest. Someone had taken great care to create the intricate design. She searched along the linen back and found two initials stitched along the seam. "*RJ*," Cory read aloud. "Reggie." She must have felt something for him to make such a beautiful vest, and Tyler had to care a little to wear it. She brushed away a stray tear that fell for no reason and tossed the vest on top of the jacket.

She had a few dresses nice enough for town and chose a yellow and white gingham frock. It buttoned nearly to her neck and the sleeves came below her elbows. Normally, she would wear a shirt beneath it, but the thought of one more layer of clothing made her rebel. The fabric was lightweight and the bell-shaped sleeves would allow air to circulate and keep her cool.

She tore off her work dress and started the laborious task of putting on all her undergarments and lacing her corset. The stiff boning created a straight line from waist to bosom and forced the extra fullness upward. Likewise, the bell-shaped crinoline created an artificial framework to drape her gown on and disguised any natural curves.

She tossed a pair of soft leather gloves and her beaded handbag into her wide straw bonnet. She examined her messy hair. Combing out the tangles was laborious, and Cory decided to braid her hair to keep it neat and in place for the trip to town. She gathered the braided strands in a chignon at the base of her neck.

Cory studied her respectable reflection in the mirror and wondered what had happened to the woman who had entered the room. She hurried downstairs and left her bonnet on the sideboard. She carried Tyler's jacket and vest into the kitchen and fetched an iron resting near the cold fireplace to heat on the stove. After breakfast, she'd press his clothes to smooth out the wrinkles.

Adelaide had finished frying the bacon and added several eggs to the bacon grease. Cory put on an apron.

"What do you want me to do?"

"Mix some dough for biscuits."

Cory added melted lard and fresh buttermilk to the flour, salt, and baking soda mixture. She kneaded the biscuit dough at the kitchen work table.

"Not so much," Adelaide warned. "I don't like my biscuits hard as rocks."

Cory patted the mound into a thick circle with flour-covered fingers. She pressed the round cutter into the dough to form the biscuits. Tyler would finish his work soon. She needed to talk to Adelaide alone while she had the chance. She took a deep breath. "Miss Adelaide, there's a man hiding in your barn."

Adelaide removed the frying pan from the stove's heat. "What makes you think that?"

"I heard the barn door open last night and investigated."

She turned. "On your own? Why didn't you wake me?"

"Tyler went with me."

Adelaide gasped. "Did Tyler see him?"

"No." Cory felt her face grow warm as she recalled why Tyler had not seen the runaway slave.

Adelaide gave her a stern look. "We need to keep it that way. Don't encourage him to stay."

"I'm not!" Cory wiped her hands on her apron and walked to the parlor. The flier Tyler had placed on the desk was still there. She took it to Adelaide. "Is the slave in the barn this one in the flier?"

Adelaide studied it. "Same description."

Cory pointed to the information. "Is his name Noah?"

"That's the name he gave me," Adelaide agreed.

"Noah."

"Tyler's slave." She felt a heavy weight in her chest. Could a heart turn to stone? "Why is he still here? Why hasn't Noah left for Canada?"

Adelaide handed her a flat pan for baking the biscuits. "He came here looking for his wife and son, but they haven't arrived."

"I didn't think slaves could marry."

"They can't, but that doesn't stop them from falling in love and wanting to be together." Adelaide lifted the eggs from the skillet to a plate. "Noah said his wife, Tess, ran away with their son, Adam, at the end of May while her master was gone. Noah followed her, but he was arrested in Akron because of that flier." She pointed at the reward offered for his capture. "He can't ask openly about them and was hoping his family came this way. But Tess and the baby never reached this station."

Cory put her hands on her hips. "Then you are part of the Underground Railroad."

"Hush," she warned. "Do you want to go to jail? That's why I don't want you involved."

"How can I have the Beecher name and not fight slavery?"

"Your name is why I've kept you ignorant of Noah's presence," she argued.

"I can't stand by and let Tyler or any chaser take a slave back to the South."

"Brave words, but do you have the gumption to back them?"

Cory didn't know the answer. She'd never been tested before.

"So you're only pretending to like Tyler?"

Cory squared her shoulders with newfound resolve. "I could never love a slave owner."

Adelaide took the biscuits Cory had placed on the baking sheet and placed them in the oven. She lifted one of the eggs left in the basket. "Your idea of love is like this egg. It's a nice egg, but you can't eat it unless you break the shell."

Cory stared. First a cow, now an egg. What would she be compared to next?

Adelaide broke the egg into the skillet. "Real love breaks the shell and makes a mess of your well-laid plans."

Cory had always believed love took time to cultivate and grew with care. She dismissed her attraction to Tyler for a fever that would pass when he left. Nevertheless, she was eager to change the subject. "I searched for Noah in the barn this morning but couldn't find him. Where is he hiding?"

"Noah hides in the woods during the day," Adelaide said. "You must have seen him coming in after dark last night. He goes out before dawn."

"How long has he been here?"

"This is the third day."

"I didn't even suspect anything."

"I've been keeping you busy," Adelaide said. "But I didn't count on all the men you attract. I might as well be running a tavern."

She resolved to do what was necessary. "I can drive Tyler into town when I run your errands. He'll be gone, and we won't have to worry about him."

"Are you going to be all right with that?"

Cory might be heartbroken for a little while, but he wasn't the only man in the world. There had to be more than one that made her heart flutter like the rapid beating of hummingbird wings.

Tyler stepped out of the barn and stood in the morning light. He looked around at the farm. Cory felt safe staring at him from the kitchen window. He was magnificent. Men weren't supposed to be beautiful, but Tyler was. It was a shame to put clothes on him. As if he could read her thoughts, he went to the clothes line, felt his shirt, and removed it.

Cory fetched clean bandages and gathered other supplies to dress his wound. She met Tyler on the back porch. "Sit down." She pointed to a backless wooden bench made from a split log. She placed a tin basin next to him and poured some warm water from a cast iron kettle into it to soak a small towel. She tried to untie the knot holding the bandage, but it had tightened.

Tyler withdrew a knife from his boot.

Cory jumped back.

"Skittish?" Tyler sliced the strip of petticoat and put the knife back in his boot.

She regained her composure. "Why do men have such awful toys?"

"To protect the womenfolk, I guess," he said in a mocking imitation of a woodsman.

"Raise your arm," she instructed.

He flexed his bicep.

He was sculptured like a marble statue, and she felt soft and yielding in his presence. But he had raised the wrong arm. "The wound is on the other side."

"The pain must be spreading." He flexed his left arm.

She squatted and balanced herself by grasping his thigh.

Tyler groaned.

"I haven't even touched it." Cory tugged on the bandage, and Tyler grimaced. The soiled rag was stuck. She wrung the towel from the basin and dampened the bandage, easing it loose from the wound. "It's beginning to heal." She wiped away a bit of blood. "Once it scabs over, you can take off the bandage."

Tyler held the square of cloth while Cory wrapped a new strip of her former petticoat around his chest. He sat motionless while she worked. "I hope you remember me fondly after I'm gone."

"I'll dream about you every night." She had meant the words to be mocking but feared the truth behind them.

He frowned. "I wouldn't want you to lose any sleep because of me."

"Then I won't." Her anger matched his and fled as quickly. She wanted their parting to be amiable. "Keep the wound clean and don't do anything strenuous until it's healed."

Tyler examined the new bandage and tested the flexibility of his arm. "Your father taught you well."

Cory scrunched her face and tossed the soiled bandages into the basin. "My sister Jennifer is much better at handling all the blood and guts. I prefer teaching."

"What do you enjoy about teaching?"

Cory smiled. "It always amazes me when one of my students puts together the words on the page and realizes it all makes sense. What about you? Do you enjoy being a lawyer?"

"I apprenticed for a Boston firm in my second year of law school. Their philosophy was to keep the rich wealthy. When a client wanted to foreclose on a poor family because they couldn't pay their rent, I wanted to quit the case. I wish I had."

"You didn't?"

"I was warned that even if I did graduate, I wouldn't have any references to find work with the prestigious law firms of Boston or New York. I saw my future evaporating and kept my mouth shut. The family was evicted from their home, and I was offered a position with Brennan, Brewster, and Waxman."

"Is that who you work for?"

"For about four months after I passed the bar exam. Then fate had other plans."

Cory handed him his shirt. "You're unemployed?"

Tyler slipped his left arm carefully into the sleeve. "I bet Douglas looks mighty tempting by comparison."

"So what are you going to do now?"

"I'm going to see what the world has to offer a young man with a good education, no responsibilities, and a lack of any moral constraints." He grinned. "Be warned, Miss Beecher, I'm a man of the world, a cad, a threat to young women like yourself."

Cory had thought the same thing last night but knew better. In a few more years, he might fulfill his self-description. She played along and shouted to a non-existent crowd. "Lock up your daughters! Tyler Montgomery is in town."

Chapter Eight

Tyler stood and buttoned his shirt. How could Cory take his confessions so lightly? If she knew the truth about his family, she wouldn't be laughing. But she didn't know his past or the burden of hiding it. He enjoyed her lighthearted teasing but wasn't going to let her think she had the upper hand.

"Your mocking will not go unpunished." He grabbed the basin of dirty water and threatened to toss it on her.

"You'll ruin my dress." She raised her hands to shield herself.

Tyler swept the pan past her without spilling a drop. "You look very pretty," he complimented. "But I don't like your hair."

Cory's hands touched her coiffure. "What's wrong with it?"

"I like a few curls hanging free to tickle my nose when I kiss you."

Cory backed against the wall as he stepped closer.

"Food is getting cold!" Adelaide called out.

"Food!" Tyler opened the door.

Cory stood where she was. "Aren't you going to…"

"Kiss you?" He shrugged. "Maybe later. I'm hungry now."

Cory stomped into the kitchen behind him and

shoved him when he didn't move out of her way. Tyler stood firm like a brick wall. He enjoyed baiting her temper to the surface. He wondered if her lively retorts were muted in parlor conversations. Did Douglas appreciate her outspoken opinions? He doubted it.

She shoved his back again. This time he stumbled forward and knocked over a chair with his vest and jacket draped over it. They fell to the floor.

"Are you all right?"

He heard the worry in her voice and felt sheepish about faking the trip. He picked up his clothes and righted the chair. "I better dress."

"I need to iron those."

"A few wrinkles won't hurt."

"It's a poor reflection on my skills," she defended.

"I have no doubt about your skills." He stood aside for her to precede him into the dining room.

"I'm sure my skills pale next to Reggie's." She nodded toward the vest. "Her needlework is excellent."

She had misunderstood his innuendo or had chosen to ignore it. "Mrs. Yoder taught her. She made it for my graduation from Harvard College three years ago."

"Her husband didn't mind?"

He recognized the sarcasm. Was she jealous? "She wasn't married then."

Cory picked at her food while Tyler attacked breakfast like it was his last meal. He debated whether to put Cory out of her misery. Reggie had only given him the vest to make her future husband jealous. He wore it as a reminder that women were liars and not to be trusted. Reggie had placed wealth and security above any feelings she had for him. She had wounded him, and he had sworn never to become emotionally entangled deeply enough to feel the blade of betrayal slicing through his heart. So why was he flirting with Cory?

He wanted Cory physically more than he had ever wanted any woman, but his feelings went deeper than the lust that erupted every time he looked at her. She made him smile with her presence, especially now when she was pouting about not being kissed. She hadn't seen Adelaide peeking out the window. Now she was jealous because of a stupid vest. He would never understand women.

****

Once the meal was finished, Tyler would leave, and Cory would never see him again. Her appetite had fled, and she toyed with the cold egg on her plate. Should she ask him to write? She could send him an invitation to her wedding. Would that amuse him? Would he laugh when Douglas took her to the bedroom and closed the door? She put her fork down and stared at her food. She felt sick. She looked up to see Tyler studying her. Or was it the food on her plate. He'd eaten everything on his.

"If your appetite is any indication, you're well enough to travel." Adelaide gathered the dishes from the table.

Tyler carried his plate and silver into the kitchen. "I can't thank you enough for your hospitality."

"Cory has some errands to run. She can drop you off in town."

"I need to repay you for your kindness."

"You've done enough," Adelaide said. "How did a lawyer learn about working a farm?"

"I lived with the Yoders. They're Quakers who

believed in hard work. Besides farming, Mr. Yoder is a blacksmith and taught me about horses, wagons, and bending iron."

"You're a blacksmith?" Adelaide asked.

"Only as an apprentice during the summers when I returned home from school."

Cory realized Tyler was seeking information, but Adelaide was tightlipped.

"I'm not the only one Mr. Yoder trained as a blacksmith," Tyler continued. "He trained a black man named Noah, who worked in his smithy."

"Your slave?" Cory finished bringing in the dishes.

"I didn't think Quakers believed in slavery." Adelaide added hot water to the basin she used for washing dishes.

"They don't."

Cory handed her the plates. "But the flier said Noah was a runaway slave."

"It's complicated," Tyler said. "I need to know if he was here."

Adelaide squared her frail shoulders. "I don't know anything about your slave."

"I have to find him."

Cory grabbed her apron from the wall hook. "We won't help you."

A loud knock on the front door interrupted their stand-off.

"Who is that?" Adelaide dried her hands.

"Wait!" Tyler looked out the window above the dry sink. "It's the Cassell brothers."

"Who are they?" Cory tried to look around him. He stepped aside. Two men stood in the front yard. They were dressed in frayed wool pants, dull gray cotton shirts, and well-worn broadcloth coats. Their hats were slouched low over their weathered faces.

"They're chasers."

Cory grabbed Adelaide's arm. "What should we do?"

Adelaide patted her hand. "We have nothing to be afraid of."

"Where's your pistol?" Tyler demanded.

"I reloaded it and put it in the desk drawer." Adelaide led the way to the parlor and retrieved the revolver from the desk. Tyler stayed back from the windows and held out his hand for the gun. Adelaide refused to give it to him.

Cory stayed out of view but looked through the panes of glass surrounding the front door. She turned to the others and whispered, "The man at the door is well-dressed."

"Blonde hair with a long mustache?" Tyler asked.

Cory nodded.

Tyler stepped into the shadows near the wall. "Don't tell him I'm here."

"Do you know him?"

"The two men in the yard are Buck and Clyde Cassell. They make a living chasing down runaways. The man on the porch is probably Edward Vandal. He's hired them in the past."

He knocked again.

"He's not going away." Adelaide looked at Cory. "Do you want me to talk to him?"

"No, I can get rid of him." Cory took a deep breath and opened the door.

Edward Vandal was dressed in a bleached white suit with red velvet piping along the edge of the wide lapels. He wore a silk embroidered vest of multi-colored birds stitched with a skill matching Tyler's vest. He had deep set eyes and an angular bump on his narrow nose.

The chasers stood back on the lawn with legs apart, arms at their sides. One of them spat tobacco juice while the other scratched at his scraggly brown beard. They both carried revolvers on their hips, and one sported a large knife sticking out of the top of his boot.

"Miss." Edward spoke in a lazy drawl as he swept his wide-brimmed straw hat from his head. He stepped back off the porch to allow room for her wide skirt as she came outside. Cory left the door open so Adelaide and Tyler could overhear.

His blonde hair was straight and reached his collar. He squinted dark eyes against the bright sun as he studied her in the shadows of the front porch. "I hope I'm not disturbing you. I do apologize." Edward had crooked front teeth below a thick drooping mustache.

Tyler had a hint of Southern regionalism in his dialect, tempered by years at Harvard, but Edward took pride in his accent and emphasized the difference.

"I'd invite you inside, but we're in mourning." Cory pointed to the wreath of pinecones with a large, black ribbon on the opened front door.

"I'm sorry for your loss." He bowed. "My name is Edward Vandal from Vandalia, Virginia."

"Vandalia?" Cory blurted out. Tyler was from Vandalia.

His face remained bland. "It's named for my family. My grandfather fought with George Washington during the American Revolution and was rewarded with land in western Virginia."

"My ancestors were blacksmiths during the Revolution. They kept the men armed against the British. I'm Miss Courtney Beecher."

"Beecher?" Edward repeated. "The Connecticut Beechers?"

"Formerly of Connecticut. My father came to Ohio as a young man to practice medicine."

"Then you're not related to Harriet Beecher Stowe?"

"Have you read *Uncle Tom's Cabin*?"

Edward looked like he was going to be ill.

Cory was accustomed to this reaction from pro-slavery advocates and had devised a lighthearted reply. "We're both related to the first white man to die in Connecticut, John Beecher," she explained. "I believe Miss Stowe is a distant cousin, but I've never met her."

"I hope you are not prone to tales of fiction like your cousin. I would like some honest answers."

Cory lifted her chin. "No one has ever questioned my honesty."

He put one foot on the bottom step to the porch. "I'm looking for a young woman. She's in a bit of trouble, and I want to help her."

"Do you mean she's in a family way?" Cory whispered.

"No!" He hesitated. "But she has a baby with her."

"Yours?"

"Of course not! She's a servant girl. About eighteen. Have you seen them?"

Cory frowned. "I don't know. What does she look like?"

"She's petite with braided black hair and medium skin color. She goes by the name of Tess."

Cory shook her head. "I haven't seen anyone like that. Have you talked to Sheriff Carter? He takes note of any strangers in Darrow Falls."

"Yes, he said no one fitting that description has been seen around town, but he'd notify me if anyone reports seeing the girl and babe."

"He believes in upholding the law. I'm sure he'll help you if he can."

"I apologize for disturbing you." Edward stepped back and made a low elegant bow.

Cory had a nagging suspicion. "Mr. Vandal, why did you think she was here?"

"A man staying at the same inn I'm patronizing inquired about Glen Knolls. Has a stranger been by? He's tall, broad in the shoulders, and has steely blue eyes. His name is Tyler Montgomery."

Cory tried not to react. "Is he a runaway?"

"He's white trash," Edward said, "but fancies himself a gentleman."

Cory shook her head. "I don't know of anyone who fits that description."

"One more question, if I may. Have you seen a tall black man? Goes by the name of Noah."

She sighed and tapped her foot against the porch boards. "Another servant?"

"He belongs to Tyler," Edward said. "Noah ran away after my girl did. They might be together."

"Mr. Vandal, this is a farmhouse with a widow in mourning not the local tavern. We see few visitors unless you count Mr. Douglas Raymond. He's my suitor and hopefully, future husband."

"Congratulations, Miss Beecher."

"That's a little premature," she corrected. "He

hasn't proposed, yet."

"A lovely woman like you," he complimented. "He'd be a fool not to."

"Thank you. I'm afraid I've forgotten my manners. Would you or your men like something to drink?"

"We must be on our way." He nodded to the chasers, and they headed for their horses tied to the post under the elm.

"Good luck with your search," she called to him. "I'm sorry I couldn't help you more."

He turned. "Well, if you hear anything about them, I'm staying at the Darrow Falls Inn."

"Say hello to Mrs. Stone for me."

He paused on the slate walkway. "Mrs. Stone?"

"She and her husband own the Darrow Falls Inn."

"Oh, yes," he said. "She likes to talk."

Chapter Nine

Paula Stone loved to gab and placed great value on being the initial bearer of any news. Tyler must have asked her about Glen Knolls, which led him and Edward here. Cory watched as the three men rode off before she stepped inside. Tyler closed the door and leaned against it. He didn't look happy. "Do you enjoy torturing men? Why did you offer him a drink?"

"It would have been rude not to," she excused. "He said he was from Vandalia. The same as you. How well do you know him?"

"Edward and I lived in Vandalia most of our lives. I'm the one who broke his nose."

Adelaide sat in her rocker, the pistol in her lap. "Why did you ask Paula Stone about Glen Knolls?"

He looked at the desk near the window. "Where's the flier I brought?"

Cory searched the drawers.

"You placed it your apron pocket," Adelaide said.

Cory fetched the flier and handed it to Tyler. "Don't you know what your own flier says?"

"I didn't print this flier. Edward did."

"Why?"

"To find Tess. Noah left Vandalia to find her, and Edward has been trailing him. He put a bounty on his head."

Cory frowned. "Why not put a bounty on Tess?"

"He did, but people are sympathetic to a young woman with a child. They're more likely to turn in a big, strong man like Noah. In fact, they did. He was smart enough to fight the Cassell brothers, and the sheriff arrested him last week."

"That was a good thing?"

"The Cassell brothers could have taken him back to Virginia and sold him as a slave."

Cory shook her head. "I thought he was your slave?"

"It doesn't matter to chasers who are willing to kidnap and lie to make a profit. The sheriff threw him in the Akron city jail. I received a telegram from a lawyer named Sam Morris and came north to help Noah. But when I arrived at Sam's office, he had already freed Noah with a *writ of habeus corpus*."

"What's that?"

"It required Edward prove he owned Noah. He couldn't. So the sheriff freed Noah, but he disappeared. Now I need to find him before Edward does."

"How did you know to come here?" Adelaide asked.

"Noah left me a message." Tyler pointed to the flier in Cory's hands. "Turn it over. He gave this flier to Sam with instructions to give it to me when I arrived in Akron." He pointed at the carefully written letters.

"*Glen knows the way*," Cory read. "That's why you thought Glen Knolls was a person."

"I thought the farm was named for the owner like Vandalia is named for the Vandals."

"Your slave needs some help with his spelling," Adelaide remarked.

"He didn't want to be too obvious and reveal an

Underground Railroad station."

"Slaves can't read or write." Adelaide remained stone-faced. "You could have written the message."

"Mrs. Yoder schooled Noah secretly." He grinned at Cory. "He can read and write as good as any Northerner."

Tyler's charm wasn't working on Adelaide. She stabbed a crooked finger at him. "He's still your slave."

"By Virginia law, he's my slave, but I'm here to help him."

"Can't you help him more by letting him reach freedom?" Cory asked.

"I don't plan on stopping him," Tyler confessed. "I want to help him find Tess if he hasn't already and reach Canada."

"You're an awfully good con man, Tyler Montgomery," Adelaide said. "You sweet talk this young woman, and now you think you can convince me to tell you something that even threat of death won't pry from my lips."

Tyler reached into his trouser pocket and showed them a small metal horse. "When I was cleaning Nell's stall I found this. Noah made it for his son. He left it in the stall for me to find. He knows I'm here. Cory spoke my name in the barn last night, and I think he heard."

"If he knew it was you, why didn't he show himself?"

Tyler hesitated.

Cory recalled the series of events. She had spoken Tyler's name, followed by a noise in the stall, and the kiss.

"We didn't stay long in the barn," he excused. "This was the best way for him to contact me."

"Are you saying you're Noah's friend?" Adelaide demanded.

"Is that too hard to believe?" Tyler retorted. "Can black men and white men be friends? The Northerners want to free the slaves, but do they want to live side by side with them in the same towns? Go to the same churches? The same schools? Even those who want to abolish slavery, don't want to create an equal society."

"They want to ship them off to Africa," Adelaide agreed. "What do you think the slaves want?"

"What everyone wants in America," he answered. "An opportunity for a better life."

Adelaide nodded. "My grandfather was a tenant farmer in England without any hope of owning any land. He sent my father to America as an indentured servant when he was nine years old. He worked as an unpaid apprentice but eventually became skilled enough to work as a baker. He bought his own shop and sent for his father and mother to come to America. You can't escape the life you're born into over there. England abolished slavery, but they didn't abolish inequality. I can't predict what sort of life blacks will have if they're free, but we'll never know until they are free."

"I think we believe in the same goals."

"Time will tell," Adelaide said. "Now what can you tell us about Edward Vandal?"

Tyler waved the flier at them. "He's the sort of man who would lie and imprison a man to find a runaway girl and her babe."

"He asked about you," Cory recalled. "He didn't seem to like you very much."

"You remember the first girl I kissed?"

"Reggie Johnston."

"She's Edward's wife."

Reggie had been more than a young boy's infatuation. Tyler had been in love with her and heartbroken when Reggie married Edward. "So this is more than a runaway slave. This is personal."

"What do you mean?"

"You were both in love with the same woman."

Tyler shook his head. "Reggie made her choice."

She caressed his shoulder. "You must have been devastated."

"Any romance was over a long time ago," he said. "But Edward thinks otherwise, and Reggie never did anything to discourage his suspicions."

"Why not?"

He shrugged. "I don't even begin to understand the workings of a woman's mind. Maybe you would know why she would want to make Edward jealous by smothering me with attention when her heart was already set on him."

She understood and smiled. "She wanted him to notice her, and a man covets what belongs to someone else, especially if he's a rival."

"Edward was the prize catch as far as husbands go in Vandalia and didn't even notice Reggie until she made a big fuss over me."

"Like making you a vest," Cory guessed. "One like the vest Edward was wearing."

"I only wear it to irk him."

"But you didn't know he would come here."

"I knew I'd meet him at some point. We're both searching for the same people."

Cory studied Tyler. "But you're a lawyer. Why

didn't Reggie marry you?"

"I'm a lawyer now. I was a poor boy with ambitions three years ago, and Edward was the owner of the Silver Pheasant."

"What's the Silver Pheasant?"

"The largest farm in Vandalia," he replied. "It grows tobacco, corn, and slaves."

Cory frowned. "You can't grow slaves."

"You can if you breed them. Old man Cyrus Vandal was proficient at it."

Cory didn't understand the implications of his statement. Did he only encourage procreation or did he actively participate in it. "He forced himself on them?"

"Some as young as fourteen."

Cory gasped, and her hand covered her mouth. Did Edward follow his father's example? "Edward said Tess' baby wasn't his."

"No master admits he's fathered a child from a slave, but for once, Edward was telling the truth. Noah is Adam's father."

"Noah must be out of his mind with worry." Cory looked to Adelaide for confirmation. Adelaide gave her a warning look. "What happens if Edward finds them first?"

Tyler's voice was firm. "That's not going to happen."

"You'd help Tess escape to get back at Edward?" Adelaide asked.

Tyler grinned. "That wasn't the original plan, but I'd be happy with it."

"What about Noah?" Adelaide asked. "Won't it hurt you to lose him as a slave?"

"Noah isn't a slave."

"Edward said he was."

"Edward is wrong."

Cory wanted to believe him. She didn't want Tyler to be a slave owner, but Edward had known him all his life. Edward would know if he owned a slave, wouldn't he? Something deeper existed between the two men. A secret he wasn't willing to share.

"Why is Edward here in person?" Adelaide asked. "Why not leave the work to his chasers?"

"The Cassell brothers are big and strong, but they can't read or write. Besides, Tess is a valuable slave," Tyler explained. "She's a young woman who has proven she can bear children. She's worth at least a thousand dollars. More to a breeder."

Cory's jaw dropped. "One slave is worth so much? A person would have to earn twenty dollars a week to make the same amount in a year."

"In the last few years, the value of a slave increased along with the price of cotton and talk of emancipation. Why do you think the South would rather go to war than free the slaves? What man wants to give away thousands of dollars?" Tyler looked out the window. "That's the reason slavery still exists. It's become a way to finance crops, obtain a loan, and hold status in the South. A man with one slave is richer than ten men without slaves."

"Then all the talk about state rights is a lie?" Cory asked.

Tyler turned and looked her in the eye. "War is always about money, whether it's in the form of land, minerals, or human lives, but no common man would risk life and limb for a soldier's pay. They need a cause, an outrage, and the rhetoric of politicians to promote a war."

"Doesn't Edward have enough money? Why does he need to take Tess and her baby back to the Silver Pheasant?"

"Edward can't let Tess run away. Besides the monetary loss, it makes him look weak. The other slaves might try to run away if he doesn't take her back and punish her. He'll have to make an example of her. He'll hurt her to teach all the slaves a lesson." His voice was hard and cold. "It won't be pretty if he finds her first. She won't have it easy like she did."

"Easy?" Cory scoffed. "What do you mean?"

"Tess worked in the house instead of the fields. She was Reggie's personal maid and wet nurse to her son, Eddie."

"Reggie has a baby?"

Tyler shook his head. "Not anymore. Eddie died a few months ago." Tyler smacked his fist against the palm of his other hand. "Edward should be comforting Reggie instead of chasing after Tess and making trouble for Noah."

Cory searched his face. "What are you going to do?"

"Edward said he was staying at the Darrow Falls Inn." Tyler ran his fingers through his hair. "I need to return to my room for my belongings. I have some papers. If he gets his hands on them, it would cause trouble for Noah and me. Something Edward would love to do."

"Well, you can't retrieve them," Adelaide concluded. "Cory will have to go."

Tyler shook his head. "It could be dangerous."

The three stood in the parlor staring at each other.

It was Adelaide who broke the silence. "Cory will run my errands. I have several dishes that need to be returned to Paula. She can retrieve your bag," she suggested. "If Cory keeps the visit sociable and lighthearted, Edward won't suspect anything."

Cory felt as if Adelaide was giving her instructions on how to deceive the enemy. Adelaide was not only a supporter of the Underground Railroad, she was an active participant. She felt a new admiration for her and realized she had never backed any of her ideals with action. "I'll do it."

"This isn't a game," Tyler warned her.

Cory put her hands on her hips. "I'm a Beecher."

"Which you proudly proclaimed to Edward. You might as well have painted a target on your chest."

Cory caught him staring at her breast and crossed her arms.

"Men always underestimate women," Adelaide excused. "I'm sure Edward will underestimate Cory. How much money do you owe for your room?"

"About half a dollar."

"Give Cory the money and write a note to go along with it."

"For what?"

"Don't question your elders, young man." She pointed at the desk. "There's paper in the drawer."

Tyler removed a sheet of plain paper and sat at the desk. He dipped the quill in the glass ink well in the corner and looked at Adelaide. "What should I write?"

"Mrs. Stone," she began. "Thank you for your hospitality. I have been called away to Cleveland on urgent business. Enclosed is payment in full for my bill. Sincerely, Mr. Tyler Montgomery."

"Cleveland?"

"Isn't that where a slave would head?" Adelaide asked. "Don't you want to throw Edward off the trail?"

"But what if Noah *is* headed for Cleveland? I could be helping Edward."

"Trust me."

"Trust works both ways." Tyler finished the note. He blew on the ink to dry it and folded the paper with the payment inside. He lit a candle and added a drop of wax to seal it. He pressed the ring he wore on his pinkie finger to leave a mark.

Cory studied the impression. "What is that?"

"When I graduated from law school last July I had the ring made. It's the scales of justice. Edward will recognize it as mine."

"Go hitch Nell to the buggy, and we'll gather the dishes," Adelaide ordered.

Chapter Ten

The dishes had been accumulating on the shelves in the pantry since the funeral. They were washed with notes of gratitude handwritten by Adelaide for each contributor.

"You can leave most of them at the church," Adelaide instructed. "And make sure to invite the Reverend and Mrs. Davis to supper tonight."

"Why?" Cory asked. "The last thing we need are more visitors."

"Tell him I need some spiritual guidance."

"Are you all right?" Cory examined Adelaide for signs of illness. "Maybe I shouldn't leave you."

She patted her hand. "I'm fine, but I need to talk with him."

Cory gathered an armload of dishes and headed outside. Tyler led Nell close to the house. The buggy wasn't much more than a two-by-four-foot box on top of wheels, but the fold-back roof provided protection from the sun. She stored the dishes on the floor in back of the two-person seat.

Adelaide carried Cory's bonnet and its contents along with a few more dishes. "These are for Paula."

Tyler put the bowls and tins under the seat. "You have a lot of dishes."

Adelaide handed the bonnet to Cory. "The people of Darrow Falls like to help."

"You're fond of this town," Tyler said.

"It's been my home for a long time." Adelaide looked around. "Hiram and I came here right after we were married. He was a surveyor and skilled carpenter. We built this place from nothing. I'm going to miss my farm."

"You're selling the place?"

"I'm moving in with my daughter at the end of next month."

Cory put on her bonnet. "You can visit."

"I can't visit if strangers buy the farm," she said. "Too bad I don't know a young couple starting out on life's journey."

"Maybe Douglas will buy it," she suggested.

"Mr. and Mrs. Raymond will have to live on the college campus."

Cory hadn't thought about that.

"The morning is half spent," Adelaide said. "You better head out."

"How long will you be gone?" Tyler asked.

Cory smiled. "Are you going to miss me?"

"I should leave as soon as you retrieve my valise."

His words wiped the smile from her face. Why was she conflicted about wanting him to stay or go? If he was leaving to help Noah, didn't that mean they believed in the same thing?

"Will you tell me where I can find Noah?" Tyler asked Adelaide.

"We'll see. While you wait, you can do some chores. The wagon wheels need greased, and the garden needs weeding." She looked at the two young people. "I have some tasks to do in the house."

Tyler turned to Cory. "Are you sure you want to do

this? I can take my chances with Edward."

She wasn't helpless. "I'm quite capable of retrieving some documents."

"I'm sorry for involving you in this. I'll be out of your life as soon as possible."

"It's not like you have any reason to stay." Cory wished he would deny it.

"You'll be glad I'm gone. You and Douglas can plan your future, and I can try to start a law practice somewhere in Canada."

"Canada? You're not going back to Vandalia?"

"When Noah left, I knew he couldn't return. I sold everything. There's nothing left in Vandalia for me now."

"What's in Canada?"

He looked around at the farm. "I bet nothing like this, but I've disrupted your well-ordered lives since I arrived."

She didn't want him to leave on unfriendly terms. "You haven't been *too* much trouble."

Tyler watched as she put on her gloves. "You've been a whole lot of trouble to me."

"What do you mean?" she demanded. "I said I shot you accidentally. Besides, it was a flesh wound. You can't hold that against me. If you hadn't grabbed the gun, it wouldn't have gone off. At least I took care of you and didn't make you walk to the inn. You ought to be grateful instead of finding fault with me."

"I'd silence you with a kiss, but Adelaide might be watching like before." He nodded toward the kitchen window.

Cory saw a movement behind the curtain. Did he think he could kiss her any time he liked? "What makes you think I'd let you kiss me?"

Tyler leaned in close. "The way you kissed me in the barn this morning."

"You kissed me," she excused. "I couldn't get away."

Tyler laughed. "Honey, you didn't try very hard."

He spoke the truth, and his overconfidence was insulting to her feminine mystique. Men needed to win a woman's affection. She'd been an easy conquest, and now he had no reason to stay. Once she retrieved his belongings, he would be gone and out of her life. Cory held out her hand. "Where's the letter?"

Tyler gave it to her along with a key. "Room three. It's off the breezeway on the first floor."

She secured the letter and key in her handbag dangling on her wrist. "Where should I look for your belongings?"

"I didn't unpack except for a few personal items on the dresser. Don't let Edward see my valise. He may recognize it. Gold-lettered initials," he explained.

"What should I do if he does?"

"I don't want you to take any chances," Tyler said. "Let him have it. Tell him I left it behind."

Cory was confused by his answer. She knew the papers were important. "Are you sure?"

He offered his hand to assist her into the carriage. "You're risking enough, darling."

She missed the metal step into the carriage as she registered the endearment he had spoken. Tyler caught her around the waist as she slipped. "I like your natural curves much better," he whispered in her ear as his hand rested against the hard corset.

Cory realized the undergarment created a sturdy

barrier between his hand and her flesh. So why was her heart beating so rapidly? She closed her eyes and wondered if he would kiss her.

"You better hurry." He helped her into the carriage and handed her the reins. "Not too fast and yield to the big wagons."

Cory frowned. "This isn't my first buggy ride."

He patted her knee. "Get going."

Cory chewed on her bottom lip. Why hadn't he kissed her? First Douglas and now Tyler. What was wrong with her?

****

Cory dropped off several empty dishes at neighboring farmhouses on her way into town. Everyone asked how Adelaide was doing. Cory made brief, pleasant talk and thanked the women for the meals. It was nearly noon before she arrived at the center of Darrow Falls where the road intersected with Church Street and River Road to form the town square. The Community Congregational Church was on the north side of Church Street. The cemetery was next to it, and the funeral parlor was beyond Mill Street, which formed the eastern side of the square. Town Hall was built facing north on River Road, the southern border of the town square. Sheep grazed on the large expanse of grass surrounded by businesses and homes.

The Town Hall was built of local sandstone and was two stories high above a cellar that served as a jail. Town meetings and business transactions were conducted on the main floor. Offices for the mayor, his clerk, and the sheriff were on the upper floor. The mayor settled most local issues. Anything more important than a drunken brawl or bill of sale was settled by the Court of Common Pleas in Akron.

Cory tied Nell opposite the church under a tree along the edge of the town square. She saw the Reverend Lawrence Davis talking with two women.

Adelaide wanted her to invite the Reverend Davis and his family for supper. She would never get away with a brief visit. The Reverend liked to hear the sound of his own voice even when he wasn't in the pulpit.

"Miss Beecher!" His voice boomed across the square.

Cory glanced around, anticipating Edward's appearance in response to the cannon-like proclamation of her name.

The two women greeted her and made excuses for leaving. Cory thought they looked relieved.

"Look at all the dishes." He examined them more closely. "They're empty."

"Adelaide is returning them," she explained. "I was hoping to leave them in the foyer where people can claim them when they come for the holiday celebration Wednesday."

"I'm working on my message for Independence Day as we speak. Mary! Beth!" he called out. "I'll have the women help you unload the dishes. I must resume my work."

Cory wondered if he would have put off writing his mid-week sermon if the dishes had contained food. The Reverend Davis was more than double the size of most men.

Mary appeared in a dull gray dress that strained at the seams. Mary enjoyed company and food as much as her husband.

Beth was the opposite of her parents in girth. She

had a willowy figure, and her dress was ill-fitted on her slender frame. Her straw-colored hair and pale complexion added to her delicate appearance. Blondes were in fashion, and Beth had the coloring and disposition to be popular. She never had a harsh word for anyone and was always the first to volunteer her services.

Cory should have hated her, especially since she had been Douglas' first choice for a wife. But Beth had turned twenty-one, a landmark age for a woman. She was considered a spinster by Darrow Falls' standards. Cory couldn't understand why she had refused Douglas when she appeared to have no other prospects.

"You're all invited to supper tonight." Maybe she'd have an opportunity to speak with Beth alone about Douglas.

The Reverend reappeared, some pages in his hand. "Supper?"

Cory recalled her instructions. "Miss Adelaide needs some spiritual guidance."

"Spiritual guidance," he repeated. "We'll be happy to come."

"I hope you don't mind the late invitation." Cory handed Beth several bowls.

"What about those?" Beth read the name on the card for the dishes stacked in the front. "I'm sure Mrs. Stone will be by Wednesday if you want to leave her dishes here."

"It's not out of my way."

"Paula has quite a few interesting visitors." Mary lowered her voice. "Strangers from the South."

The two biggest gossips in town had probably spent hours discussing Edward Vandal and his men.

"Maybe they're in town for the holiday," Cory suggested.

"Not these men." Mary carried a few dishes inside. "Chasers if you ask me."

Cory feigned surprise. "Chasers?"

The pastor's family lived on the lower level of the church. Mary arranged the dishes on a narrow table in the foyer between the twin staircases to the second floor sanctuary. "I don't like it one bit. We're a peaceful community. Why can't they stay home where they belong instead of coming to our town and upsetting everyone?"

Beth patted her mother's plump hand. "They'll be gone soon enough, Mother."

****

Dinner and an hour later Cory took the short ride along Darrow Falls Road to the corner of River Road. Darrow Falls Inn was a two-story building painted a bright red with an abundance of gingerbread trim. An open breezeway provided access to private rooms on the first floor. One of them was Tyler's. To the left was the main entrance with a kitchen and large dining room. A wrap-around porch provided an area for boarders to sit and chat with travelers on the roads through downtown.

Darrow Falls Inn was a scheduled stop for the stagecoach traveling east to west along River Road. A barn with stables and a corral was behind the inn. The nearby train depot added to the clientele. The public house attracted travelers and the latest news.

Paula Stone greeted her. She was a stout woman with a face full of freckles and a high round forehead. "Jennifer Beecher." She waved as she bustled down the steps.

"No, I'm Courtney."

"But you're one of the Beecher girls, right?"

"Yes. I'm the oldest."

"I never can keep you girls straight."

"No one can." Although each one of them had a different hair color, they were grouped together as the Beecher girls. Even Paula, who had witnessed them traveling from the Beecher farm past her inn to the downtown for years, failed to match a name to a face. What happened to one Beecher girl, happened to all. And as the oldest, Cory set the example for her younger sisters.

"What brings you to my humble abode, Courtney?"

Cory hardly considered Darrow Falls Inn humble. Paula was known for her hospitality. Her elaborate meals filled the dining hall with diners from far and near.

"I'm staying with Adelaide and wanted to return some of your dishes. She was grateful for the meals you sent." She handed Paula the note inside one of the empty bowls.

"I figured she wouldn't eat unless someone put something in front of her." Paula took the dishes and placed them on a table. "Why don't you stay for lunch? I always make plenty."

"I've already dined with the Reverend Davis and his family, and I should return to the farm and help Adelaide." She looked around. Edward and his men weren't among the guests sipping coffee and eating dessert.

Paula read the lines Adelaide had penned. "Such a lovely note. It's such a shame she has to move away now that Hiram has passed."

"She's going to miss Darrow Falls and all her friends." Cory lowered her voice. "Would it be all right if I used your outhouse before leaving? It's a long drive back to Glen Knolls."

Paula looked at her hooped skirt. "You could use one of the chamber pots in an empty room."

"The outhouse is good enough." Cory pressed in the collapsible crinoline to show she could fit inside the privy. "Behind the barn?"

"Near the hollyhocks. If your skirt doesn't fit, there might be some clean pots nearby. Or do like I did when I was a girl and squat in the weeds."

Cory headed for the outhouse. Once out of sight, she turned toward the open hallway. The number three was painted in white against the red door. She reached into her purse and removed Tyler's key. She glanced around and listened for any footsteps on the wooden floor. Hearing none, she inserted the key, turned it, and entered.

Chapter Eleven

Tyler's valise rested on a storage chest at the foot of the bed. "*TGM*" were imprinted in gold letters on the brown leather. The case had hinges like her father's medical bag and opened wide to expose the contents. Several ties and socks were on top of a white shirt. A brown packet was stuck along one side. She reached in, hesitated, and retrieved it. Inside were legal documents. Tess' name was on the top one. The legal language was confusing, but the paper appeared to grant her freedom.

Several signatures were on the bottom of the document. One was Tyler's. Another was Regina Vandal's. She folded the documents but hesitated to return them to the valise. She unbuttoned her dress and forced the packet beneath her corset cover.

She gathered a brush, razor, soap, and toothbrush near the washstand and added them to Tyler's bag. The dresser drawers were empty. She left Tyler's note and payment on top of the dresser with the key.

Cory cautiously opened the door, saw no one around, and headed for her buggy. She put Tyler's bag on the floor and spread her skirt over it. "Giddy-up." She slapped the reins against Nell's hindquarters and directed her down the drive.

Edward and his two companions nearly collided with her when they turned onto the curved path toward the inn. Their horses startled Nell. Cory struggled to calm her. "Easy, girl."

Edward grabbed Nell's harness until she quieted. "I'm so sorry we startled your horse, Miss Beecher." He tipped his hat.

"We usually don't have this much traffic on the road." She hoped her voice didn't sound as nervous to Edward as it did to her.

"Out for a ride?"

"I was returning some dishes," Cory explained. "So many people provided meals for Mrs. Thomas after her husband died. This was my last stop. Mrs. Stone is an excellent cook. You must know that since you're staying here." She was rambling.

"She is a good cook, but not as good as my wife."

The pride in his voice startled her. "Is she traveling with you?" She knew the answer but was curious about Reggie.

"No, my wife is home in Vandalia," he said. "We recently lost our child."

"I'm sorry. That can be a difficult time for a couple."

"How would you know? Have you ever lost a child?"

His angry outburst frightened her, but she quickly defended her words. "My father is a doctor. I've helped with patients, especially during childbirth." She recalled a birth last spring. "In April I delivered a stillbirth. We tried everything, but the baby never took a breath. It's the last thing a couple expects after nine months of happy expectations."

Edward studied her. "I'm sorry for my rudeness. Our son died from a fever. Regina was inconsolable after Eddie's death. How do you comfort someone who only wants to mourn?"

Cory hesitated to answer, but the pain in his voice evoked her empathy. He was Tyler's enemy, but she offered some advice. "Everyone mourns differently, but don't let Reggie shut you out. Whatever her feelings, she needs to share them with someone. It's the only way she'll be able to deal with her grief. And someday, you'll have more children."

Edward had a strange expression on his face. Was he surprised by her sage advice? Or had she said something wrong? She'd called Regina, Reggie, the name Tyler used for her. She looked at Edward, met his gaze, and knew she had betrayed Tyler.

Edward nodded toward Buck, who circled the buggy. He stopped behind Cory. "Mr. Vandal, there's a bag under the seat."

"Grab it."

Buck dismounted. He was a bulky man with thick hairy hands and stubby fingers. He climbed on the carriage step and tugged at Cory's skirts.

"What are you doing?" She kicked at him, but he grabbed her foot and jerked her body aside. He reached for the valise beneath her seat.

Cory looked around for something to defend herself and grabbed the buggy whip from its holder. She smacked Buck with the long wooden handle. "Get off!"

"Clyde!" Edward called the man with a white scar on the side of his face.

Clyde reached from his saddle and wrenched the whip from Cory's hands, nearly unseating her. He handed the whip to Edward. He broke it in two and tossed it on the ground.

Cory caught her breath as she clung to the side of the buggy. No wonder Tyler disliked Edward. All his polite manners hid a nasty stray dog. She glanced around for help but saw no one.

"Got it?"

Buck pulled out the leather bag and jumped to the ground. He handed it to Edward, who searched through the contents. He tossed the clothes and personal articles on the ground until the valise was empty. He shook it at her. "Where did you get this?"

Cory trembled at the violence of their actions. Why did men have to use brute force to take what they wanted? No wonder men were eager for war. Cory calmed her nerves and thought of a lie for her possession of Tyler's personal belongings. "Mrs. Stone gave me the bag to donate to the Community Congregational Church." Her words were rushed. "She said the tenant left without it." She climbed down and began gathering the discarded clothing and items. "No one is going to want to wear them if they're all dirty."

Edward dismounted and held the empty valise open. She hastily folded the suit and shirt and dropped the remaining items on top. He snapped the brass clasp and shoved the bag under the seat. He held out his hand. She ignored it and turned to board the carriage.

"Your purse." He pointed to the handbag dangling from her wrist.

"I hardly think there's anything of interest in my handbag."

Edward snatched the purse and opened it. Cory grabbed for it, but he turned his back and rifled through the contents. He faced her and returned her bag.

Her fingers trembled, but she counted the coins

inside. It was a small gesture to show him how she felt about his behavior.

"I'm not a thief." He offered his hand to assist her into the carriage, but she refused again.

Cory's bonnet had fallen back during the confrontation. She rearranged it and tied the ribbons. The men still surrounded her buggy. "May I leave now?"

Edward rested his hand on Nell's harness. "What was the name of the tenant who left behind his valise?"

She'd betrayed Tyler with her overconfidence. She needed to be cautious, or she could put everyone in jeopardy. "Ask Mrs. Stone if the owner's name is important to you."

"I will, but I think you know his name."

Cory looked straight ahead. Her voice trembled. "Why do you say that?"

Edward pointed at the bag. "Those initials belong to the man I asked about. He calls my wife, Reggie. The same as you did a minute ago." He patted Nell's shoulder. "I like you Miss Beecher, and I'm going to give you some advice. Stay away from Tyler Montgomery. He's no good for you or any woman."

Cory gripped the reins. "Are you an expert on character, Mr. Vandal?"

"Oh, I'm a very good judge of character when it comes to Tyler Montgomery," he warned. "Don't let him seduce you with his lies, Miss Beecher. Has he told you he's a Harvard educated lawyer? Or has he regaled you with the story about being raised by Quakers? Tricks of deception, Miss Beecher. An education and peace-loving guardians have done nothing to make him a gentleman. No one knows about his father, but everyone in Vandalia knew about his mother." Edward snorted. "Ask him about a woman called Miss Olivia. Ask him about the Dunking Witch. Tyler Montgomery is a bastard, a liar, and not fit for the company of decent folks. You should stay clear of him."

Cory felt numb by his revelations. It couldn't be true. "Those are harsh words, Mr. Vandal."

"You better heed them, Miss Beecher." He released Nell and moved aside.

Cory wasted no time urging Nell forward. She started to cry and swiped at her wet cheeks. Tyler had a past he hadn't revealed. All his teasing and playfulness seemed tainted. Tyler had warned her no decent woman would marry him, but she hadn't taken his words seriously. What sort of man was Tyler, and what did she truly know about him?

Anger replaced her tears. How could she be so stupid? He was a slave owner. That alone was reason enough not to become attached to him. How could she have kissed him? She was a fool. Douglas may be boring, but he was honest. He would never deceive a woman with hopes of love or pretend he was something he was not. Thank goodness she hadn't fallen in love with Tyler. She would gladly hand over his belongings and send him on his way.

****

Cory reached Glen Knolls and saw Tyler in the garden, hoeing the rows to remove the weeds. It was something she hated doing and had neglected. He raised his head and smiled at her. It took her breath away. Why was he so handsome? Why did her heart jump for joy every time she looked at him? And why did Edward's words make her so troubled?

Tyler strode toward the barn and slid open the wide door for her to drive Nell into the upper storage area. He grabbed Nell's harness to halt her. "Any problems?"

Cory had calmed her nerves on the ride home but was glad it was dark in the barn. She had proven she was an incompetent liar with Edward and would have to tell Tyler the truth. She struggled to steady her voice. "Edward and his men stopped me as I was leaving the inn."

Tyler jerked around. "Did he harm you?"

"No. His men scared me, and Edward broke the whip." She pointed at the empty holder.

He unhitched Nell from the buggy. "Anything else?"

"They searched your bag and threw your clothes everywhere. I'll clean them," she promised.

"I never should have allowed you to go into town alone," he shouted. "This isn't your battle."

"Allowed me?" Cory's anger matched his. "I volunteered."

"What happened to my bag?"

She lifted it from the floorboard and handed it to him.

He opened it and felt inside. "Does Edward have the papers?"

Cory turned to step down from the carriage. "No, they're in a safe place."

Tyler grabbed her around the waist before she could jump down. His hands caressed her corset as he lowered her to the ground. "I think I know where you hid them."

She stepped away. "I almost put them back in the valise."

"So you read them?"

"I'm not very good at Latin."

"All those old phrases are for job security," he explained. "I spent two years learning legal jargon to confuse clever school teachers like you."

"You think I'm clever?"

"Clever enough to keep Edward from finding the documents. Now are you going to hand them over, or do I have to go on a treasure hunt?"

Cory should have been shocked by his suggestion, but after Edward's revelations, she wondered if Tyler talked to all women the way he had been teasing and flirting with her. Tyler Montgomery was a rake. She toyed with the top button of her gown. "Turn around."

Tyler obeyed. "You know I've seen you in your nightie."

"It was dark."

"Not that dark."

She slapped the packet against his shoulder. "So what are the papers for?"

He pointed at her dress. "You missed a button."

She fastened it. When she looked up, he was staring at her bodice. She directed his attention to something more important. "The papers?"

"This makes it clear Noah is a free man."

"Why didn't you give them to Noah in Vandalia when he left to look for Tess?"

"He was in a hurry. I didn't have time to draw up legal documents like these. I wrote him a pass stating he was free, but as I said before, it doesn't mean much if chasers knock him out and take him south where he can be sold for several thousand dollars."

Cory wasn't sure she had heard correctly. "How

much?"

"Noah is a skilled blacksmith. He's strong, smart, and could be sold for three thousand dollars or more in an open slave market. That's why it's so dangerous for him to be on his own. I should have come north with him to look for Tess, but I knew he'd need money. I stayed behind and sold off everything we owned."

"We?"

Tyler smacked the packet against his thigh. "Noah had his own workbench and tools in Mr. Yoder's blacksmith shop. I sold some and crated the rest. Once Noah is settled, I'll have Mr. Yoder ship them to him."

Cory looked at the document in Tyler's hand. "And this proves he's free."

"This is a legal document the local authorities won't question. I can't say the same about the commissioners."

"Why not?"

"Commissioners are paid ten dollars to say a black man is a slave. They're paid five for saying he's not a runaway. It's amazing how an extra five dollars will put shackles on a free man."

"How unfair!"

"That's why the Fugitive Slave Law is such an abomination. A free black can be forced back into slavery. They've been doing the same thing in Virginia since 1806. If a freed black man or woman doesn't leave the state within a year, freedom is revoked."

"You're lucky Sam Morris stopped Edward from taking Noah."

"I owe him," Tyler admitted. "Sam said the local sheriff is more sympathetic than federal marshals. That's why the commissioners have the power to fine local judges and sheriffs if they don't comply with the law." He grinned. "But they don't like being strong armed."

"So Noah is safe," Cory concluded.

"If chasers find him with Tess, he can be arrested for aiding a runaway." He tapped on the packet. "These papers should convince any chasers except the Cassell brothers that Noah and Tess are free. The problem is the flier Edward sent out. A hundred fifty dollar reward for news about Noah would tempt any man. That's why Noah can't search for Tess in the open, but I can."

"Won't you lead Edward to Tess?"

"I don't know where Tess is." He studied her. "Do you?"

"No." Did he believe her? She wondered about something in the packet. "I saw a paper with her name on it. It had Reggie's name on it, too. Did she set her free?"

"That's the problem. Only Edward can legally free Tess and Adam, but I was hoping the documents would fool local inquiries."

"Won't having the false papers cause trouble for you?"

Tyler didn't answer. He didn't have to.

Chapter Twelve

Cory felt emotionally drained. Tyler was a slave owner who had given Noah his freedom. He was defying the law, the very thing he had trained for and sworn to uphold, to give freedom to Tess and Adam. And the one person determined to stop him was Edward Vandal. And she was caught in the middle of it. "But you could lose your right to practice law. Why would you risk that?"

"I know what I'm doing." He removed Nell's bridle and replaced it with a halter to lead her out of the barn. "It's you and Adelaide I'm worried about. Don't you know how much of a risk you're taking helping runaways?"

"Six months in jail and a thousand dollar fine if we know the person is a runaway," she replied. "Otherwise it's Christian charity."

Tyler opened the gate to the pasture. *"Actus reus non facit reum nisi mens sit rea."*

"What does that mean?"

"Same thing you said, but doesn't it sound more important in Latin?"

Cory looked around. "Won't Edward fetch the sheriff now that he knows you're here?"

Tyler froze. "Does he know?"

Cory's shoulders sagged. "I used the name Reggie instead of Regina when I spoke to him." She sighed.

"I'm not clever after all."

Tyler led Nell inside the fenced pasture and released her halter. "I won't put you or Adelaide in danger. I should leave immediately."

Cory accepted his inevitable departure but needed to discover the truth. His character would determine whether his kiss would be banished or cherished in her memories of him. "Edward slandered your name."

Tyler secured the gate as Nell grazed. "That doesn't surprise me. You heard him call me white trash, but if he's the measure of a gentleman, then I'm glad he doesn't consider me an equal. He's arrogant and cruel."

Cory didn't know any way to ease into the topic. "Who's Miss Olivia?"

Tyler ran his fingers through his hair, a nervous habit she was beginning to recognize. "What did Edward say about her?"

"He said to ask you about her. Is she your mother?"

****

Tyler kicked the fence post so hard some of the bark fell away. "She *was* my mother." He wrestled with what to tell her. He wanted Cory to like him. He didn't want to see the look of disgust he had seen on women's faces when he had confessed the truth before. Even Reggie had looked at him differently after the revelation of his ancestry.

"I told you there were reasons no respectable woman would marry me. Miss Olivia was one of them."

Cory rested her hand on his arm. "You don't have to tell me."

Tyler searched her eyes for a sign of understanding. He paced with the nervous energy of a caged animal. "If I don't, Edward will. He delights in revealing my sordid family history." He jammed his fists into his pockets. "When I was seven, my father, Grayson Montgomery, abandoned us."

"Why?"

"The reason doesn't matter." Tyler paused when he saw Cory's confused expression. Half-truths were no better than lies. "Miss Olivia lied to him about something he couldn't forgive."

"Oh," she gasped. "I understand."

Tyler doubted she had guessed the truth. "You understand what?"

"Another man."

She was wrong, but her mistake was easier to accept. He walked along the pasture fence, and Cory kept pace. "Miss Olivia didn't have many choices," Tyler remarked quietly. "She had run away from home when she was fifteen and couldn't go back. When she left, she took some jewelry and her personal maid, Lydia. She sold the jewelry and hired Lydia out after Noah was born to pay the rent and bills. Then she met Grayson Montgomery."

"Were they married?" Cory asked.

Tyler cocked an eyebrow. "Edward called me a bastard, huh? He enjoys spreading false rumors. My parents were married. Grayson was a quiet, respectable banker, and we had a comfortable life. I remember he was a good father, then."

"What happened?"

"There was a scandal involving missing funds at the bank. Grayson lost his job."

"Was he guilty?"

Tyler shrugged. "I don't know, but others thought

so. He couldn't find work and started drinking. Grayson wanted to sell Lydia and Noah, but Miss Olivia refused. Then one day we returned from the store, and Lydia was gone. Grayson had sold her. It was his right," he explained.

"He wanted to sell Noah, too, but Miss Olivia wouldn't allow it. They fought, and Grayson hit her." Tyler recalled the images of the nightmare. "I remember Noah and I tried to stop the beating, but he shoved us outside and locked the door. We could hear her screams as his fists connected with her flesh. We thought he was going to kill her and fetched a neighbor. When we returned, Grayson was gone, and Miss Olivia was covered in blood, barely alive."

The memory angered him. "No man, drunk or sober, has the right to harm any woman. Grayson left town and took all the money he'd received from the sale of Lydia. We couldn't buy her back."

"Poor Noah. Did he ever see his mother again?"

Tyler hesitated. "No. We moved to Vandalia. It was a small secluded town in western Virginia where no one knew us. Noah and I moved in with the Yoders."

"And your mother?"

Tyler grinded the words out. "She found a job."

"At the Dunking Witch?"

He sucked in his breath. "You and Edward had quite a talk."

"What kind of place is the Dunking Witch?"

It was the moment of truth. "A saloon and a whorehouse in a mining town where the men outnumber the women five to one." Tyler watched the myriad of emotions cross her face. It was too late to stop now, and no reason to sugarcoat his story. She would be glad when he was gone. "There aren't many ways a woman can make a living." He shook his head. "My mother entertained men at the Dunking Witch. She eventually became its owner." How much detail did she need? "I never saw her."

"Never?"

"Nearly never," he amended. "That's the way she wanted it. The Dunking Witch was across the river from town. You had to ride the ferry to reach it. When Miss Olivia left Noah and me with the Yoders, she ordered us never to use the ferry. She dropped her surname so nobody knew Miss Olivia was my mother except for the Yoders, and they kept her secret. They offered to take her in as well, but she wouldn't accept charity. She paid the Yoders to care for Noah and me so we wouldn't be a burden."

"But didn't you work for him?" she recalled.

"The Yoders didn't believe in sloth. The money paid for our food and clothes, but we worked around the farm, and Mr. Yoder taught Noah to be a blacksmith."

"Didn't you work as a blacksmith in the summers?"

He chuckled. "Do you remember everything I say?"

Cory blushed.

He was flattered by her interest. Most people listened to conversations only to add comments or switch to a topic of their own. "I learned enough to help out when I came home from school, but Noah was a craftsman."

"Did Mr. Yoder get into trouble for teaching a

slave a trade?"

"It's not against the law, and blacksmiths are valued in any community," he reminded her. "It was one of the reasons Miss Olivia chose the Yoders to raise us. She was intelligent about some decisions," he conceded.

"Then Noah was never treated like a slave," Cory realized. "Is that why you said he wasn't a slave?"

What should he tell her to explain Noah's status? Tyler debated his answer. "I explained a freed slave has to leave Virginia. An adult can petition the court to remain. By the time Noah was twenty-one, it was easier to be a slave."

"Why would he want to be a slave?"

"Vandalia was Noah's home. He was learning a respected trade, and the Yoders offered protection from being sold."

"What about Tess?" Cory asked.

He'd forgotten the most important reason. "Tess and Adam kept him in Virginia until she ran away."

They had reached the end of the fence. "How did Edward find out Miss Olivia was your mother?"

Cory was relentless in her pursuit of answers. Tyler turned back toward the house. "Edward's father, the great Cyrus Vandal, was a frequent visitor to the Dunking Witch. When I was fourteen, Cyrus decided he wanted to marry Miss Olivia. I guess she thought she wanted to marry him, too, because she claimed me as her son. Cyrus told Edward he was going to have a stepbrother." He snorted. "One big happy family."

Tyler chose his words carefully. "Only problem was Edward didn't like the idea of having a whore as his stepmother and made his feelings public. He was almost three years older, but I stood up to him. I don't know why. I hadn't acknowledged the existence of Miss Olivia in seven years, but I demanded an apology. He refused. I threw a lucky punch and broke his nose. He started pounding on me, and Noah pulled him off. That's when Cyrus took a whip to us. All three of us."

****

Cory didn't know what to say. Edward and Tyler had almost become brothers. Then they had been in love with the same woman. Now, they were searching for Noah and Tess. Edward would take Tess back to Vandalia. If he did, Tyler and Noah would follow no matter what the risks. She was a spectator in a drama that had been playing for a long time.

Tyler shrugged. "I lost the battle but won the war. The marriage was called off. Edward became my sworn enemy, and everyone knew Miss Olivia was my mother."

"Didn't the truth make it easier?"

"Easier being a pariah? My number of friends shrank considerably when mothers deemed me unsuitable as a playmate." He headed for the pump to wash. "After the fight with Edward, Miss Olivia decided it was time for me to attend a good academy for a proper education. She wrote me every month. I only opened the missives because she enclosed money with each one." He stopped at the pump, worked the handle until water flowed, and splashed some on his face and neck. "I wasn't a very good son."

"She put you in a difficult situation."

"I was ashamed of her. How can a son be ashamed of his mother?"

Cory had helped her father care for a prostitute

who had been brutalized by one of her customers. Although prostitution had been around since the beginning of time, society was beginning to sympathize with women who had to earn a living by selling their bodies. Beautiful young women became mistresses or courtesans to wealthy benefactors. Brothels supported unfortunate women who had no home but were still attractive enough to demand money for their companionship. The old, deformed, or diseased women walked the streets, hoping a man would part with a few coins for a moment of pleasure.

"You said it yourself. Society doesn't give a woman a lot of choices, especially if she doesn't have a father or husband to take care of her." Cory recalled his words. "You said she *was your* mother. Is Miss Olivia dead?"

"She died in January. When I spoke of the fate that took me from Brennan, Brewster, and Waxman, it was a letter from Mr. Yoder telling me she was ill and asking to see me. I informed the law firm I needed to go home, but they asked for an explanation. I didn't want to answer their questions so I quit."

"Wouldn't they have understood?"

"You forget the requirement of moral character for a lawyer," Tyler said. "In Boston it applies to a lawyer's father, mother, and wife. Any hint of scandal and no job."

"That's ridiculous."

Tyler shrugged. "It doesn't matter. I returned to Vandalia and spent Christmas with Miss Olivia. She filled in the blanks of her life I had been too young to remember or understand. I didn't know how to feel. I hated and loved her at the same time." He ran his fingers through his damp hair. "I made the funeral arrangements. I figured it would be poorly attended."

Tyler looked out over the yard. "I was wrong. No one cared she was a fallen woman but me. In fact, everyone loved her. Not in the carnal sense," he added when she gasped. "She had a strength I didn't understand or appreciate."

"What do you mean?"

"I know respectable women think saloons and whorehouses are the devil's playhouse, but she knew her customers better than they knew themselves. Men with tempers spent the night at the Dunking Witch instead of going home and slamming their fists into a wife or child. She would take half the pay from a man and give it to his wife before he drank or gambled it all away. Then there were the miners. She provided showers and made special soap to scrub the coal dust off before they returned home to one room shacks so their skin wouldn't break out in sores. She fed the hungry and gave shelter to any woman in trouble. The preacher in Vandalia admitted the Dunking Witch did more good than his church."

She didn't believe him. "You're joking!"

Tyler crossed his heart. "She was loved by everyone but her son."

Cory understood why his story had been difficult to share, and she knew it had been true except for the last part. "Liar. You're proud of her."

Tyler shook his head. "If I'm so proud, why didn't I tell you about her? You had to hear it from Edward."

"We've only met," Cory reminded him. She thought of his warnings, his outrageous behavior, and his kisses. "Maybe you wanted to make a good impression."

"Oh, I made a great impression calling late at night, scaring you into shooting me, and then putting you in the middle of my fight with Edward. I'll wager Douglas' family has no shocking revelations."

Cory didn't answer. She knew so little about Douglas. She wondered if Beth had turned down his proposal because of some dark secret he had confided. A secret he had not shared with her. Cory was equally apprehensive about Tyler. Why had he bothered sharing so much of his life with her? It was unfair. Tyler had a mission, and she was a minor distraction in his quest toward his goal. He would be gone soon, and she would be left alone to pick up the broken pieces of her life.

"I shouldn't have said anything. A respectable woman can only overlook so much. The women in New England overlook nothing. They pride themselves on long family histories and family wealth. They look for the same in husbands," he said. "Even Reggie wouldn't settle for a poor country lawyer with questionable parentage. She wanted a rich farmer like Edward with ancestors back to the American Revolution."

"I prefer honesty to lies." Cory heard Adelaide call her name from the back doorway. "I better help Adelaide with supper. The Reverend Davis will be arriving soon."

Chapter Thirteen

Cory heard the Reverend's loud voice outside as he called "whoa" to his team of horses. She studied her image in the mirror over the sideboard. Her braids weren't as neat as they had been earlier, but she didn't have time to redo her hair. She examined her dress and found a stain on her sleeve. Maybe nobody would notice. She felt exhausted from the day's activities and prayed the Reverend and his family didn't stay long after supper.

Cory heard Tyler's footsteps on the stairs. He wore the dark suit Edward had thrown on the ground. Between cooking and cleaning, she had brushed the wool clean and pressed it free of wrinkles. His long hair curled about a clean white shirt. She admired the tall, wide-shouldered man. No matter who his parents were, they had produced a handsome son.

"I bought this suit for court," Tyler excused. "Do I look overdressed?"

"Not at all." She wished she had something nicer to wear. Her day dresses showed the scars of repeated use. She'd have to make some new ones soon.

He stared over her head in the mirror. "Is my tie straight?"

"No." She took the ends and retied it. Tyler smelled of soap. He had shaved the stubble from his chin and upper lip, and Cory stared at his mouth in between. He had a delicious mouth, and she recalled what it felt like to have his lips crushed against hers. She tried to image Douglas making love to her. Nothing. Maybe if she closed her eyes and kissed Douglas, she could pretend it was Tyler. That seemed dishonest. Did men imagine they were kissing other women when they kissed her?

She heard footsteps on the porch and a knock at the door. "Our guests are here."

"Miss Adelaide and I worked out a story to explain my presence unless you want me to tell them I'm sleeping in the room next to yours."

"Don't you dare! Mary Davis may be a preacher's wife, but she loves sinful behavior. In others," she amended. "I'll die an old maid."

"I doubt that, but I have no intention of ruining your good reputation. I know how hard it is to regain once lost."

She knew he referred to his own and disagreed. "A reputation is earned. You're not born with it."

Cory opened the door and greeted the Reverend Davis, who removed his hat and returned her greeting. He was followed by his wife and daughter. Beth wore a new dress that flattered her slender frame. Cory looked at her own dress and felt dowdy by comparison.

Beth lifted a pie basket. "I made some fresh pies." She placed the basket on the sideboard along with her bonnet and gloves.

"Thank you." Cory began to close the door, but a familiar figure filled the opening. "Mr. Raymond."

"I hope I'm not intruding." He rotated his hat in his hands. "I saw you had guests, but it's urgent. I've misplaced my keys, and I've looked everywhere for them. I thought maybe I left them here last night."

Cory stepped back to allow him to enter. "You know the Reverend Davis and his family." He reddened when he saw Beth. She appeared equally uncomfortable. Cory turned her attention to the sideboard. "There are no keys here."

Douglas searched the sideboard and lifted the candlesticks, Beth's pie basket, and the vase of wilted flowers. He repeated the process.

"Mr. Raymond." Beth pointed at his jacket. "Do you have a hole in your pocket?"

Douglas smashed his hat on his head and jammed both hands into his jacket's pockets. "I could have lost my keys anywhere." He began to hyperventilate. "Those keys open the doors to all the buildings at the college. I have to find them."

"I don't think you lost them," Beth said.

He waved his arms like a windmill. "Of course I lost them! They're gone!"

"Calm down." Her voice was soothing. "May I?" She lifted his jacket near the back. "I believe your keys are inside the lining of your coat."

Douglas twisted around so quickly, he tore the jacket from Beth's fingertips. He searched for the keys.

"Stop," Beth ordered. She found the keys and massaged them forward to the front beneath his pocket. "I think you can reach them now."

Douglas plunged his hand into his pocket and retrieved the lost keys. He sighed. "They've been there the whole time."

"You need a wife to mend your jacket," Tyler remarked from the hallway.

Cory wanted to kick him, but the others were

staring at the stranger. "This is Tyler Montgomery," she introduced.

"He's my lawyer." Adelaide entered the hallway from the dining room. "He's helping me settle my affairs before I move in with my daughter. Come in. We don't want supper to grow cold. Mr. Raymond, please join us. There's plenty to share."

Cory had to admire Adelaide. She was a cool bird under fire, but why did she have to invite Douglas? She didn't even like him. How was she ever going to isolate Beth and ask her why she turned Douglas down?

"It was nice of you to invite us to supper," Mary remarked as they passed through the hallway and into the dining room. Cory grabbed another table setting from the hutch. Tyler seated Adelaide at the head of the table, and the Reverend sat opposite her on the other end. Mary sat to his right with Beth next to her. That left Cory seated between Douglas and Tyler.

"It's good to have guests again," Adelaide remarked. She passed the dishes of chicken, green beans, corn on the cob, and potato slices around the table, the clinking of serving spoons breaking the initial awkwardness of a social gathering. "I hope you enjoy the meal. Cory made the biscuits," she added.

Tyler took one from the bowl and noticed the bottom was nearly black.

Cory cringed. "Don't eat the bottom if it's burnt. The oven was too hot."

"You should take lessons from my Beth," Lawrence said. "Her pie crust is so flaky it could float in the air."

"I look forward to tasting it." Normally she was a fair cook, but nothing had gone right in the kitchen. Her mind had been busy pondering too many other matters to concentrate on baking biscuits.

"I hope you had a pleasant visit with Paula Stone," Mary remarked to Cory.

"Very pleasant," she answered quietly.

Tyler leaned forward to grab a bowl and whispered in her ear, "Liar."

"Where are you from, Mr. Montgomery?" Beth asked.

"Please call me Tyler. I spent most of my life in Virginia except for six years at Harvard."

"I'm a Yale man," Douglas said. "My father always believed in a good education."

"So did my mother."

Douglas held his spoon midair. "Your mother paid your tuition?"

Everyone stared at Douglas. It was impolite to discuss personal finances.

Tyler dismissed his rudeness by answering. "Yes. She was a successful business woman."

"How unusual," Beth said. "What sort of business was she in?"

"She passed away," Cory interrupted before Tyler could answer. "Recently," she amended to explain her bluntness.

Beth touched her hand to her heart. "I'm so sorry."

"My mother's death was the reason I returned home," Tyler replied. "It put my legal career on hold, temporarily, but family is the most important thing in life."

"Of course," Beth gushed. "I'm sure she was a wonderful mother."

What was Tyler doing? Did he plan to reveal his

entire family background? "She was known for her charity work," Cory added. She put her hand on Tyler's thigh to signal his silence.

"A religious woman?" Lawrence asked.

"She had strong convictions." Tyler's voice was high as he moved Cory's hand back to her skirt.

"And your father?" Mary asked. "Is he living?"

"He was a restless man. He died looking for gold in California."

"Like so many," Lawrence agreed. "The Good Book warns us not to store up treasures here on Earth. No good can come from greed."

"And greed attracts the most heinous creatures," Mary remarked in a hushed tone. "Two big hairy men spat tobacco juice all over the church entrance while their master talked to Lawrence before we came here."

"Master?" Adelaide asked.

"Mr. Vandal was looking for runaways." Lawrence said. "The two men were his hired chasers."

"Someone has to track down lost slaves," Douglas excused. "The law requires property should be returned to its owner."

"For a nice profit," Tyler added.

"That's an odd comment from a Southerner," Beth said.

"I'm representing a black man chasers claimed was a runaway," Tyler admitted. "They printed fake fliers seeking information about him."

"Nasty business," Lawrence agreed. "With so many forged documents about, it must make your job difficult."

"I'm not afraid of the documents," Tyler revealed. "It's the informants who lie and the chasers who kidnap innocent men and women to make a dollar who are the real threat."

"I blame it on that book, *Uncle Tom's Cabin*!" Douglas shook his finger. "A fictional account of slavery that has everyone in an uproar."

Cory paid extra attention to the potatoes on her plate. Douglas didn't know about her connection to its author.

"Cory has been reading *Uncle Tom's Cabin* to me. You know her cousin wrote it."

Cory tried not to groan. It was just like Adelaide to throw that bit of news in his face.

Douglas stared as if he had never seen her before. "You're one of *those* Beechers?"

Before Cory could reply, Beth spoke. "You said you were from Virginia, Tyler. Have you read *Uncle Tom's Cabin*?"

"I've read it," he admitted. "It's popular in Massachusetts."

"So what do you think?" Beth asked. "Is it an accurate account of slavery or purely fictional?"

Tyler looked around at his audience. "One book could never capture the full impact of slavery on our society, but it did start a dialogue that, for better or worse, has changed the attitude toward slavery."

"I think slaves should be returned to Africa," Douglas announced between bites of food. "Colonization is the answer."

"Are you competent with figures?" Tyler asked.

Douglas gagged. "I teach mathematics. What do numbers have to do with slavery?"

"How many slaves are in the United States?" When Douglas hesitated, Tyler answered. "Nearly four million. Now calculate how much it would cost to send four million people to Africa. Calculate the loss in man power for Southern farmers. Calculate the loss in profits when those slaves need to be replaced by paid laborers. The numbers add up to a bad idea."

Cory felt trapped between two raging bulls. Both men had forgotten the niceties of polite society and had turned the evening into a heated debate.

"What other solution do you propose?" Douglas asked. "Should we follow the abolitionist John Brown's example last year and arm the slaves?"

"John Brown was a preacher," Tyler countered. "Maybe the Reverend Davis should answer your question."

Lawrence had nearly cleaned his plate, but paused to reply. "Our forefathers believed they had to fight the British to gain their freedom. Maybe John Brown wasn't a traitor but a patriot. It all depends on the outcome."

"And the winner rewrites history," Tyler concluded.

Cory felt an obligation to defend Douglas. "I wonder what they will write about those who owned slaves?"

"Not all slave masters are Simon Legree," Tyler defended. "Some are even friends with their slaves. I know it's a strange concept. A hundred years from now all slave masters will be portrayed as cruel and inhumane, and all slaves will be victims of abuse and starvation. It's not that black and white."

"Slavery has been with us since Biblical times." Douglas looked to the Reverend Davis, who nodded in agreement. "It will still be here in a hundred years."

"Hopefully not in this country," Tyler argued. "I hate to say slavery is good anywhere, but slaves, serfs, or servants provided the hard manual labor to create civilizations. But once civilized, society needs to free them."

Douglas pounded his knife on the table. "But at what price?"

"I know some slaves who are willing to risk everything for freedom," Lawrence said.

"With a war?" Douglas demanded. "Or a slave uprising?"

"Harriet Beecher Stowe captured some aspects of slavery, but unlike John Brown, she didn't promote violence," Tyler argued. "Uncle Tom is a young black man who refuses to fight. He practices something in law we call civil disobedience. It's where someone disobeys the law because they believe the law is wrong."

"Like Tom not betraying the whereabouts of the two women at the end of the novel," Beth said. "Even though the law requires it."

Tyler smiled at Beth. "That's right."

"But Legree whips Tom to death," Cory reminded them. Beth was paying far too much attention to Tyler. "So much for peaceful disobedience."

"Disobedience has consequences and resisting violence with non-violence can be dangerous," Tyler agreed. "Tom was a fictional character, but there are many real slaves who have died not only for breaking written laws but unwritten ones."

"They're fools," Douglas said. "Decent citizens obey the laws. All the laws."

"Then how are bad laws changed?" Beth asked.

"Did Uncle Tom change anything?" Douglas demanded. "He died for nothing."

"He didn't die," Tyler corrected. "Uncle Tom is ink on paper, but even a fictional character can change the world. Otherwise we wouldn't be discussing slavery now."

"We can discuss it until we're blue in the face," Douglas said. "It won't change anything."

"Change is inevitable," Tyler argued. "Nothing remains static. Someday someone will rally the blacks to change the laws, hopefully, through non-violence. It will take a special person, and it will take more than one person. Civil disobedience only works when a large group of people protest something they feel is wrong and needs to be challenged."

"Like if all Northerners refused to return slaves, the Fugitive Slave Law wouldn't matter anymore." Beth looked directly at Tyler. "Two years ago a black man named John Price was offered work. Only it was a trick by chasers, who kidnapped him with the help of U.S. marshals. They planned to put him on a train at Wellington and return him to Kentucky. They didn't succeed. Are you familiar with the incident, Tyler?"

Cory could feel the excitement in Beth's rushed words and watched as Tyler leaned forward toward Beth. She wanted to tear them apart.

"I studied the case. A group of men stormed the hotel where they were holding Price and removed him to Oberlin and then Canada. A federal grand jury indicted thirty-seven of the rescuers. To obtain their release, state authorities arrested the federal marshal and the men involved and charged them with kidnapping Price. To avoid going to jail, they dropped charges against all but two of the thirty-seven rescuers."

"Simeon Bushnell served sixty days and Charles Langston served twenty days," Beth confirmed.

Cory pouted. No one existed but Tyler and Beth. What was going on?

"Langston made a very impactful statement in court," Tyler recalled. *"I must take upon myself the responsibility of self-protection; and when I come to be claimed by some perjured wretch as his slave, I shall never be taken into slavery."*

"I can't believe the Ohio Supreme Court upheld the Fugitive Slave Law as constitutional," Beth complained. "At least the Republicans want to repeal it."

"Republicans want war," Douglas argued. "Change brought about by violence is not the answer."

"I agree," Tyler said. "A war might change the laws, but slavery is a state of mind. If a slave refuses to act like a slave, others begin to see him differently. They may even see him as a man."

"Do you believe blacks and whites are equal?" Douglas asked.

"They could be," Beth answered quickly before blushing. She cleared her throat and continued. "We live in a country where poor people have an opportunity to better themselves, own land, even become wealthy. No other country in the world offers the same."

Adelaide nodded in approval, and Cory wondered why she hadn't chosen Beth as a companion. They had more in common than she'd realized. Both men were focused on Beth now. Cory could slip under the table and disappear, and no one would notice.

"You're an idealist, Beth," Tyler spoke gently.

"And reality has a way of smashing our dreams with tough choices. When I attended Harvard, I saw plenty of men who believed they were chosen by God to be the leaders of the world. Only they possessed the wisdom and character to make decisions for this country. Not only was it their right but their duty to govern the people and control the commerce of the nation." He glanced toward Douglas. "I don't underestimate the white elitist in the world who clutch their power and wealth with both hands. They will go to war or die to keep society status quo."

"There has always been a hierarchy in every society," Douglas argued. "There are leaders, and there must be followers. And the followers must submit to the leaders or chaos results."

Cory was tired of being ignored and didn't bother to hide her irritation. "You don't need to talk to women about submission. We're trained in it from childhood."

"As we are in cooking, cleaning, and being a good hostess," Adelaide interrupted. "How would you like to see if Beth's pie crust is as flaky as promised?"

Chapter Fourteen

The women gathered the dishes after dessert, and the men stepped outside on the porch to finish their discussion of impending war. The sunlight filtered through the treetops, and the air felt cooler when the women joined them.

"It's a beautiful evening." Lawrence looked to the sky. "The breeze is from the north and should cool things off."

"Why don't you young people take a stroll down the road," Adelaide suggested.

"Sounds like a lovely idea," Beth agreed.

Everyone gathered hats and bonnets before heading down the drive toward the road.

"How long do you plan to stay with Miss Adelaide?" Beth asked Cory. They walked side by side with Douglas next to Cory and Tyler next to Beth.

"Until school begins."

Douglas turned to Tyler. "Miss Beecher teaches children their ABCs in a little one-room school house."

His remark sounded condescending, and Cory defended her job. "It may not be as important as your work at the college and preparatory school, but the children think I'm a wonderful teacher."

"I think it's marvelous you're so accomplished, Courtney. I can barely manage to teach a Sunday School class," Beth confessed. "Sometimes the children are so unruly. How do you manage them?"

"I have five younger sisters," Cory reminded her. "Anything is easier than controlling their behavior."

"They're quite spirited," Beth agreed. "Didn't one of them fight with a boy and give him a black eye?"

Tyler chuckled.

"Your father should exercise a firmer hand with your sisters," Douglas said.

Cory twisted her handkerchief in her hand. Tyler had ignored her, Beth's delicious pie had emphasized her burnt biscuits, and now Douglas dared to criticize her family. How much was a woman to take in one night? She snapped out her defense. "So my sisters aren't perfect. Who is?"

Douglas jumped back. He looked afraid. All the weeks of being demure and ladylike undone in a careless shrewish outburst. She needed to apologize, but the words stuck in her throat.

"They're lovely girls." Beth's calm, quiet response neutralized any unpleasantness. She turned to Tyler. "May I take your arm? The road has so many ruts in it, and I'm so clumsy."

Tyler offered his arm. "You're the picture of grace."

Cory should have been grateful for Beth's intervention, but as Beth leaned into Tyler, all her fury returned. She glared at the back of Beth's head. She was being far too charming for a casual acquaintance. Did she think Tyler husband material? If Beth knew what she knew about Tyler Montgomery, she wouldn't be clinging to his arm. She'd run like all the other women in Tyler's life. But two could play Beth's game. She turned to Douglas and smiled. "How is your work at the college?"

His face brightened. "Wonderful. Although I have a difficult group of young men. Some of them don't know how to apply themselves."

They rejoined Tyler and Beth. "Don't the students go on break soon?"

"The seniors are taking their exams for college admissions July 10."

"Don't you mean college graduation?" Tyler asked.

"No, as an instructor, I teach the preparatory students at the academy. We have forty-four students this year and forty-eight attending the college."

"What do you plan to do on break?" he asked.

"I plan to pursue personal interest during the interim."

"What interests are those?" Cory asked.

"Matrimony." He looked surprised. "Why do you think I've been calling?"

"You're looking for a wife?" Tyler asked.

Cory glared at Tyler.

"There comes a time when a man benefits from marriage." Douglas puffed out his chest. "After all, marriage is about gain. Both parties should feel they are improving their lives."

"How will you benefit?" Tyler asked.

"Marriage increases my chances of promotion to a professor."

"That's a good reason to get married," Tyler said.

Cory knew he was being sarcastic. "I think some men cling to any excuse not to marry," she argued. "They're content being roguish bachelors."

"I think if the right woman came along, any man could be persuaded to change his mind." Tyler patted

Beth's hand. "But it's the woman who makes the final decision."

"I believe a man chooses a wife," Douglas argued.

"You don't think the woman picks a husband?" Cory asked.

"I believe marriage should be entered into logically and not emotionally," Douglas said. "Only a man has the temperament to make such an important decision."

"I'm sure a few women lose a night's sleep over the same question of matrimony," Beth replied briskly. "And wonder if they've given the correct answer to a proposal."

Beth's words sounded like a personal confession. Did she regret turning Douglas down?

"In the South a woman likes to be asked more than once," Tyler revealed.

"By the same man?" Beth asked.

"That's ridiculous," Douglas said. "A woman should know whether a match is suitable and give a prompt answer."

"But we're so emotional!" Cory cringed at her outburst. What was wrong with her tonight? She composed herself before explaining. "There are so many factors to weigh and consider when making a match. After all, it is for a lifetime."

"Yes," Beth agreed. "A woman needs time to make up her mind. She doesn't want to have any regrets."

"True enough," Douglas said. "As a future professor, I must choose a wife that is not only respectable but will help advance my career."

"In what way?" Cory asked.

"A professor's wife has a prestigious position at Western Reserve College. She works with the other wives to promote intellectual and social causes, and of course, she promotes her husband. Although I consider that an easy task for me." Douglas chuckled in a high pitch like a bird call. "In addition, there are her responsibilities to the staff and the students."

"Students?" Cory asked.

"The wives are surrogate mothers to the students. After all, they are away from home. They cook for them, clean the common areas, and do the laundry."

Cory nearly gagged. "For all of them?"

"No." Douglas chuckled like a bird, again. "There are three dormitories on campus. About half of the students live in them. The others live in private homes near campus."

"I would think grown men could take care of themselves."

"They need their time freed up for studying."

"It's one thing to care for a husband but a dozen men?" Cory asked. No wonder Beth had turned down his proposal. "It doesn't leave much time for your wife to pursue her own interests."

"I would hope her interests were the same as mine," Douglas replied.

"It gives a woman a unique opportunity to participate in her husband's work." Beth studied Douglas. "They can truly be partners."

Cory looked from Beth to Douglas. Maybe she was wrong about the reason for Beth's refusal. "Shouldn't two people marry because they're in love?"

"Is that how you plan to choose a husband?" Beth asked.

Cory didn't answer. She wanted to marry for love, but she had to be practical, too.

Douglas filled the void in conversation. "Romantic nonsense is not part of the equation. Marriage is too serious a commitment to be based on emotions. That's why a woman should not clutter her mind with frivolous drivel."

"Do you believe in romance, Beth?" Tyler asked.

"I am a great fan of Jane Austen," she proclaimed. "I think she wrote the most wonderful romance novels. I'm reading *Sense and Sensibilities* now."

"Nonsensical fluff," Douglas dismissed. "How does reading a novel like that improve your mind or character?"

"It has nothing to do with improvement." Beth smiled broadly. "It's like sunshine on your face or the sound of laughter. It's for pure enjoyment."

"I like reading, too." No one paid attention to Cory's confession.

"I know Austen's works are reputed to be a great accomplishment for a woman, but as a man, I prefer more serious readings," Douglas countered.

"I think we should allow the ladies their simple pleasures in life," Tyler said.

Cory counted on her fingers. "Between the cooking, cleaning, laundering, ironing, sewing, canning…"

Tyler's laughter interrupted her list. "I'm exhausted, Miss Courtney." He turned to Beth. "I see the house ahead. Can you make it, Beth?"

"Your strong arm has taken the burden from me." Beth released his arm as they entered the yard. "I thank you for lending it."

"Any time," Tyler answered.

Cory stared daggers at the two of them. Why was

Tyler being so nice to Beth? And so familiar? Did he flirt with all women the way he had been flirting with her the past two days? He had called her Miss Courtney and ignored her except for a few crumbs of attention. Didn't he like her anymore? Maybe he didn't care for her at all. He'd played with her affections until the next woman came into his life. He was a cad.

The Reverend Davis was loading the pie basket into his carriage. "We better return home before dark."

Tyler helped Mary and Beth into the carriage.

"Aren't you coming?" Mary asked Tyler.

Tyler looked confused.

"I asked them to drop you at the Red Pony Tavern," Adelaide said. "That *is* where you're staying? Unless you'd rather walk the mile down the road."

Tyler climbed in next to Beth. "I hope I'm not crowding you." The Reverend Davis urged the team of horses forward.

Cory heard Douglas talking, but her attention was on the receding carriage with Tyler and Beth looking cozy in the back seat.

"I was hoping to have some time alone with you."

Cory spun around to face Douglas. Was he going to propose now? She looked for Adelaide, but she had retreated into the house. All his talk of logic and common sense toward marriage had cooled any interest in becoming Mrs. Douglas Raymond. But maybe he was right. He had shared the benefits marriage would provide for him. She thought of the advantages marriage would provide her. She would have a roof over her head along with a dozen young men. She would socialize with intellectuals, but they would never think of her as an equal. A teacher of ABCs is how

Douglas described her. But was that enough to turn down a proposal?

Marriage for love was all good and well except when the man you loved was riding away with another woman. Tyler had brazenly flirted with Beth all night right in front of her. She'd prove her heart wasn't broken by accepting Douglas. She smiled warmly. "We're alone now."

He cleared his throat and ran his fingers under his collar. Shy and nervous. Would he find the courage to kiss her? She needed to know how it felt. She smiled and leaned forward to encourage him.

"I am looking for a wife. I think I made my reasons quite clear tonight. I want to clarify my decision is not based on anything personal."

Cory stepped back and frowned. Marriage was the most intimate relationship between two people. How could it not be personal?

"I know I have called several times, and the pursuit of making a match was sincere, but I was unaware of your family's background." He cleared his throat, a habit that set Cory's nerves on edge. "Attending Yale, I am quite familiar with the Beecher family. Their political support of abolishing slavery is something I cannot overlook. If we were to make a match, I would require you to give up your family's politics and support mine."

"I believe many at Western Reserve College sympathize with abolitionists," Cory argued. "I don't think my family's beliefs would jeopardize your career."

"But I would want my wife to support my viewpoints. All of them. Any disagreement would be looked upon as a weakness on my part. You need to be clear about your duty to support me completely. I hope I have not wasted my time considering you for a wife."

Wasted your time! A jumble of words collided on her tongue. All the Sundays she listened to his arrogant boasting was a waste of time. Complimenting him on idiotic statements as if they were pearls of wisdom was a waste of time. Thinking he had the potential to be a loving, caring husband was a waste of time.

"Cory!" Adelaide stood on the porch. "It's late."

Douglas patted her shoulder. "I will give you some time to think over my requirements."

Cory didn't need any time to consider whether or not to become a mindless, head bobbing puppet of Douglas Raymond.

"Perhaps this will help with your decision."

Before she could react, he kissed her on the mouth or a close proximity. It was wet and made her shudder with repulsion. She wanted to wipe the dribble from her chin but forced her hands to remain limp at her sides until he was astride his horse. Her swipe became a wave when he turned his head to say good-bye and rode down the drive.

She had her answer. Even if she was willing to forsake all her dreams and plans to meet his requirements, she could never marry Douglas. If she couldn't even bear a kiss from him, how would she endure intimacies required between a husband and wife? She only craved one man's touch, and he was enjoying a cozy ride with Beth.

She burst into tears.

Chapter Fifteen

Tyler didn't mind the short walk back to Glen Knolls after the Davis family dropped him off at the Red Pony Tavern. It gave him time to think about Cory. He'd been outraged when Douglas had shown up uninvited and talked about marrying a woman who could advance his career. Cory was an asset to any man, but her talents and charm would be wasted on an insolent man like Douglas. Tyler had flirted with Beth all night to anger Cory. By her stormy expression when he left with Beth, he had hit a mark. Yet, it provided no satisfaction.

Why were relationships so complicated? Even his relationship with Noah was far from simple. If only he could find him and talk to him. He knew Adelaide had seen him, maybe knew where he was hiding, but the old woman didn't trust him.

He couldn't blame her, especially if Cory had shared any of the information he had confided in her. But Cory had whitewashed his past during supper and instinctively, he knew his secrets were safe with her. As long as he hadn't made her too mad.

He walked around to the back of the house and glanced at Cory's window. Was she looking out the open window? He wouldn't mind seeing her in her nightie one more time. One more time? He'd never grow tired of looking at her in her nightie or anything else.

He could barely keep his eyes off her all evening, and she'd been dressed in a prim and proper gown. He had to exercise every ounce of self-control with her sitting so close to him at the table. When she had innocently placed her hand on his thigh, he thought she was going to discover how much his self-control could be taxed. He'd nearly dragged her onto his lap and made her dessert.

Why did men like Douglas always win the girl? Couldn't Cory see he was all wrong for her? She'd be bored, even on their wedding night. It made his blood boil to think of someone else touching Cory.

But he had no right to claim her. His father had abandoned his family, his mother had turned to a profession no decent woman practiced, and he had no lucrative prospects for employment.

Cory was only being polite in her tolerance of his presence. She would give a cry of relief when he finally left. But before he left, he wanted to do something noble, something to win her respect. Winning her love was out of the question after revealing so much, but he wanted her to know he was above his base breeding. He wanted her to know that deep down he was a decent man.

He was ready to open the back door when he heard the barn door slide open to the threshing floor. He turned. Was it Cory? His heart quickened at the thought of a repeat of their actions last night. He hurried to the barn. "Cory?"

"I hate to disappoint you," a deep masculine voice replied. A black man the same height and build stepped out of the shadows into the moonlight shining through the open door.

"Noah!"

"I heard you were looking for me." Noah stepped forward and embraced Tyler in a bone cracking bear hug.

"Easy." Tyler gripped his side. "I was shot."

"Chasers?"

"Courtney Beecher."

"Serves you right after what you did in the barn last night."

"How much did you see?"

"You're lucky the barn didn't catch fire." He grinned. "I didn't want to interrupt. I left the toy I made for Adam in the stall so you'd know I was here."

Tyler reached into his pocket and handed him the small metal horse. "I wasn't sure if you were still around."

"I hadn't planned on staying this long." Noah examined the miniature before putting it in his pocket.

"You don't know where Tess and Adam are?"

"I know she was in Akron the day I was arrested. I convinced one of the conductors who visited me in jail to confide about where she was heading. That's why I left the flier with *Glen knows the way* on it with Mr. Morris. I figured you would find us or know we had headed for Canada. Only she never arrived here."

"I came here to help, but Adelaide refuses to tell me anything."

"She's bull-headed about not betraying her guests. She came out to the woods where I hide and asked about you. I convinced her you were trying to help."

"I may have caused more trouble by coming." Tyler paced along the floorboards of the barn. "Edward knows I'm here. He came snooping around earlier today with the Cassell brothers."

"You let him follow you?"

Tyler cringed. "I'm new at this Underground Railroad secrecy, and I had to ask a lot of questions."

Noah looked out the door. "I have to find Tess and Adam before Edward does."

"We have to find them."

Noah shook his head. "You should go back home."

"I sold the Dunking Witch. I knew you could never go back to Virginia, and I had no reason to stay. Your money is safe in an Akron bank."

"Half is yours."

"I don't have your responsibilities."

"I won't have those if Edward takes Tess and the baby back to Virginia." He swiped at tears on his cheek. "I can't lose them."

"You won't." He patted him on the back. "How did you know Tess was the one for you?"

"One day she was all grown up, and I knew."

Tyler rubbed his wounded side. "Did it feel like a kick to the gut?"

"Only when Edward refused to let me marry her. It took nearly a year before he gave us permission."

"I didn't know that," Tyler said. "What made him change his mind?"

"Miss Regina convinced him Tess needed a man."

"Reggie always liked you."

"She likes Tess," he corrected. "That's why I didn't understand why she ran off. And why didn't she tell me? I would have gone with her."

"Reggie told me she made her leave," Tyler explained. "You left in a hurry when you followed her trail, but I had a long talk with Reggie after Edward headed north after Tess. She was sorry for the way she did it, but one morning she woke to Tess playing with Adam, and it broke her heart. She said something snapped inside of her. She ordered Tess to pack a bag and drove her to the river. She put her on the next boat north. Tess only left because Reggie promised to tell you what happened."

"Three days later," Noah complained. "I've been following her trail ever since."

"Does Adelaide have any idea where they are?"

"Miss Adelaide said Tess refused to leave Akron while I was in jail and couldn't reach Glen Knolls with Edward snooping around. She's been hiding in the church on the square. Miss Adelaide is working on a plan to bring them here."

"No wonder she wanted Cory to invite the Reverend Davis to supper," Tyler realized. "He must be a part of this."

"Who was the other fellow? I saw him calling Sunday night."

Tyler grunted. "Douglas Raymond. He's courting Cory."

Noah smacked a mosquito. "You're worried about *him* as competition?"

He hung his head in despair. "I have nothing to offer. I told her about Grayson running off and Olivia being the madam of the Dunking Witch. I'm out of contention as a husband."

"Now, why did you tell her all that?" Noah demanded. "They're dead. Nobody cares anymore but you."

Tyler disagreed. "Edward tipped her off when she

was in town."

"Is his nose still out of joint about who's the better man?"

Tyler laughed. "Crooked as the day I broke it. But he hasn't learned his lesson. The man won't stop meddling in my life."

"You're lucky Miss Olivia didn't marry Old Man Vandal, or he'd have every right to play big brother."

Tyler met Noah's gaze. "One big brother is enough."

****

Tyler entered the kitchen through the unlocked door and crept up the stairs as quietly as possible. He cringed when one of the steps creaked beneath his weight, but no sound came from the occupied bedrooms. He was about to open the door to his room when Cory opened hers. She stepped into the hallway, illuminated by a candle in her hand.

"Is something wrong?" he asked when she didn't speak.

A smothered sob escaped her lips.

He took a step closer. "Have you been crying?"

Cory swiped her cheek. "I have a cold."

"In July?"

"It's a summer cold."

"Probably from running around in your nightie." He noticed she wore no robe and her feet were bare. Her dark hair cascaded in a turbulent wave nearly to her waist. She swept it back behind her shoulders in a habitual gesture. Her breast jutted out against the thin white fabric. Tyler felt an instant hardness and cursed the woman. Why did she have such a strong effect on him? All he had to do was look at her, and he was aroused. Did she enjoy torturing him on purpose?

"Did you kiss her?"

Tyler wasn't sure he had heard the question. "Kiss who? Whom," he corrected.

Cory took a deep breath. "Beth Davis."

The deep breath undid Tyler. His fascination feasted on her taut nipples, his fingertips yearning to caress them, his mouth watering in anticipation of devouring their pink loveliness. His answer was a casual dismissal. "Does it matter?"

"Oh, you did!" Cory's words were a horrified shriek. Both glanced toward Adelaide's room. The door remained closed.

Tyler was baffled. "I only met her tonight," he excused. "Why would I kiss her?"

"You kissed me within hours of meeting," she reminded him.

Tyler thought about it. Had it been so soon? "Do you think I go around kissing every woman I meet?"

"You cad!" She turned and slammed the door.

Tyler was astounded. Did she honestly think he could seduce a woman mere hours after introductions? Or that he would want to? All his carnal actions were prompted by Cory. He had kissed her because she had put her arms around him and whispered words to distract him from Noah hiding in the barn. He had taken full advantage of an innocent diversion and recalled her reaction and subsequent description. *His kisses were anything but chaste.*

He wanted her, but it would be a small conquest if she did not match his desire. Neither one of them was experienced, but discovery would be the sweetest adventure lovemaking could give them. Tyler turned the knob of the door and entered.

****

Tyler shed his clothes and quietly slipped into bed. The ropes creaked beneath his weight, and Cory stirred, turning toward him in her sleep. She nestled her warm body next to his without acknowledging his presence. His hand brushed against the smooth skin of her thigh, eager to explore uncharted territories. Fingertips danced down to the indent at the back of her knee and upward to the curve of her hip.

She moaned and turned to her other side. "Go to sleep, Juliet."

"It is Romeo, not Juliet, who shares your bed," Tyler whispered in her ear. He kissed her neck.

Her eyes flew open. He crushed her outcry with his lips and pinned her beneath his body. His rough grip softened as her tense body relaxed beneath his ministrations. He kissed her temple, forehead, nose, and returned to her lips, urging her to respond. When he knew she wouldn't reject him, his fingertips danced from her shoulder to her collarbone and over the fullness below. The succulent fruit of her body ripened beneath his clever fingertips. Her breathing quickened to match his.

She tugged at the cotton barrier between them. "Help me take this off."

He was impatient to see her nakedness and ripped the nightgown free with a violent split of the fabric.

She sat up. "My nightie!"

He tossed it over his shoulder onto the floor. "You'll never wear a nightie again."

The moonlight bathed her nakedness, and he stared at the twin peaks perfect in shape and form. Nothing was more beautiful than her body.

"Are you going to do something other than look?"

She was bossy. Another man would put her in her place, but he knew her frustration from lack of power. He wanted to give her control. He belonged to her. "What do you want to do to me?"

"I want on top." She rolled him to his back and dangled twin fruits in full ripeness before his gaze. He reached, and she moved away. She was taunting him. He would not go hungry tonight. His mouth brushed against a pink nipple and teased the taut peak with his tongue. He latched on and feasted until her body rocked with orgasmic spasms.

He heard her moans and nearly went mad with wanting her. Even inexperienced, he knew he had to control his own need for satisfaction. Hers came first.

His fingers discovered the differences between them. It was a slow, sensual journey as he scoped the details of the landscape and gathered information on what pleased her.

Her hands sought an equal exploration. Fingertips danced all around until they played lightly along the smooth length of him. Her touch was torturous, but he steeled himself to remain still. But when her gentle fingers took ownership of his manhood, he groaned.

"Am I hurting you?"

"No." It was barely a gasp. He didn't dare speak, move, or think. He was ready to explode, but he couldn't take pleasure without giving in return. His hand stroked her flat belly and fumbled between her thighs for the hidden treasure. It was her hand that guided him into virgin territory.

His fingers trembled. He began a rhythmic beating.

She moaned and arched against his hand. He moved within her, and she became stiff. Was he doing something wrong? Was he even in the right spot? Then suddenly, she cried out, arching her body to his dance. She grasped his hair. "Don't stop, please, don't stop," she urged.

He covered her body and replaced his hand with a stronger tool. Slowly, carefully he pressed inward as he sought his way into this strange land. He felt her warm embrace as it drew him inward, deeper, and tighter. He advanced and retreated, her body matching his own in a battle both could win, building to a climax…

Tyler woke up in a sweat. He felt for Cory next to him, but he was alone in his bed. The dream had seemed so real. He swung his legs over to the edge and stood, his arousal evident. He pulled on his trousers and boots and grabbed the blanket from the bed. He carefully opened the bedroom door. Cory's room next door was too close. He might be tempted to act on his thoughts in the middle of the night. Then Cory's accusation would be true. He kept telling himself he was doing the right thing, but why did being noble seem so foolish?

Chapter Sixteen

The clock in the parlor tolled one in the morning. Tyler hesitated at the top of the stairs and looked over his shoulder at Cory's door. He half expected her to open it and give him a come-hither look. Nothing. He reluctantly headed outside, stopped at the pump, and opened the barn door to the upper level. Noah was already settled on a bed of straw in the corner away from the smell of the animals below. Tyler threw down the blanket next to him and plopped on top of it.

Noah groaned. "Hey, I thought you were going to sleep in the house."

"Change of plans."

"Miss Courtney throw you out?"

"No."

Noah rolled toward him. "So what happened?"

He ran his fingers through his damp hair. "I had a dream about her. It was so real." His body reacted to the memory. "I don't trust myself in the room next to hers."

Noah studied him in the moonlight streaming through the glassless windows. "Why is your hair wet?"

"I stopped at the pump."

"One of those dreams," Noah mumbled.

It was impossible for Tyler to sleep. "What am I going to do?"

"What men have been doing since the beginning of

time," Noah said. "Pay a whore or take a wife."

"Your advice is a little late. I already sold the Dunking Witch," Tyler reminded him. "And no woman would marry me."

"Not every woman is Miss Regina." He sat up. "Besides, you don't propose to a woman on her wedding day."

"It would have been too late the day after," Tyler defended.

"You weren't in love with her."

"She was making a mistake."

"It was her mistake to make." He sank into the straw bed.

Tyler considered his words as he struggled to get comfortable. "Why do women want to marry the wrong man?"

"Are we talking about Miss Regina or Miss Courtney?"

"She plans to marry Douglas, and she's not in love with him. Doesn't that sound like Reggie? She married Edward for his money."

"You can tell yourself that if it makes you feel better, but I've seen them together in Vandalia while you were away at school. She loves him."

"How? He's Cyrus Vandal's son."

"And you're Miss Olivia's son. Do you want people to judge you by your parents? I spent a lot of time at the Silver Pheasant to be near Tess. I saw Edward struggle with harsh decisions. I don't think he wants to be like his father, but Cyrus casts a long shadow. He's a lot like his mother, too. She was always cold and aloof. Miss Regina brings out the best in him. He doesn't like you because he's afraid of losing her."

Tyler was startled. "To me?"

"Miss Regina has always been fond of you, in a big brother way," he amended. "And Edward likes to have a firm grasp on his possessions."

"Are you talking about Reggie or Tess?"

Noah leaned forward, his head in his hands. "He's here to claim his property. Control is an ugly thing when it feeds a man's power over someone who is helpless. It results in beatings, rapes, and murders."

"He's not going to find them," Tyler vowed.

"Only over my dead body."

"I have a better way. Reggie signed papers for Tess and Adam. You can travel in the open with them."

"Legal papers?"

He hesitated. "Only Edward and the Cassell brothers would know they're fakes."

"And I thought all the years you spent in school made you smart. We can't use them."

"I don't care if I never practice law again."

"I am not going to be the reason you stop being a lawyer. I never saw anyone prouder than Miss Olivia when you graduated from Harvard. Then you attended law school, and she reminded everyone you were her son. She died in peace believing you were successful and happy. Don't you dare disappoint her now."

"Disappoint her?" Tyler demanded. "How could I disappoint a whore?"

Noah raised his fist. "I ought to hit you for that. She loved the wrong man. Men," he corrected. "But she didn't let her mistakes define her. She may have had to sneak around at night to deliver food and medicine to the needy, but no one ever slammed the door in her face or turned down a gift from her. I thought you knew that when you saw all the people at her funeral."

"I saw them. They loved her better than I did."

"Edward wouldn't have a crooked nose if you didn't love her," Noah reminded him. "She knew even if you never said the words."

"She was so beautiful," Tyler recalled. "She could have had any man."

"True." Noah relaxed on the straw. "She could have married for wealth, but she didn't. She was always true to her feelings. Maybe you should be true to yours."

"But how is any woman ever going to look beyond my past?"

"The past isn't the problem." Noah stabbed his finger in Tyler's direction. "You need to stop being ashamed of the past and look toward the future. You're a Harvard lawyer. Start acting like it."

"Why do you think I'm here? I'm taking care of you."

"By breaking the law? Burn the documents."

Tyler wasn't done arguing. "You might want to keep the one granting your freedom."

"Another fake document."

"It's not like you have a birth certificate proving you weren't born a slave."

"I won't need proof once I reach Canada."

Tyler turned his back to him. "You were always free, Noah."

"You and I know that, but a man isn't free when the world thinks of him as a slave."

"The world is changing."

"But not fast enough. I don't want my son to be a slave," Noah confessed. "Promise me, you'll guarantee

Adam never wears shackles."

Tyler didn't hesitate. "I promise."

****

Tyler was dreaming about Cory when someone started to shake him. It was dark, and he felt disorientated by his strange surroundings.

"Wake up!" Noah nudged him.

Tyler bolted upright. "What is it?"

"Someone is in the barn."

Tyler heard a match struck and focused on a flash of light as someone lit a lantern.

"Why are you sleeping out here?" It was Adelaide.

"We had a lot of catching up to do." Noah stood. "Is something wrong?"

"It's nearly dawn, and I didn't want you to hide in the woods before we talk about the plan to move your wife and son out of the church tower and here to the farm." She stared at the two men who towered over her. "Edward and his chasers have been checking wagons and carriages passing through town."

"How are you going to get them out?"

"A distraction." Adelaide pointed to the big wagon in the middle of the barn. "Tyler will drive the wagon to Akron with enough hay on it to make it appear he's hiding someone. I've arranged for Orva Miller to drive it back tomorrow with beer and supplies for the Fourth."

"How is that going to help?" Tyler asked.

"We're hoping Edward or a chaser follows you out of town. We're hoping one of them follows Cory as well."

Tyler shook his head. "I don't want Cory in any danger."

"She'll be safe riding the train into Akron," Adelaide said. "She's going to run errands. Her grandfather is in town and can bring you back by boat."

"There are three of them. What if one stays behind?"

"The Reverend Davis will take care of him," Adelaide said.

"What do I do?" Noah asked.

"Stay hid. That flier about you is still circulating, and the Reverend said he saw a new one with Tess on it. I want to review some maps so you'll know which route to take to Sandusky."

"Sandusky?"

"Too many chasers in Cleveland. A boat will take you to an island where a fisherman will take you to Canada."

"When will we leave?" Noah asked.

"Tonight if Tess is ready to travel," Adelaide said. "Edward is too suspicious for you to remain here at the farm."

Tyler glanced at Noah and back to Adelaide. "When do I leave for Akron?"

"You can milk the cows and eat breakfast first. Then you can hitch up the buggy for Cory and the draft horses for your trip."

****

Breakfast was awkward. Cory wouldn't even look in his direction. Tyler was worse. He couldn't think of the right words to change her opinion about him. Douglas was a saint contrasted against the sordid picture he'd painted about Gaylord and Olivia. How was he going to convince her she should marry him instead?

If only he hadn't talked about his parents. What did it matter if they had been less than stellar citizens? Noah was right. They were dead. She should judge him on his own merits. But what were those? He was an unemployed lawyer. And if anyone found out he had created and witnessed illegal documents, he wouldn't even be a lawyer. But he hadn't destroyed them. Noah might change his mind about needing them.

Adelaide broke the silence. "If either one of you is having apprehensions about doing this, there's no shame in backing out. You know the penalty."

"I'm not afraid," Cory replied.

Tyler didn't answer. He'd heard ugly rumors about Buck and Clyde. If one of them caught Cory alone, her reputation wouldn't be the only thing in jeopardy. "Maybe we should leave Cory out of this." Tyler studied her innocent countenance. He didn't want it scarred because of him. "This isn't her fight."

"Tess is a woman. I'm a woman. This is my fight."

"I can distract Edward and his men alone."

"There are three of them. You'll be lucky to have one of them follow you."

"I'm wearing Reggie's vest. That should make Edward mad."

Cory hadn't missed the fact he wore the embroidered vest Reggie had made him. Was he still in love with her? Was that why he flirted outrageously with every woman he met? Would no woman measure up to his first love?

Cory was still mortified by her behavior last night. She had been jealous of another woman. Never in all her years of being courted had she fought over a man. In fact, she had stepped aside several times when another girl made it known she was interested in one of her beaus. There had always been another man to take his place. Only, she didn't want another man. She wanted Tyler.

"Well, you ought to attract at least one man in that dress," Adelaide remarked.

Cory hadn't been paying attention. Was there something wrong with her dress? Tyler was studying the gown of red, white, and black plaid. She hoped others noticed the bright colors in the pattern, and the lightweight material floated over her tightly cinched figure. It was practical on a hot day. She smoothed the white lace collar that outlined the square cut neckline and hinted at her curves. "I've worn this dress to town before. What's wrong with it?"

"You look beautiful."

Cory studied Tyler. Why was he complimenting her? Was he practicing for Beth or some other girl?

"Have you forgotten your manners?" Adelaide asked. "He gave you a compliment."

"Thank you," Cory muttered.

Tyler stood. "I'll take some breakfast to Noah."

"Take it in the milk bucket in case someone is watching the farm," Adelaide said.

Cory realized the meaning of their words. "Why is Noah still in the barn?" She fought her hysteria. "Isn't he supposed to hide in the woods?"

"I need to talk with him." Adelaide placed some food in the milk bucket.

"But if someone finds him in the barn," Cory warned.

"You're not helping a runaway," Tyler reminded her. "And Edward and his men will be following us."

"I forgot." Cory placed her hand over her pounding heart. "I'm guess I'm a little scared."

Tyler took the bucket but paused by the door.

Cory waited for him to speak. She needed a word of reassurance. He grinned. It was lopsided and marred his perfect features, but it vanquished her anxieties.

"Better hurry," Adelaide said. "You'll have to leave soon."

****

The draft horses were hitched to the wagon, and Tyler was securing Nell to the buggy when Cory and Adelaide came out into the yard. Cory tied her bonnet while Adelaide gave her final instructions.

Adelaide looked at the two vehicles. "It didn't take you long to ready them."

"Noah helped."

Cory looked toward the barn but saw no one.

"He stayed out of sight," Tyler explained. "He found something that might be useful." He led her to the back of the wagon. Tyler pointed to an old boot sticking out from the straw.

"That ought to attract a chaser," Adelaide said.

"How am I going to attract a chaser?" Cory asked.

"You don't need any help attracting a man."

Another compliment. He was oozing with charm. What was Tyler up to?

"When you're done shopping, can you meet me at the law office of Sam Morris?"

Sam was the Akron attorney who had helped Noah. "Where is it?"

"On Main Street next to the Town Hall above the dry goods store. An outdoor staircase leads to his door."

"I can find it." Cory opened her purse and checked

the contents. She didn't know what to say to Tyler.

Adelaide headed for the barn. "I need to talk to Noah."

"Are you still mad at me?" Tyler asked.

Cory closed her purse. "I'm not mad. I'm embarrassed. It seems every time I'm around you, I make a fool of myself."

Tyler furrowed his brow. "When?"

"Acting like a schoolgirl about Beth. It's none of my business if you want to talk with her."

"Too bad. I was hoping to make you jealous."

Had he been manipulating her or... "Why?"

"I didn't like Douglas pawing all over you."

"Douglas pawing all over me?" She stomped her foot. "Who was clinging to your arm because she might trip?" Cory batted her eyes and imitated Beth. "You're so strong, Tyler."

"I was being a gentleman. You didn't expect me to let her fall, did you?"

"She's as sure footed as a mountain goat," Cory argued. "She risked no injury."

He raised an eyebrow. "You have a bit of a temper."

"It's one of my faults," she snapped. "One you won't have to put up with much longer."

"That's reassuring."

She pouted. "You don't have to be so happy about it."

"I thought you'd be glad to be rid of me."

Cory feared she would cry into her pillow the way she had last night. She squared her shoulders. "Why wouldn't I be? In fact, I'll be quite busy being courted by Mr. Raymond with summer term ending next week."

Tyler snarled. "Won't that be wonderful!"

Why was Tyler so angry? He had no intention of courting her. "Delightful."

"So he didn't propose last night?"

"No." Cory tried not to think about his kiss, but trembled involuntarily.

"What happened?"

Why did he need to know every intimate detail of her life? Why did he care? And why should she? She stuck out her chin. "He kissed me."

Tyler kicked the buggy wheel, startling Nell and Cory. He grabbed Nell's bridle to calm her. "Well, here you are accusing me of kissing Beth, and you're smooching Douglas."

He had no right to be angry, but she didn't want to mislead him. "It wasn't a very good kiss." Cory made a face.

Tyler clenched his fist. "I'm sure he'll improve with a little practice."

"Time to go," Adelaide called out.

Cory wondered how much she had overheard. They had nearly been shouting at each other. "I plan to leave the buggy at the livery." Cory raised her skirt to board, but Tyler lifted her in his arms and swung her up into the seat.

"Tell the blacksmith to put a couple of nails in the mare's back right shoe. Noah said it's loose." He handed Cory the reins. "I'll see you at noon. Try not to kiss any more men before then." Tyler smacked Nell's hindquarters.

Cory glanced back and saw Tyler climbing into the wagon. Who was he to tell her not to kiss anyone? But the more she thought about it, the more she smiled.

Chapter Seventeen

The trip into town was uneventful. Cory passed the butcher, the grocer, the baker, the cobbler, the tailor, and the harness maker before reaching the livery. Lou Smith was the owner. He bragged he was older than the flood, and no one argued. He was wrinkled on every part of his body except the smooth cap of his bald head. Lou took Nell's bridle as Cory climbed down from the buggy.

"I'm taking the train to Akron and won't be back until late." Cory recalled Tyler's instructions. "Nell needs a couple of nails put in her right rear shoe."

He sighed. "I'll try to find time."

Lou looked tired. "You should hire someone to help you."

"I'm too old to train someone, and it's impossible to find a good blacksmith."

"I know a good blacksmith," Edward Vandal announced from the shadows of the livery. He stepped into the bright light of the yard. Cory saw Buck and Clyde hovering behind him like rats on rafters ready to leap on unsuspecting prey.

"Do you?" Lou asked. "Is he a hard worker?"

Edward was referring to Noah. If he didn't have to worry about being dragged back to Virginia and sold into slavery, he could work for Lou. She almost argued her point before remembering Edward was looking for

Noah to find Tess. He was baiting her to discover if Noah was at Glen Knolls. "Lou has wanted to retire for years. Perhaps this blacksmith can take over for him."

Edward stared at Cory. "Do you know where I can find him?"

"How would I know?" Was he suspicious? Maybe her nervousness would work in her favor. She wanted someone to follow her. She jumped when she heard the train whistle blow. "I have to buy my ticket." She gathered her basket and purse from the buggy. "Good day." Clyde and Buck stepped out into the light. They didn't look any less menacing.

The livery stable was opposite Darrow Falls Inn. Cory headed west on River Road toward the train depot built on a rise above town. She focused on the small rectangular building, afraid she might glance toward the church tower and reveal Tess and Adam's hiding place. She wasn't good at disguising her true feelings. No wonder Adelaide had hesitated to tell her about Noah. She'd never done anything this dangerous, and although baiting the chasers was part of the plan, her heart was beating at a frantic pace.

She bought her ticket and boarded the train. Her seat was on the opposite side of the depot and gave her an overview of the town. Edward stood in the livery yard, holding the reins to a horse. His chasers were missing.

The sheep that grazed on the square to keep the grass shorn were absent today. Several men were cleaning up the center of town in preparation for tomorrow's holiday. Businesses would be closed, and shoppers were busy making last minute purchases. Tomorrow a new flag with thirty-three stars would be displayed on the front of the Town Hall to mark the Fourth of July. Cory glanced toward the church. Somewhere inside Tess and Adam were preparing for their final flight to freedom.

She spied Edward and Clyde riding south on Darrow Falls Road. Where was the other one? She turned to show her ticket to the conductor and saw Buck Cassell seated in the rear of the passenger car. She quickly faced front. At least one of the chasers was following her.

The train gave a long blast on its whistle and chugged out of the station. Cory saw Edward and Clyde race down the street to Akron and cross a covered bridge. As the train left them behind, she spied their prey. Tyler drove the draft team at a fast clip on the dusty road to put some distance between him and the chasers. The train would beat all of them by at least an hour, but Cory had some shopping to do while in town. She hoped Buck wouldn't mind.

****

Akron was built on a steep hillside with Summit, Broadway, High, and Main streets running parallel between the train tracks at the top and the canal below. Exchange, Middlebury, State, and Center streets crossed them in a grid with every corner a coveted spot for businesses. Churches with towering steeples were the centerpieces of neighborhoods scattered on the hillside and beyond. Cory led Buck along Center Street to the downtown area.

She explored several establishments before she reached a general store on Main Street. Buck stayed hidden behind bags of feed while she examined some cotton diapers. Cory bought a dozen along with a baby gown, booties, and a cap. She added pins and a blanket.

"When are you expecting your baby?" the woman behind the counter asked.

Cory was startled by her question. Did she look like she was expecting? "It's a gift. I'm not even married."

"What's wrong with young men today?" She wrapped the items. "You're too pretty a young lady not to be married."

Cory wondered. There were plenty of women younger and more attractive, and men weren't lining up to propose. Tyler had given her plenty of reasons he couldn't marry her, and what if Douglas didn't ask? What if he did? Would his kisses improve over time? Maybe life as an old maid wasn't as bad as it appeared. She enjoyed teaching, and her students could be substitutes for no children of her own. But children weren't the only reward of being married. It had been different the last few days with a man in her life. Tyler shared the chores and provided lively companionship. But would it be as nice if the man was Douglas?

Cory debated the merits of becoming Mrs. Douglas Raymond as she shopped. She marked off the items on Adelaide's list: Plain white buttons, white thread, black ink, matches, salt, and sugar. Most of the items could have been purchased in Darrow Falls, but Buck didn't know that. He kept a watchful eye on her at a discreet distance while she filled her basket.

It was around eleven, and Cory needed to find Grandpa Donovan. She headed for Exchange Street, which crossed the canal to Lock One. Boat captains had to pay the toll at Lock One to travel on the canal. The collector would know whether the Irish Rose had reached the lock.

She was still three blocks away when a stocky white-haired man with sparkling blue eyes hailed her from a group of men in front of the Thirsty Lizard Tavern. "I thought it was you, darlin'!" He picked her up and twirled her around like she was six years old.

"Grandpa!" She hugged Captain Michael Donovan in return.

"Orva Miller said you'd be in town and needed a ride." He looked inside her basket. "I see you didn't pack a lunch. Where would you like to eat, darlin'?" he asked in an Irish brogue forty years in the states had failed to erase.

She glanced around. "Where would you suggest?"

"The Thirsty Lizard has a steak three inches thick."

She inhaled the cornucopia of smells, some pleasant like meat sizzling on a grill behind the restaurant and others putrid like the garbage tossed into the waterway. "It's awfully close to the canal."

"I like to keep an eye on the Irish Rose."

Cory knew the history of the canal and her family's role in it. Michael Donovan had traveled to Ohio in 1825 to help build the Ohio Canal. He worked from sun-up to sun-down for thirty cents a day, a jigger of whiskey, food, and shelter. Armed with picks and shovels, workers dug a hole twenty-six feet wide at the bottom, four feet deep and forty feet wide at the top. Men cleared trees and brush twenty feet on each side of the canal for towpaths.

Stones were cut and hauled from the quarry near Peninsula for the walls, and white oak was used for the miter gates. A balance beam attached to the top of each gate opened and closed the double doors for a watertight seal.

Michael Donovan was able to buy his own boat a few years later. He moved his family aboard and began his life as captain on the Ohio Canal.

Cory wondered where the Irish Rose was now. "Is she still docked?"

"The pilot is taking her down through the staircase. Charging me fifty cents. I'd do it myself, but the man needs the money. He has nine children."

Cory looped her arm through his as he led her to the tavern. "You have a generous heart, Grandpa."

The dining room was filled with canal boat captains and crew members. Whole families lived aboard canal boats, and many of the patrons were women and children. Grandma Donovan had worked along with Grandpa and their children for years, but now Caroline Josephine Donovan ran an inn in Peninsula, half way between Akron and Cleveland. The Irish Rose docked at night to split up the run between the two cities. The inn provided income for off season when the canal was shut down for repairs and dredging.

The Thirsty Lizard was dark but a cool retreat from the heat. Michael greeted several other canal captains as he entered. "You remember my granddaughter, Courtney Rose, don't you?"

A man with a gray-streaked beard tipped his hat. "You've grown into a lovely lass."

"Where's your grandson Zeke?" he asked.

"He's working at the butcher shop on Howard Street. He'll give you a good deal on meat. Tell him I sent you."

"Butcher, you say?" Grandpa grinned at Cory. "Good catch for a girl. Never go hungry."

Cory didn't need to worry about finding a husband as long as Grandpa was around. They sat near a window overlooking the canal. South was Lock Three where a dry dock was located for building and repairing boats. A tannery was located to the north at Lock Four. All along the canal route's waterway, mills for lumber, flour, and machinery had sprung up like wildflowers. Basins at locks Six and Seven allowed for loading coal and grain.

Fifteen locks stepped down the water route through Akron from Exchange Street to beyond North Street. The closely-placed locks were difficult to maneuver, and special pilots took the boats down the steep incline the city was built upon.

"When will the Irish Rose reach Mustill Store?" Cory asked. The waiter served two steaks layered with sliced onions and green peppers. On separate plates, he served diced potatoes seasoned with fresh herbs and corn on the cob swimming in butter. A loaf of wheat bread on a cutting board was placed between them. He gave each of them a mug of cold beer.

"My granddaughter doesn't drink beer." He placed his hand on her mug when the waiter tried to remove it. "I'm thirsty enough to finish both. Serve her some lemonade."

He looked at Cory. "The pilot guaranteed me two o'clock. Are you going to ride down the canal with me?"

"How long will it take to reach River Road?"

"Be there by suppertime if traffic is light."

"Then I'll meet you at Mustill Store after I go to Sam Morris' office."

"Who's Sam Morris? A beau?"

"He's a lawyer."

"A lawyer?" He lowered his voice. "Are you in trouble, darlin'?"

"I'm meeting someone at his office. He had some business to take care of before we head back to Darrow Falls."

He raised a bushy eyebrow. "He?"

"Tyler Montgomery is your other passenger."

He studied Cory and then glanced at her steak, half untouched. "Aren't you going to eat that?"

"I'm full."

"I'll have them wrap it up along with all the other food you barely touched. Your cousins will want it."

She didn't know what was wrong with her appetite, but the food wouldn't go to waste. "Thank you for buying me lunch."

"It's a bribe," he said. "Jessica and Colleen are helping your mother put up preserves, and Jake wants to stay in town and spend the holiday with his steady girl, making me short-handed. Can this fellow handle a pike?"

"He's a lawyer, too."

"I don't know what you girls see in those mollycoddles. Probably have to tether him to the deck so he don't fall overboard."

Cory smiled. He'd find out soon enough Tyler wasn't a milksop.

The waiter wrapped up the food as Grandpa paid the bill. Cory turned to the door and saw Buck waiting outside.

"What are you hesitating for?" He looked around.

She leaned in close to Grandpa. "See that burly man outside with the droopy hat and long beard?"

"The one with a pistol tucked in a holster on his hip."

Grandpa didn't miss a thing. "When we pass him, say to me, '*I'll deliver your package to Cleveland.*' Can you do that?"

"What sort of mischief are you plotting, darlin'?"

"The less you know, the better."

They took no notice of Buck. Grandpa spoke his line and left her with a kiss and a wink.

Cory made her way along Main Street to Sam's office. She climbed the steep staircase on the exterior of the building and opened the door. Inside was a small waiting area and beyond two offices. The door was open to Sam's office on the left. The shelves were filled with books. Tyler sat in a padded leather chair facing a large desk cluttered with stacks of paper and more books. Sam sat facing her. He was in his forties with a thick mustache and thinning hair. Cory stepped forward. Sam stood and removed his spectacles.

Tyler turned, stood, and made introductions. "Sam helped me straighten out my legal matters with Noah."

Cory frowned. "I thought you were a lawyer?"

"I am, but I haven't passed the bar exam in Ohio. I told Sam I'd take it at the end of July and help him with his caseload. It's the least I can do for all his help."

Cory wasn't sure if she had heard correctly. "You're going to work for Mr. Morris?"

"I don't want to go back to Boston, and I can't go back to Vandalia," he excused.

He was staying in Akron. Cory couldn't digest the news Tyler wasn't leaving. She nearly missed his next comment because her mind was boggled with possibilities she hadn't dared entertain before.

"He's holding my legal papers," he explained. "We agreed it would be best."

Cory didn't answer. She had barely comprehended the fact he had a job in town.

Tyler ran his hand through his hair. "One close call was enough."

"If Noah is apprehended again, remind him to make enough ruckus, he's arrested," Sam said.

"He knows. He's worried they'll take Tess quietly and sneak her back to Virginia."

"Once she's over the border, I can't do anything to help her. Legally," he added. Sam walked them to the door. "Pleasure meeting you, Miss Beecher."

Cory took Tyler's arm as they headed down the stairs. "I'm so clumsy, I might fall," she excused.

He chuckled but stopped suddenly.

She spied Buck with Edward in the street.

"Our shadows have joined forces."

One was missing. "What happened to Clyde?"

"Turned back about half way. I hope it gave the Reverend Davis enough time to move Tess and Adam out of the church."

"Let's put some distance between them and us," Cory suggested.

"How?"

"We'll head up town and circle around to Mustill Store. Grandpa is waiting for us there." She led Tyler up the hill away from the chasers.

Chapter Eighteen

They headed for the county courthouse, built less than twenty years ago on High Street. It was a stone building with two pillars supporting a frieze and pediment gable. A small open dome rose above the roof. Cory led the way inside, across the rotunda's foyer, past the county offices, and out the opposite door, which opened onto Broadway Street.

They passed the jail on the other side of the street opposite the courthouse. It had been built in 1843 of local sandstone. The soft stone had to be reinforced with steel rods after prisoners dug their way out and escaped the new building. The three-story structure had small bars in each window except those in the living quarters for the sheriff and jailer.

The train tracks ran parallel with Broadway Street. "Are we heading for the depot?" Tyler asked.

"We want Buck and Edward to think we are. Then we'll head back downtown to the canal."

"But I thought we wanted them to follow us."

"We do, but we want to give Grandpa time to get the Irish Rose underway."

"Can your grandpa lose them on the river?"

"It's a canal boat not a river boat," she corrected. They headed west on Quarry Street. "We can't outrace them. That's why we need some distance. Once we're underway, it won't be easy for them to board."

"Is your grandpa what they call a muleskinner?"

"Of course not!" Cory needed to educate him before he offended someone. Canal people solved insults with their fists, and she was rather fond of his face. "A muleskinner drives mules along the towpath to pull the canal boats through the canal. Children do that."

He studied her. "Have you ever been a muleskinner?"

"The whole family helps out on a canal boat," she excused. "My mother and her brothers lived on the canal boat when they were younger. But now Uncle Padrick owns an inn in Peninsula with Grandma Donovan, and Uncle Clive has a farm for mules. My cousins and my sisters take turns working for Grandpa. Cole and Jess are helping this year, but with me at Adelaide's and Jem working for Papa, my mother needed them to help with picking berries and making jam this week."

He chuckled. "So you were a muleskinner."

"Mule driver. It's a lot easier than jumping on and off the boat to move it through the locks. But I always hated clearing the snakes."

He grimaced. "Snakes?"

"They like to sun themselves on the towpath. Makes the mules skittish," she explained. "You throw the garter and black snakes in the grass, but you have to kill the rattlers."

"At least rattlesnakes warn you of a strike. We have copperheads in Virginia. They like to coil up and wait for you to step on them."

"Let's hope Edward is more like a rattler."

Tyler turned around. "How far back is he?"

"Far enough." Only if the Irish Rose was down the fifteen-lock staircase, and Grandpa was ready to get under way. "Let's run!" She grabbed his hand and rushed into the crowd on Main Street. They wove their way down the steep hill to Howard Street. Although this part of the street was home to legitimate businesses, farther north it was known for gamblers, drunkards, and the Unfortunate Maiden whorehouse.

They headed for Mustill Store. The two story market sold everything from groceries and fresh meat to dry goods and traveling provisions. A narrow road separated the store's porch from the canal. Like many of the businesses located on the edge of the man-made ditch, it relied on the canal for moving goods. But Mr. Mustill also owned a closed delivery wagon for taking merchandise to customers in town. His son, Tom, was loading it.

The Cuyahoga River, which ran north of North Street, had a series of waterfalls and large boat-damaging rocks that made it impractical for ship travel. The canal ran solo from Summit Pond to North Street, then parallel to the Cuyahoga River until it reached Lake Erie. The canal provided a calm man-made waterway for shipping from Cleveland to Akron. Unfortunately, the eight-year-old railroad connecting the same cities could carry passengers more comfortably and travel faster, putting the canal in jeopardy of becoming an unprofitable transportation route.

Mills dotted the banks of the canal and kept captains busy hauling wood, paper, and coal. Farmers still sent their wheat, oats, corn, flour, cheese, and whiskey north to Cleveland and bought nails, glass, cloth, salt, coffee, tea, and other manufactured goods in exchange.

Although this was the third Irish Rose, all Captain Donovan's boats were eighty feet long and fourteen feet wide to fit through the fifteen-foot wide locks. Every canal boat ran shallow with a draft of three feet fully loaded.

When Captain Donovan owned a packet version of the canal boat, his sons served as the steersman and bowsman. Maureen drove the mules, and his wife, Caroline, cooked for the passengers. Now he operated an open freighter boat with no need for a cook, and his grandchildren drove the mules and served as crew.

The Irish Rose was waiting for its turn to enter Lock Fifteen where Captain Donovan would man the tiller. Cory waved to Grandpa and her cousins Ethan and Paddy. They had red hair and blue eyes. Ethan was fifteen, tall and wiry, while Paddy, two years younger, still had enough baby fat to make him look stocky.

The pilot, who had navigated the Irish Rose through the locks, tossed a rope to Paddy. He tied it around the snubbing post in the ground to stop the boat in the lock chamber. The pilot jumped off and collected his fee from Captain Donovan. He ushered everyone aboard when two men closed the back gates of the lock. "Hurry up, girl!"

Cory handed her basket to Grandpa, who took her arm and hauled her to the top of the stern cabin. Tyler gave her a boost on her backside. She glared at him when he joined her on the cabin roof.

Three separate cabins were connected by a catwalk along the roofs. The stable cabin was in the center. Three mules were stored inside to replace the three tied in tandem to the towline pulling the boat. The open midship area was loaded with cargo.

Ethan climbed aboard after Tyler. "Who's this?"

"Tyler Montgomery." Cory made introductions while Ethan ran across the bow cabin and jumped to the other side of the lock.

"Take over the tiller, darlin'." Captain Donovan grabbed an eight-foot long wooden pole with a metal tip called a pike. "Open the paddles."

Ethan gripped a long metal wrench and turned a rod that ran from bottom to top on the wooden gate. It opened a small paddle door in the bottom of the gate and water rushed out. Paddy did the same on the other side.

"She's a bit bumpy when we release the water." The captain shoved against the stone wall to keep the boat from hitting it.

Tyler grabbed Cory as the boat dropped along with the water level.

Ethan and Paddy closed the paddles when the water in the lock reached the level in the lower canal. Ethan jumped on board, and Paddy released the line on the snubbing post. He tossed it to Ethan. Then he tossed the team's line to Ethan, who attached it to the boat's deadeye on the bow deck. The two men who had closed the back gates, opened the front gates by pushing on the balance beams.

"We're ready to go down the canal," Ethan shouted.

Paddy urged the mules to move and the boat jerked forward.

"Isn't Cleveland up river?" Tyler asked.

"You'd think," Cory answered. "But the Cuyahoga

means crooked river. It flows south, hooks when it hits the high ground of Akron, and curls around to head north, emptying into Lake Erie." She made a hooking motion with her hand.

The mules plodded along the well-worn towpath and pulled the boat through the canal water at a slow and steady pace. Bullfrogs and crickets serenaded them as butterflies danced to the music. "Is this as fast as the boat goes?" Tyler asked.

"They're mules not race horses." Cory swatted at a fly buzzing by her head.

Ethan gripped the edge of the board with his toes as he scurried along the catwalk. Captain Donovan handed Ethan the pike and took the tiller handle from Cory.

Tyler still had his hands around Cory's waist. "You can let go of my granddaughter." Captain Donovan looked at Cory. "Not much of a sailor, is he?"

Cory shrugged. "I told you he's a lawyer."

"He don't look like a bookworm," Ethan said. "Might be worth training him to be a boatman."

"He might be able to earn his fare."

"I'm a fast learner." Tyler winked at Cory.

"You can store your things in the bow cabin. You'll want to take off that fancy coat if you're going to help crew the boat."

"How do we get down on deck?" Tyler looked at the lower level covered with crates and barrels in the front and cords of wood for the paper mill in the back.

"We are on the deck. That's the hold you're looking at."

"This single board is the deck?"

Cory walked along it to the stable cabin. He

followed at a slower pace.

"Don't worry about falling." Ethan stepped aside on the stable cabin roof and allowed them to pass. "With all this cargo, you won't have far to go. But don't bounce and land in the canal. It's nasty this time of year."

"Why is it green?" Tyler asked.

"Duckweed. It's what's under the duckweed you have to worry about."

Tyler stared at the green covering. Cory waited for him at the bow cabin. He planted each step before taking another toward her. "Now what?"

Cory lifted a trap door and climbed down a ladder nailed to the wall. Tyler followed her down into the tiny cabin at the front of the boat. There were wooden bunks built along one wall for sleeping and a small galley for preparing meals. "This is the crew's cabin." She sat down on the lower bunk and removed her gloves and shoes.

"What are you doing?" Tyler watched her remove her garters and stockings.

"You're going to want to remove your jacket and boots. It's easier to walk the catwalk barefoot."

"Why didn't you tell me that before I crossed the gangplank of death?"

Cory snickered. "Once you've fallen a few times, you'll get the hang of it."

"I have no intention of falling into that cesspool you call a canal. Does it always smell so foul?"

"It's July." She turned her back and untied her petticoat and crinoline at her waist and wiggled out of them. "The city uses the canal as its sewer. It's cleaner away from downtown."

The trap door above them opened. "Stop canoodling and help on deck," Ethan said. "There's a shallow spot ahead."

"What does he mean?"

Cory retied her bonnet. "You don't know what canoodling is?"

Tyler grabbed his hat and followed her on the ladder. "I'll canoodle you in front of the whole crew," he threatened. "What does shallow mean?"

"The state keeps cutting money for maintaining the canal. A shallow is where silt builds up and grounds a boat. It means you can practice your balance." They reached the deck, and she closed the trap door.

Ethan handed each of them a pike. "You two take the catwalk, and I'll take the bow."

Tyler frowned. "Why does he take the bow?"

"He's going to measure the depth and tell us which way to push." She made her way to the stable cabin. "I'll go in front and you can follow. Do exactly what I do."

Ethan plunged his pike into the water. "Push off on the starboard side."

Cory flipped her pike so the metal tip was on the right side and plunged it into the water. When it hit bottom, she pushed and ran forward along the catwalk. Tyler followed her example but nearly lost his balance when the pike stuck in the mud on top of the clay bottom.

"Pull it," Ethan ordered. "We can't afford to stop and go back for it if you lose it."

He yanked the pike free and ran to the bow cabin where Cory was waiting. "Now what?"

"We go back and do it again." She motioned for

him to turn around and shoved him along the catwalk.

"Slow down," he warned. "I'm not a monkey."

"We'll be grounded if we slow down," she warned. "I would think a big strong man like you would find this easy."

"A big strong man on a little piece of wood," he excused. "Why can't the mules pull us through the shallows?"

"It's hard enough for them to pull a loaded boat through deep water. If the boat becomes stuck, we'll have to jump in and push."

"I think we should have taken the train back to Darrow Falls."

"We wanted to keep Edward and his men busy."

"How do we know if they're following us?"

"Look over at the road beyond the river."

Tyler saw Edward and Buck on horseback. "Can they reach us?"

"Not for a few miles. Cuyahoga Street follows the river not the canal, and it swerves away from us ahead. They can't reach us until the road to Tallmadge intersects Cuyahoga Street."

Chapter Nineteen

Tyler followed Cory along the catwalk. His balance improved with each run. He enjoyed the view of Cory's hips swaying as she preceded him. It was a hypnotic movement that trained his feet to move in a mirrored dance of her footwork.

"Hey, I'm pretty good at this." He lost his footing and began waving his arms like a fledgling on the edge of a nest afraid to fly.

"Stop fooling around. We're coming up on Lock Sixteen."

Tyler regained his balance and wiped the beads of sweat from his forehead with a kerchief from his pants pocket. "Does that mean a break?"

"Locks are not breaks," Cory informed him. "Everyone has a job to navigate the boat through a lock. There are usually five in a crew."

"We're the crew?" Tyler did a quick head count. "Do we have to go all the way to Cleveland?"

"No. My cousin Colin is in Peninsula. That's Lock Twenty-nine. He'll board for the rest of the trip north."

"The Mary Louise is coming south," Captain Donovan called out from the stern. "We'll be able to make headway and not wait for the lock to fill."

"Headway?" Tyler watched as the wooden gates of the lock opened, and another boat headed toward them.

"It means we can go straight into the lock without

waiting for it to fill."

"Fill with what?"

Cory pointed to the canal. "Water. The water is higher on this side of the lock. The Mary Louise came into the lock on the lower side. Once inside the lock, the doors are closed on both ends and the lock is filled with enough water to make the boat rise to this level. Once she passes, we can go in, and we lower the water like we did before."

"Headway!" Captain Donovan hollered.

Paddy pulled up on the mules and let the towline go slack to the bottom of the canal. Paddy kept his mules to the far side out of the way of the mules pulling the Mary Louise as she passed. As soon as she was clear, Paddy moved the mules forward. The towline grew taut and pulled the canal boat toward the lock.

"Use your pike to keep the boat from hitting the gates or walls," Captain Donovan ordered.

"You take the starboard side." Cory prepared to push on the leeway side.

Captain Donovan manned the tiller to line up the boat with the lock, letting it glide in. Tyler and Cory poked with the pikes enough to keep the rub rails on the side of the boat from smashing into the large cut quarry stones and jarring them from their precarious perch.

Ethan jumped to the lock's edge and wrapped the bow line around the snubbing post to stop the boat as it reached the end of the chamber of the lock.

"The tender shed is empty!" Ethan called out.

"We'll have to tend the lock," Captain Donovan said.

Tyler looked at the abandoned shed. "What happened?"

"They fired all the lock tenders in March except those at feeder gates. The two men at Lock Fifteen work at Mustill Store. Most captains didn't start the season until the end of May this year because of flooding. Now there's talk of leasing the canal." Cory lowered her voice. "Everyone thought the railroad would put the canal out of business, but the state's lack of funding is ruining it."

"Is the captain losing money?"

"Not as long as he has grandchildren working for him." Cory nodded toward Ethan. "Think you can help with the gate so Paddy can stay with the mules?"

Tyler jumped off the boat opposite Ethan and mimicked him. Each turned a balance beam attached to the miter gates. Once the back gates were closed, they ran to the other end of the lock and turned the paddle control to open the sluice door in the bottom of the gate wall. Water rushed out, and the boat lowered with it.

Once the boat was level with the water outside the gate, Ethan and Tyler closed the paddles and opened the front miter gates using the balance beams. Ethan released the bow line and jumped on board the Irish Rose. Tyler leaped onto the bow deck, and Paddy tossed him the towline. Tyler slipped the hook through the deadeye, and Ethan signaled Paddy to move the mules.

The boat hit the side of the gate. "Look lively!" Captain Donovan called out. Cory shoved against the wall. Tyler grabbed a pike.

"Push against the stone. You could damage the lock if you break the wood."

"And I thought a blacksmith's job was hard," Tyler remarked. "One lock and my shirt is soaked. Are we going all the way to Peninsula? That would be thirteen more locks."

The boat cleared the lock, and they stopped pushing. "River Road is at Lock Twenty-four. Do you think you can handle it that far?"

He let out a gasp. "How long has the captain been doing this?"

"More than thirty years, right Captain?" Cory asked.

"Made the run from Akron to Cleveland and back again every summer except for the year I broke my leg," he said. "That's the year your father met your mother."

"Are you sure?" Cory met Tyler's gaze and winked.

"I remember it well. The summer of 1839. Canal captains were highly respected back then. Fortunes were at stake. Tempers were hot and fights common. Danny O'Hara cut the Irish Rose off to beat me into the Deep Quarry Lock. He was the dirtiest fighter in these parts, but I didn't take nothin' from nobody back then. I had headway, but O'Hara closed the gate and took my turn. We scrapped for more than an hour on the bank with so much sweat pouring off of us; we could have filled the lock with it. Then he knocked me down onto his boat. I scrambled up the wall but slipped. His boat smashed against my leg and broke it in two places."

He made a breaking motion with his hands. "It looked so bad, CJ called for a doctor. Your pa came to set it. He had me cursing his name when he put the bones back where they belonged, but he set it straight. I don't even have a limp. He ended up in a whole lot more pain than I did."

Tyler looked at Cory. "Pain?"

"Mother."

"Maureen Rose Donovan was sixteen and the prettiest lass in these parts," Captain Donovan explained. "Had plenty of men trying to wed her, but she turned them all down. She was waiting for the right man to come along and ask her. She decided Doctor Sterling Beecher was the right man. Only he never proposed. He kept calling to check on my leg but never courted her. Unfortunately, it healed."

Tyler was being treated to a family yarn and urged the Captain to continue. "Unfortunately?"

The captain grinned. "He didn't have any reason to call anymore. I took matters into my own hands and laid down the law. No man trifles with my daughter." He waived his finger in Tyler's face. "I told him if he likes what he sees, then put a ring on her finger."

"I bet that was an easy decision," Tyler said.

"It wasn't as easy as you think. He didn't have many patients and marrying a canal brat lost any chance to gain more."

"Mama wasn't a canal brat!"

Captain Donovan snorted. "High society types thought otherwise, but true friends remained loyal. They lived at Glen Knolls with Hiram and Adelaide until you were born."

"Most of his patients paid bills with produce or livestock. He had so many cows and chickens, he decided to buy land in Darrow Falls and farm it. The price for wheat had tripled since the canal opened and corn was nearly double. He'd still be a farmer except for the fire in '45. A lot of people were hurt, and your father took care of them. He earned the respect of everyone in the area and gained plenty of patients."

"Papa said he owed a favor to Hiram and Adelaide," Cory said.

"They were generous folks," Captain Donovan said. "Never turned anybody away who needed help. I was sorry to hear Hiram died."

"To think I was born at Glen Knolls," Cory remarked to Tyler. "I guess that's why I'm so fond of the place."

"It holds some pleasant memories for me, too." Tyler watched Cory blush. He wondered if either one of them could settle for nothing more than memories.

****

By the time the boat reached Lock Nineteen, Tyler had become proficient at treading the catwalk. He gripped the board with his toes and stepped back and forward in a rolling gait. "Maybe there's some privateer blood in me," he confessed. "Miss Olivia's folks lived along the coast."

Cory laughed. "More likely pirate blood."

"Then you can be my wench." He grabbed her around the waist and threatened to make them fall. They came out of the woods into a clearing with a road ahead. He saw two men on the bridge over the lock and released her. "Looks like Edward found us."

Cory turned around on the bow cabin. "Edward and Buck."

Edward gave his horse's reins to Buck and stood on the edge of the wooden planking of the bridge.

"That ugly fellow looks familiar," Captain Donovan announced from the stern. "The fancy dressed one looks like he wants to jump on board."

Tyler knew a confrontation was imminent. "Is

there a way to go through the lock faster than a tortoise's pace?"

"Rushin' don't get a lad any place sooner than he ought."

"Then it looks like he's going to board," Tyler called back to Captain Donovan.

"Let 'im board. We'll give him a nice welcome and then hurry his departure, with your help, laddie."

Tyler grinned at Cory. "I like the captain."

"I'm rather fond of him, too."

"Stay here with Ethan." Tyler hurried back to the stable cabin.

Edward jumped aboard. He landed on the roof in front of Tyler. Captain Donovan didn't let the additional passenger stop him. He steered the boat through the gates of the lock. "Look lively," he called out.

Ethan jumped off the boat and tightened the bow line around the snubbing post. The boat slowed.

"I have the mules." Cory jumped off with the towline. She took the mules' reins, and Paddy helped Ethan with the gates.

"Where is she, Tyler?" Edward looked below into the stable cabin.

Edward thought Tess was aboard the boat. Tyler glanced back at the stern and walked backwards along the catwalk. He bluffed. "You can't have her."

Edward followed. He took one step on the narrow plank and stopped. "She belongs to me! Hand her over."

Tyler showed off his new prowess. He agilely danced back along the plank, daring Edward to follow. He held the pike out equally on each side for balance.

When Edward refused to follow, he charged forward. Edward backed up to the front of the stable cabin.

"With that staff, it's not much of a fair fight, but then a ruffian like you wouldn't know about honor."

It was as if they were boys again. "I broke your nose when you had the advantage. I can break it again."

Tyler saw the Donovan boys opening the paddles on the gates. He hoped Edward lost his balance as the boat dropped with the outpouring of the water. He didn't.

Edward looked around. "What's happening?"

"It's a canal lock."

"You can have your duel once we're out of the lock," Captain Donovan announced.

Ethan and Paddy opened the front gates. Ethan helped Cory back on board and secured the towline.

"Give him a pike."

Cory handed Edward the long pole and backed up to the bow.

Tyler squared off with Edward.

"Tess is my slave." Edward took the pike in both hands. "The law requires you return her to me." He swung the pole upward and caught Tyler's pike in a jarring collision.

Tyler exerted his greater strength. "You own other slaves. You don't need Tess."

"I gave Tess to Regina as a wedding gift." Edward pushed against Tyler, but he didn't budge. "She was born on the Silver Pheasant, and she'll die there."

Tyler backed up, hoping to draw Edward out onto the catwalk and off the stable cabin roof. "She's not going back."

Edward charged, and Tyler battled back. Each

blow of the wooden staffs echoed in the still, humid air.

"Reggie doesn't want Tess." Tyler swung the pike around to knock Edward off balance. "She sent her away."

"Liar! She'd never do that." Edward stepped back and then lunged forward with the pike. They locked the pikes in primitive battle.

Tyler needed to convince him of the truth. "I talked to her after you left."

Edward stepped back. "Who do you think you are calling on my wife?" He charged forward on the narrow plank. He lost his balance and swung the pike up and down to regain it. The pole smacked Tyler on the cheekbone and nearly toppled him.

Tyler felt burning pain along his eye and the side of his face. Anger blinded him as he lunged. He locked Edward's staff with his own.

"You had no right to be alone with her!" Edward shouted. "She told me about your proposal on our wedding day. You were trying to steal her away from me!"

Tyler needed to reason with him. "She turned me down." He shoved Edward away. "Maybe if you had talked to her before going off after Tess, you would have saved yourself a trip. Adam reminded Reggie too much of Eddie. She packed Tess and the baby up and put them on a boat heading north before she realized how much trouble it would cause. Do you think Tess would leave Noah?"

Edward gasped for breath. "He followed her." He swiped the pike at Tyler's head.

Tyler ducked. "To find her. He's her husband. He knows his place is beside his wife. Unlike you."

"Don't tell me how to treat my wife or my servants!" Edward swung the pike like a club.

Tyler jumped back. His pike flipped upward and smacked Edward on the side of his head. Blood flowed down his face.

"I want Tess back." He stumbled on the plank.

"It won't change anything!" Tyler knocked the pike from his hand. It fell into the cargo hold. Edward charged and threw a wild punch. Tyler took a couple blows to the face before he dropped his pike. He punched Edward and knocked him off balance. Edward fell on the cords of wood below, rolled several times, and splashed into the canal water.

Tyler looked back to see Edward's wet head surface in the shallow muddy water.

Captain Donovan tied off the tiller and made his way to Tyler. "Are you all right, boy?"

Tyler's head felt like a bee hive. "I'm fine."

He grabbed his face. "A leech will take care of the swelling around your eye."

His other eye widened. "A what?"

"Leeches." Cory opened the trapdoor to the bow cabin. "There's plenty in the canal. The captain keeps a jar for bleeding bruises."

Chapter Twenty

Tyler was shaken by the battle with Edward. The man was driven. He was blinded to the truth. Tyler had hoped he could use the money from the sale of the Dunking Witch to buy Tess and Adam but doubted Edward would consider any offer now. He had to make sure Edward never found them.

"Go on, son." Captain Donovan returned to the tiller. "I figure that fight earned yah a kiss."

Ethan had retrieved both pikes and Tyler's hat from the cargo hold. Ethan handed him his hat. He turned when Cory called his name. It was like a siren luring him to his death. She was going to suck his blood out.

Tyler looked at the other men. He didn't want them to think he was a coward. He descended into the cabin. Cory was holding a jar with thick black leeches in it. He felt sick. "You're going to put that on my face?"

"It won't hurt." Cory examined his eye. "And it will take down the swelling."

"I don't mind a few bruises." Tyler put his foot on the ladder to make a hasty exit. "You are not putting a blood sucking creature on my face."

"I bet you would do it for Reggie."

Tyler paused. "What does she have to do with this?"

"You fought over her."

"I wasn't fighting for Reggie," he countered. "I was fighting for Tess."

Cory put her hand on her hip. "You proposed to her on her *wedding* day?"

How was he going to explain? "It was a desperate measure to prevent her from doing what I thought was a mistake." He ran his fingers through his hair. "I didn't love her. And from what Noah says, she loves Edward. I guess I was too mad at him to think anyone could love him."

"How do you know you don't love her?"

He looked at the jar of parasites in her hand. "I would never let her put a leech on my face."

"Will you let me put a leech on your face?"

He stepped closer in the tight quarters. "Only you."

****

Cory felt flattered by his admission, but it was a far cry from a declaration of love. She shoved him toward the bunk. "I won't let the big bad leech hurt you."

"It better not suck my eyeball dry."

She saw blood seeping through the vest Reggie had made. "You're bleeding." He unbuttoned his vest and removed it. His shirt was red above the gunshot wound.

"How am I going to keep your shirts clean if you keep bleeding on them?"

He pulled the shirt free from his trousers.

"Sit." Cory put the jar of leeches on the floor by the bed and examined the wound. "It opened up."

"Can't you put a fresh bandage on it?"

"That won't be enough."

He looked at the jar. "Leeches?"

"Stitches."

"Do you mean a needle and thread?"

198

"What else would I use for stitches?"

"I hope we're talking about mending my shirt."

"The wound won't heal properly without stitches now that it's opened up." Cory searched for some bandages.

"You're not going to do it now, are you?"

"I don't have the proper needle." She found a roll of cloth. "I'll use this to bandage it temporarily." She folded a strip for a compression bandage and a long strip to secure it as she lifted Tyler's shirt out of the way. When she was done tying off the bandage, she picked up the jar of leeches.

"My eye is feeling much better now."

"Your eye will close tight if I don't leech it." She opened the jar. "The key is to concentrate on something else."

Tyler stared at the jar of swirling black bloodsuckers.

Cory's father had used leeches and maggots for medical reasons, but he was careful to prevent the patient from seeing the repulsive creatures at work. She had to distract Tyler. She unbuttoned the top two buttons on her bodice. "It's hot in here." She had his attention.

"Lie back." She leaned over him, giving him a hint of her cleavage as she put the leech on his skin. Why were men fascinated with two lumps of flesh on a woman's chest?

He shuddered as it tickled his skin, but his attention remained on the opening on her bodice.

Her chemise covered most of her bosom, but what he could view, kept him riveted. "You're doing fine." She stroked his hair back from his face. The fight with

Edward had left the scent of sweat and blood on Tyler's skin. Instead of repulsing her, it aroused her senses. Her body responded in a way conquered women have responded since men fought to possess them. She wanted to yield to him, to climb into bed with him, but common sense won.

She poured some water on a towel and cleaned his face. "See, it's not so bad." The plump leech fell off. Cory snatched it off the bed with the towel and dropped it back into the jar.

Tyler leaned on his elbow. "Is that it?"

She secured the lid to the jar. "You want another leech?"

He looked at the trap door. "Captain Donovan said something about a kiss."

Cory felt her body respond to the deep tone of his voice, urging her to comply. She wanted to kiss him. She wanted Tyler to kiss her. But she worried about where kissing would lead. She wasn't sure if she could stop herself once she surrendered. "Haven't you kissed enough women?"

"I didn't kiss Beth." He frowned. "And you're still ahead of me. And I don't care what you say about it, I'm still counting Douglas."

Cory carried the jar to the shelf. "What about Reggie? I know she was the first girl you kissed, but when was the last time you kissed her? Maybe you're ahead of me on number of kisses."

Tyler stood and tucked in his shirt. "That was it."

"Not even when you proposed?"

"It was more of an ultimatum than a proposal."

"How can men be so unromantic?" Cory thought of Douglas and his logic in choosing a wife. She closed the cupboard and secured it.

"We're beasts." Tyler closed the small space between them and pressed against her back. His hands encircled her waist. He leaned down, and his lips tugged on her earlobe. "Wild, untamed beasts."

Cory's breath caught in her throat. She felt her body tense in anticipation of his lovemaking. What was he doing to her?

"Tame me." He nuzzled her neck, lingering in one spot and waited.

Her emotions warred between yielding to her immediate desires and resisting his affections in order to spare her heart more pain once he left. He would surely leave to help Noah and Tess, but what about his job with Sam Morris? Was that a temporary repayment of a debt or something more permanent? Did his future plans involve her, or was she deluding herself with romantic dreams? "We need to talk."

Tyler released her and backed away.

Cory was surprised by his sudden change. He looked hurt.

The trap door opened above them. "We're coming up on Lock Twenty-four," Captain Donovan shouted down. "I hope you got your kiss."

Cory snatched her belongings but hesitated to dress in front of Tyler. He shoved his feet into his boots and grabbed his clothes. "I guess our talk will have to wait." He climbed the ladder and left her alone.

Tyler had sounded angry. What had changed his mood so abruptly? A girl had a right to say no to a kiss. Cory dressed and hurried on deck. She turned to Grandpa. "Are you coming to Darrow Falls for the fireworks?" Cory arranged her bonnet and smoothed her hair around the opening.

"I'm docking in Peninsula for the night. There's always a big celebration on the Fourth. Mostly canal folk. You ought to join us."

"Thank you for the invitation, but we have our own celebration in Darrow Falls."

"A picnic and dance, and everyone returns home after the fireworks. We don't start celebrating until the sky is lit up."

"Be careful if you see Edward Vandal or one of his chasers," Tyler warned. "He thinks his slaves were hiding on this boat."

"I know how to handle any brawlers," he replied. "I think you missed the coach, but you ought to be able to catch a ride on one of the freight wagons traveling River Road." He pointed to the steep incline away from the river. "You don't want to walk that hill in this heat."

"Thank you, Grandpa." Cory kissed him on the cheek and hugged her cousins.

Tyler shook hands. "Pleasure meeting you, Captain Donovan, Ethan, Paddy."

"Come back anytime," Captain Donovan invited. "You ain't like most lawyer types." He winked at Cory.

Tyler and Cory rode with Darrow Falls' baker, Sydney Robinson. He had a wagon load of flour, newly milled in Peninsula and shipped south on the canal. They hopped off when they reached the Beecher farm.

Tyler's hand went to his side.

"How bad is it?"

"Not bad. I don't think I'll need stitches after all."

"Let me see."

Blood had seeped around the makeshift bandage. "Papa will stitch you up."

"I wouldn't want to bother him."

"Haven't you had stitches before?"

"No, and I've never been shot or had a leech put on my face."

"What a sheltered life you've led," she said. "Look at everything you missed before meeting me."

"How can you be so beautiful and cruel at the same time?"

Was he teasing? She wondered how he truly felt about her.

He looked toward the house. "Tell me about your sisters. Five of them, right?"

"Yes." Cory counted down on her fingers. "There's Jennifer, Colleen, Jessica, Cassandra, and Juliet. Each of us is about two years apart in age. I'm twenty and Juliet is nine."

"Any reason why your names begin with C and J?"

"After Grandma Caroline Josephine."

"That's who CJ was. I didn't want to interrupt the captain's story to find out."

"You shared your family history. I thought you'd enjoy hearing mine."

"I did, Cory. Do your sisters have nicknames?"

"Jem, Cole, Jess, Cass, and Jules."

"Sounds like boys' names."

"Just nicknames. I don't think any of us wanted to be boys. But we wanted the fun they have."

"Seems to me girls have all the advantages."

"Advantages? Girls are instructed to be quiet, gentle, and obedient. Boys don't have to follow such silly rules."

"What part of quiet, gentle, and obedient do you practice?"

Maybe she didn't follow society's customs all of the time, but neither did he. "You don't obey any rules in your behavior toward me."

He laughed. "I threw out all the rules when you shot me."

"Don't tell my parents I shot you. They'd be horrified by my recklessness."

"I won't tell them you shot me if you don't tell them I kissed you." He stopped. "Nice house."

Cory stood next to him as they studied the big white farmhouse she called home. Her parents had purchased a two-room cabin but had expanded it to accommodate six children and a medical practice. Hiram had helped with the additions, and it resembled Glen Knolls. A Greek pediment divided two wings. Each wing had porches with ornate moldings.

"Welcome to the Beecher homestead." Cory noticed the green shutters were faded. "The shutters need painted."

"Your hired hands have grown lazy without you."

"Hired hands?" She held up her arms. "These are the only hired hands. It's a family farm. That's why Adelaide chose me to help at Glen Knolls. I can milk a cow, kill a chicken, and drive a buggy."

"I can understand why you look forward to becoming the wife of a college professor."

Cory didn't answer. She had never longed for a life of social gatherings and vain luxuries. "I don't mind the work. Not when it's my home."

They reached the slate walk to the front door. It was decorated with chalk drawings.

"Looks like one of your sisters has some artistic talent."

"Cass likes to draw." She pointed out several horses drawn in detail on the slate.

Cass and Jules ran around the side of the house, screaming. They hid behind Tyler. "Help us."

Jess followed with a green garter snake in her hand. "It's going to get you!"

"Stop waving it around," Cory ordered Jess. "You're scaring it."

"He likes me." Jess let the snake wrap around her hand. She had blonde curls that escaped from a single braid. "It's a little thing."

"I don't like snakes." Cass poked her head out from behind Tyler. Cass was eleven with dark hair like Cory's, but it lacked any red highlights. Her hair was worn in two braids, and her eyes were the same green as Cory's.

"I like snakes." Jules stepped forward and tentatively touched the snake's body. She had strawberry blonde hair worn in a ponytail of curls that framed blue eyes.

"Then why did you run?" Jess demanded.

"I like screaming."

"Jules is the dramatic one," Cory explained. "Put the snake back in the grass where it belongs."

"Cory!" Cole rushed out the western porch door and down the sandstone steps. She was wearing a huge crinoline with a new dress draped over it. The dress hem was pinned on one side and hung too long on the other side.

Jem followed with a pincushion in one hand and measuring tape in the other. "Don't you dare dirty my dress," she threatened.

Jem and Cole both had red hair and blue eyes.

Jem's hair was darker and more bronze in color, while Cole's was as bright as copper.

Cory examined Cole's gown. "Is that a new crinoline cage?"

"Six feet wide," Jem bragged. "I borrowed it for the dance."

"Why can't I wear a crinoline like this?" Cole demanded. "I should make a good impression at my first dance."

"Sit." Jem pointed to a wooden bench beneath a nearby tree.

Cole marched over, turned, and sat. The crinoline shot up to her face and exposed her underwear underneath. Cole struggled to lower the cage.

"That, little sister, is why you start out small," Jem said. "You have to acquire some coordination to wear a crinoline."

"That's not the only hazard," Cory revealed. "Last Christmas when Jem wore a crinoline to a dance, she caught her dress on fire standing too close to a fireplace."

Jem laughed. "That was the night Ben Collins came to my rescue and beat the fire out with his new coat. We both looked like chimney sweeps."

Cory knew her family's budget. "Do you think Ben warrants a new dress?"

"Grandma bought a sewing machine and insisted upon making ball gowns for us for the holiday dance. Yours is upstairs. Mama hemmed it for you, but I'll never finish mine if Cole doesn't stand still."

"Why can't you wear the dress, and I'll pin it," Cole suggested.

"You can't pin a straight line."

"All they do is fight." Jess looked at Tyler. "What's your name?"

Cory made the introductions.

"Where did you find him?" Cole studied him. "You're pretty."

"Men aren't pretty," Jem corrected. "They're handsome."

"Then he's pretty handsome."

Cass squinted. "He's awfully tall."

"Your eye looks funny," Jess remarked. "Did you get into a fight?"

"There's blood on his shirt." Jules pointed at the stain.

"We came from the Irish Rose. Tyler had a little altercation."

"With Grandpa?" Jules demanded.

"No. It was with a man named Edward Vandal."

"Did you win?" Jess asked.

"The other guy is still swimming in the canal," Tyler bragged.

"Nobody swims in the canal," Jess argued.

Tyler laughed but suddenly clutched his side.

"We better go inside and take care of your wound." She ushered him toward the door. "Is Papa home?"

"No," her sisters echoed together.

Chapter Twenty-One

They entered through the door on the left porch. It opened into a family parlor with a large brick fireplace on the left wall and the kitchen and pantry to the rear. A stool was in the middle of the room with a wicker sewing basket nearby. Cole took her position on the stool, and Jem circled until she found where she had left off pinning the hem.

Cory led Tyler into the main foyer. A staircase was centered in the middle with hallways on both sides leading to the dining room and back of the house. The cherry banisters ended in opposite spirals. Color rectangles shimmered against the wall from the sunlight streaming in around the main door. It was fancier than the foyer of Glen Knolls, but Hiram had wanted to improve on the original. Another doorway opened on the opposite side into a formal parlor with a piano and sofas arranged for entertaining. Two rooms were off the parlor. Cory entered the one on the left.

A large oak desk was situated to one side with a matching oak chair. A black leather book for recording births and deaths was on top of a ledger for her father's accounts. An ink well and several pens were beside it. Clean and neat. To the side was a wooden case with sliding glass doors on top of a chest of drawers. Inside were medicines and supplies. Cory searched for needles and bandages.

"What happened, Cory?" Maureen stood in the doorway. Her mother had the same ginger tresses as Cole and blue eyes. Her figure was fuller after bearing six children, but her face showed few signs of aging. "Are you all right, sir?"

"His name is Tyler Montgomery, and he was in a fight," Jules announced from behind her mother.

"It looks like he lost," Jess added from behind Jules. "But he said he won."

Maureen turned. "Go find something useful to do." She turned back to Cory. "Your father is taking care of one of the Herbruck boys. He broke his arm."

"He only needs a few stitches." Cory shrugged. "I can handle it."

"Well, if you need anything, your sisters are within earshot." She quietly closed the door.

Tyler sat down on a bench along the wall and examined his wound. "She trusts me to be alone with you?"

"Earshot means the other side of the door," she explained. "Get undressed."

His head jerked up. "What?"

Cory shook her head. "From the waist up."

He chuckled. "You're no fun at all."

Cory heard giggling on the other side of the door and quickly opened it. Jess and Cass stumbled inside.

"I'm going to need some water." She shoved a pitcher at Cass. "And you can ask mother for one of Papa's old shirts."

Jess stared at Tyler's bare chest. "Do you think it will fit?"

Sterling Beecher was tall and thin. Cory had to agree with her sister's assessment, but he couldn't walk around half naked. She took Tyler's bloody shirt. "Go rinse this out and hang it on the line. He won't have to wear Papa's shirt for long."

Cory laid out several odd shaped needles and strung them with thread.

Tyler examined a needle. "Don't you have any smaller ones?"

"Haven't you ever had stitches before?" Cass poured water from the pitcher into a basin on the table.

Tyler returned the needle. "No, and I don't look forward to becoming a pincushion for your sister."

"Papa stitched me up lots of times." Cass showed him a scar on her forehead near the hairline. "See."

Tyler swallowed. "Did it hurt?"

Jess returned and sat down in her father's chair. "Did I miss anything?"

"She hasn't stuck him, yet," Cass said.

"You two are the most morbid creatures I know." Cory removed Tyler's bandage.

Cass pointed. "Look at all the blood."

"Who cares about that? I want to hear him scream."

"Why would I scream?" Tyler turned to Cory. "How much does this hurt?"

"You want us to hold him down?" Jess asked.

"Didn't I ask you to find a shirt?"

"Mama is looking." Jess stood. "He looks like a fighter. Are you sure we shouldn't tie him down? Ethan showed me how to tie knots on the Irish Rose."

Cory snarled. "I want you to leave and close the door behind you."

"We want to help," they said in unison.

Cory pointed at the door, and they shuffled out.

Tyler nodded toward the door. "How loud should I scream?"

"Raise your left arm and brace it with your other hand behind your head so I can reach the wound."

Tyler did as he was instructed. "I'm ready." He nodded toward the door.

Cory swiped the blood from the wound and pinched the torn edges together. She stabbed through the two pieces of flesh with the needle.

Tyler yelped.

"Hold still!" She pulled the needle all the way through and knotted the ends.

"That wasn't funny!" he gasped.

Cory wanted to be gentle but knew it was better to join the wound as quickly as possible. "Only two more."

Tyler's fingers tightened on his left arm, and he clenched his teeth.

She finished the final stitch and knotted it. "See, that wasn't so bad."

He released the grip on his left arm but didn't move. Tyler looked pale.

Cory felt his forehead. "Are you all right?"

"I didn't think anything could be worse than being shot," he gasped. "I was wrong. I would never hurt you this way."

She turned away. "I'll remember that when I'm giving birth to our children."

"What?"

Cory froze as she realized what she had implied. "I didn't mean we…" she stuttered an explanation. "You said you were not a marrying man."

"I never said that." Tyler struggled to breathe

normally. "I said no woman would ever marry me."

"It's the same thing."

"No, it's not."

Cory realized he was right. But did he mean he would marry a woman who overlooked his background? Beth might overlook it, but her parents were moralists. She doubted they would approve the marriage. But would a doctor and a canal brat approve of Tyler? By the end of their visit, she'd know. She cleaned the needles and put them away in the medical cabinet. She picked up a bottle and gasped.

"What's wrong?"

She showed him the bottle as tears welled in her eyes. "I forgot the morphine."

Tyler gagged. "That would be the pain killer?"

"I'm so sorry. My sisters distracted me."

He walked toward her on unsteady legs. "Don't worry about it."

She opened the bottle and applied some morphine to a cloth. "This should help dull the pain." She rested her left hand against his shoulder and placed the damp cloth against the stitches.

He shuddered. "That's much better." His hand rested on her back.

"I keep burning the biscuits." She straightened and found herself in his embrace.

Tyler raised an eyebrow. "Biscuits?"

"I never burned the biscuits before you arrived," she confessed. "I can't seem to do anything right when you're around. What's wrong with me?"

Tyler pulled her close against his chest. He brushed a stray curl away from her face. "We were interrupted on the boat, but I think you owe me a kiss."

"It sometimes helps to ease the pain," she admitted, feeling guilty for her mistake. Cory's eyes widened as he lowered his head and brushed his lips against hers. His touch ignited a spark that lit up her body like a glowing ember. Her fingertips gripped his shoulder. She felt her knees go weak, and her body yielded to his control. She craved to learn all the secrets two people could share and wondered if she could wait. Her body was impatient, and her heart was in turmoil from denying the truth. She loved him. She gasped for air as he pulled away. Only his arms kept her from collapsing.

"I think you owe me two." She nodded in agreement, but a knock at the door tore them apart.

Cory grabbed a roll of bandages as Cole entered with a shirt. She had changed from Jem's ball gown to a plain cotton dress. "Mama wants to know if you'll be staying for supper." She stared at Tyler.

He held out his arms so Cory could wrap the bandage around his chest over the stitches.

"Close your mouth," Cory reminded Cole.

****

The dining room table was large enough to seat ten. Tyler sat to the right of Maureen and next to Cory. Jess and Cole served. They carried the bowls from the kitchen and handed them to Maureen, who passed them around the table. "I'll be glad to return to Grandpa's boat after all the work we've had to do around here," Cole said.

"Me, too," Jess agreed.

"How much jam did you put up?" Cory asked.

"I haven't counted all the jars, but I'm sure we'll have extra to sell," Maureen said.

"I hear Papa!" Jules ran to the window. They could

hear the sound of a horse and buggy on the gravel.

"Do you mind waiting?" Maureen opened the door. "Leave the buggy hitched," she called out before turning back to Cory. "You do want a ride, don't you?"

"It's better than walking."

Sterling Beecher entered with his medical bag and hat in hand. He had dark brown hair with a touch of gray at the temples. He was tall with an intelligent face etched with laugh lines.

Maureen greeted him with a kiss, and his daughters greeted him with hugs and kisses.

"Cory." He kissed her. "What brings you home?"

Maureen looked toward Tyler. Sterling greeted the young man.

"Tyler Montgomery." He stood and waited for everyone to be seated before sitting down. "It's a pleasure meeting you, sir."

"Is that my shirt?"

"Medical problem." Maureen passed the dishes. "Cory took care of it. How is the Herbruck boy?"

"Nasty break," Sterling replied. "The ulna and radius jammed together, and I had to separate and rotate them to set the arm."

"Did Arthur scream?" Jess asked.

"It was Harry, and you'd scream, too," he answered. "It was very painful."

"I like Harry. It's Art who is always making fun of me in school."

"Maybe he likes you," Cole said. "Boys that age act stupid when they like a girl."

"Well, I don't like him, and he knows it."

"Is he the boy you hit?" Tyler asked.

Jess glanced toward her father and lowered her

voice. "How do you know about that?"

"I saw Arthur's black eye. You are not allowed to fight with any boys," Sterling warned from the end of the table.

"Sorry," Tyler whispered to Jess. "I didn't know it was a secret."

"Nothing I do remains a secret for long." Jess turned to her father. "Why can't I hit him? He's bigger than me."

"Because he's not allowed to fight back."

"And any fighting includes girls," Maureen added.

"There are other ways to beat girls," Cole said.

"Nasty words are equally unacceptable. I hope you're not plotting anything, Colleen. You wouldn't want to miss your first dance."

Cole squirmed in her seat.

Maureen turned to Cory. "You better try on the dress Grandma made you and make sure it fits. Unless you plan to take it with you and make your own alterations."

"You're not staying the night?" Sterling asked.

"Adelaide is expecting us."

"Us?" Sterling looked at Tyler. "Are you staying with Adelaide, too, Mr. Montgomery?"

Tyler tugged the collar on his borrowed shirt. "I'm meeting a client at Miss Adelaide's tonight."

Cory saw her parents exchange secretive glances. "Why don't I try on that dress?"

Jem stood to join her, but Maureen spoke. "I'll help her."

Cory hurried up the stairs as her mother followed more leisurely. Cory found the dark green silk gown spread out on the bed she shared with Jules. "It's beautiful."

"Grandma was always talented with a needle, but with a sewing machine, she made dresses for you, Jennifer, and Colleen in a few weeks." She helped her undress and put on the new gown. "So tell me about Mr. Montgomery."

Cory shrugged. "There's not much to tell."

"You light up like a flame every time he looks at you." Maureen pulled back her hair to hook the ball gown. "Is this a love bite?"

"What?" Cory stared in the mirror at the bruise in the shape of a mouth. Tyler had left a mark. She groaned.

"What have you been up to Courtney Rose?"

Cory began with the knock on Adelaide's door two nights ago and nearly everything up to the trip on the Irish Rose. She left out the kissing in the barn and in her father's office.

"He's afraid no woman would marry him because of his parents. Do you think that's a good reason not to marry someone?"

"The members of our family have never had easy love lives. Your father's family didn't approve of me, and Grandma's family didn't approve of Grandpa."

Cory wanted to confess her fears to her mother. What if Tyler didn't want to marry her? What if he was flirting with her until some new girl came along? What if he left and never came back? A sigh escaped her lips.

"What's bothering you?"

"What would you have done if Papa hadn't married you?"

Maureen seemed startled by her question. "I think I would have eventually married someone else."

"But you love Papa."

"We like to believe love is eternal, but it can grow or die. You can build on your initial feelings for each other or look elsewhere for happiness."

Cory didn't want to look elsewhere. "He's taken a job with Sam Morris. What does that mean, Mama?"

"I think you should find out." She helped her remove the new gown and put on her day dress. "Do you want to take it with you tonight?"

"Can you bring it tomorrow?" Cory gathered up her formal gloves, fan, and some hair ribbons and added them to the box with her dress. "You'll have more room in the wagon."

Maureen stroked her hair. "Before your love grows too much, you need to find out where you stand with this young man. If you don't, your father will."

Cory agreed. Tyler liked teasing her. He enjoyed kissing her. But did he love her? Was he over any feelings for Reggie, or was she clinging to false hope?

When they went downstairs, her sisters were putting away the dishes. "Where's Tyler?"

"Papa is talking to him in his office."

Had her father taken the initiative to question Tyler? And what had he answered?

"Here's his shirt." Jem had pressed it. "I don't think the blood stain is coming out."

She took the shirt and headed to her father's office.

Tyler had his borrowed shirt off, and Sterling was replacing the bandage. "I examined his wound," he said. "The stitches should hold as long as he doesn't exert himself."

Cory handed Tyler his shirt and helped him maneuver his left arm into the sleeve. He gathered his vest and jacket from the bench.

"Looks like a gunshot made that hole." Sterling looked at Tyler. "You're not in any trouble, are you, young man?"

"No, sir." Cory helped him with his jacket. "It was an accident."

"Keep the wound clean." Sterling looked at Cory. "Are you ready to go?"

"I left Adelaide's buggy at the livery." Cory gathered her basket and bonnet and led the way through the house to the back door. She gave everyone a hug. "See you tomorrow."

Chapter Twenty-Two

The buggy was built for two, and Cory had to practically sit on Tyler's lap. His hand rested familiarly around her waist. She disguised any unease with a steady flow of conversation. Sterling broached the topic of Douglas.

"I heard Mr. Raymond called at Glen Knolls. Most young men wouldn't call on two ladies alone, especially with one in mourning."

"He called to check on Miss Adelaide."

"Every Sunday?"

Cory rarely had to explain her actions to her father but still felt nervous every time he asked questions. "The last few calls were to visit me, but Miss Adelaide was chaperoning."

"Isn't he a professor at the college?"

"Not yet."

Tyler snickered.

Cory frowned. She knew what he was thinking. Douglas wouldn't be a professor until after he married.

Sterling looked at Tyler. "Do you know him?"

"I met him yesterday when the Reverend Davis and his family came for supper," Tyler replied.

"Douglas was only looking for his keys," she explained. "He thought he'd lost them, but Beth found them. Miss Adelaide invited him to join us."

"Sounds serious. I think it's time I ask Principal

Gregory about him. See what his prospects are."

Cory cringed. "You don't have to do that."

"A father has responsibilities," he answered. "A man with daughters has to make sure a man isn't trifling with their affections or their reputations. Adelaide is an adequate chaperone, but if he doesn't intend to marry you, he won't be welcomed at Glen Knolls or here. Courtship has rules, or a man would throw a woman over his shoulder and carry her off."

Her father wasn't talking exclusively about Douglas. Tyler hadn't followed any rules of courtship. Wait until her mother told him about the love bite.

An awkward silence ensued until they reached the livery. Tyler helped Lou hitch up Nell. Sterling kissed Cory and shook hands with Tyler. "Stay out of trouble, young man."

Tyler swallowed. "I intend to, sir."

On the ride to Glen Knolls, Cory explained how her mother found his mark. "Look!" She pulled back her hair. "What were you thinking?"

"I didn't know it would bruise."

She was too amused by his boyish innocence to be mad. Her chuckle turned to a scream when Clyde stepped out from the woods across from the farm and grabbed Nell's harness.

"Let go there, Clyde," Tyler ordered. "You're scaring the horse."

"What are you hiding?"

"Nothing."

Clyde circled around the buggy. "Mr. Vandal don't want to involve federal marshals, but he will if you don't turn over Tess and her brat."

"How is Mr. Vandal?" Cory asked.

"Do you know there were leeches in the canal?"

Tyler groaned.

"Buck and I don't give up." Clyde moved aside to let them pass.

Tyler handed Cory the reins when they reached the barn and jumped down to slide open the door. He led Nell inside and closed the door before lighting a lantern. "Noah!" Tyler looked around. No reply.

"Maybe they're in the house."

"Noah wouldn't leave without saying good-bye." Tyler hung up the harness. He led Nell outside and around to the back to put her in a stall.

Cory waited for him by the side door to the lower level, and they crossed the yard together to the back door.

Adelaide was heating some water on the stove. Dirty dishes were piled in the dry sink. Her apron was wrinkled, and her normally tight bun was loose.

Cory put her basket down on the table and looked around. "What's wrong?"

"One of the chasers came back to town and almost discovered Tess and the baby hiding in a wagon. Then he set up camp across the road to watch for them. Beth had to lead them through the woods, and it took longer."

"We ran into Clyde out front. He's still watching the house and road. Where are Noah and Tess?" Tyler asked.

"I put them in Hiram's office."

Hiram's office was off the hallway opposite the dining room. It had been closed up since his death. Tyler and Cory found Noah seated next to Tess on a red horsehair sofa. Tess was holding their baby.

"What's wrong?" Tyler asked.

Noah stood up. "The baby is sick."

"He won't suckle." Tess covered her breast. "I don't know what's wrong."

Cory studied the family. Noah was a big man with muscles honed from hard labor. His hair was cut short, a black mass of tight curls. His features were those of a black man with a smooth round forehead and high cheekbones, but his nose was not as flat on the bridge. The white race was more evident in Tess. Her skin was lighter, and her nose was narrow. Cory studied her face, looking for any similarities to Edward Vandal.

"I bet you don't meet many slaves in Ohio," Tess said quietly.

Cory was embarrassed for being caught staring. "I am sorry for being rude. You're quite beautiful," she added.

"What?" Tess hid her face.

Cory turned her attention to the baby. He was quiet. He opened his big round eyes but didn't seem interested in his surroundings. Cory placed her hand on his forehead. He was warm to the touch and listless, neither crying nor smiling.

"Let me see your hand, Tess."

She held out her small hand palm up.

"I'm not going to hurt you." Cory turned it over and saw fresh briar scratches. She pinched the loose skin on top before releasing it. The skin remained peaked before smoothing out. "Have you eaten?"

"Miss Adelaide fed us when we arrived."

"What about before that?"

"We had some breakfast, but Adam hardly nursed. It's been so hot in the church."

"You're overheated." Cory looked at Adam. "It can be deadly."

Tess held Adam closer.

Noah stroked his son's head. "Can you do something?"

"He needs fluids."

Tess choked back tears. "He won't nurse."

Cory cleared a table. "I'll start by giving him a bath to cool him down."

"Will my son be all right?" Noah asked.

Cory didn't want to lie to them. She didn't know. Dehydration from the heat could kill an adult in hours and less time for an infant. "You need to start drinking water, milk, anything we have," Cory instructed Tess. "Otherwise, you won't have any milk for Adam."

"I'll go milk Bessie." Tyler hurried out the door.

"You have a cow named Bessie?" Noah asked.

His grin was familiar. Cory didn't have time to wonder why. "He calls all the cows Bessie." She opened the door. "I'll fetch some water."

Cory found Adelaide in the kitchen. "The baby is overheated, but well water will be too cold for a bath. What did you do with the hot water you were heating?"

"I used most of it to wash the dishes, but there's some left in the pot. Is it enough?"

Cory lifted the pot. "Enough to take the chill off."

Cory headed for the pump and filled a pitcher. In the kitchen she added the hot water from the stove and tested the temperature. She gathered up bathing supplies and entered the study. Tyler entered with a pail. "How much milk did you get?"

"About half a pail."

"Have Tess drink as much as possible."

Cory filled a basin with water and laid the towels on the table before she turned her attention to Adam. He wore a soiled gown made from a flour bag. She helped Tess remove it and watched as she undid a piece of string holding a triangle of burlap lined with cotton that served as a diaper.

Cory felt the diaper. "It's dry." She looked at the others. "That's not good."

"Help him," Noah urged her.

Cory cradled Adam in her arm and lowered him into the water. She gently bathed him with a sponge.

Noah and Tess held hands as they looked on.

"Don't forget to drink the milk, Tess." Cory nodded toward the pail Tyler had placed on Hiram's desk. "You'll need to be ready when this young man becomes hungry."

Tyler crowded behind Cory. "Is he any better?"

She continued to wet down the baby's dry skin. Adam stared. "You're wondering who I am, aren't you? All these new places and strange people. You've had quite an adventure." He reached for her. "You are too pretty for a boy. Look at those long lashes. Where did you get such pretty eyes?"

Adam smiled and revealed four small white teeth.

Cory looked up. "I think he's feeling better. He's flirting with me." He slammed his fist in the water and splashed her. "Now, I know he's better."

"I can't believe how much he's grown." Noah reached his finger out, and Adam grabbed it. "He can sit up and feel that grip."

Tess finished a cup of milk and joined them. Adam reached for his mother and fussed.

Cory wrapped him in a towel and handed him to

Tess. "Try nursing him now."

Tess looked around. "Where did I put his diaper?"

"I have something better." She left, found her basket in the kitchen, and returned with her packages. "I bought some items for the baby." Cory unwrapped the bundle.

"You don't even know me," Tess said.

"I've heard a lot about you." Cory placed the diapers and pins on the table.

"I certainly can use these. I've worn out every bit of cloth I could find to put on him."

Cory held up the gown and cap.

Tess touched the soft fabric. "It's beautiful."

"I'm glad you like them."

"That was real nice of you, Miss Beecher," Noah said.

"My students call me Miss Beecher. You better call me Cory."

"Miss Cory," Tess corrected. "It's a sign of respect."

"Thank you, Miss Tess."

"Oh no. I'm Tess."

"You traveled all the way from Virginia with a baby, and you don't deserve respect?" Cory demanded. "I could never do what you did."

"I've caused a lot of trouble," Tess said. "That's what I've done. I should never have left, but Miss Regina didn't give me a choice."

"She's sorry for what she did," Tyler said. "But you can't go back."

"Them chasers have other plans."

"Don't worry about Clyde and Buck." Tyler looked at Noah. "We can handle them."

Adam fussed, but Tess didn't unbutton her dress.

"Let's give them some privacy." Cory herded Tyler out of the room.

"You were good with him in there." He followed her into the kitchen.

"Babies are easy to take care of," Cory said. "It's grown men who cause the most trouble."

Adelaide was making coffee. "How are they doing?"

"Better."

"Is that the truth?" Noah had followed them into the kitchen. "I won't leave if it's going to risk their lives."

"Let's see how the baby is doing after nursing," Cory said. "Has Tess slept any?"

"She's been too worried about Adam."

Tyler grabbed a slice of blackberry pie left from last night's supper. "We only saw Clyde in front. Any sign of Edward and Buck?"

"No, but Beth rang the church bell when she returned to the square," Adelaide said. "It means all is clear."

Cory frowned. "Why did Beth bring them? I thought the Reverend was going to do that?"

"Beth always does the traveling," Adelaide said. "Nobody ever notices her."

Cory felt new respect for Beth. Underneath her quiet, demure exterior was a warrior. Maybe her support of the Underground Railroad was the reason she refused Douglas' proposal.

"There's a lot more to her than I thought," Cory conceded.

"I'm sorry we involved so many people," Noah

226

said. "I thought it would be easy to find Tess and head north. I never expected Edward and his chasers to be so relentless."

Tyler looked outside. "No lights in the house until we can put some distance between us and Edward Vandal."

"Us?" Noah demanded. "You're not traveling with us."

"I can help. I have a letter of credit from the bank, and I can vouch you're my slaves if we're stopped."

"You will end up in jail if Edward finds you with us," Noah said. "You can help us by staying out of trouble and arguing my case if I get caught with Tess and Adam."

Noah and Tyler stared at each other.

"Do you think you'll be able to find the next stop in the dark?" Adelaide asked. "It's going to be cloudy tonight. Maybe you should wait."

"Every minute we stay puts all of us in danger," Noah said. "I'm surprised Edward has waited this long. I can't thank you enough for the help you've given me and my family."

"You should sleep some before you set out," she advised.

Cory recognized the signs of fatigue in Adelaide. "Why don't you rest, too?" She took her arm and led her upstairs to bed. Once Adelaide was settled, she checked on Tess and Adam. They were seated on the couch. Tess stood.

"Sit down." Cory sat opposite her. "How is he doing?"

"He's wide awake." Tess yawned. "I think he wants to play."

"Well, I'm not sleepy. I'll wear him out while you sleep."

Tess handed over Adam. "Send my husband in if you see him." Tess spread a quilt on the floor. "I miss him."

"The bed upstairs would be more comfortable, but you'd be trapped if the Cassell brothers decided to pay a visit. If there's any trouble, the back door is right there."

"I've been sleeping in the woods and in barns, Miss Cory. This is pure luxury."

Cory found Tyler and Noah in the kitchen drinking coffee and eating pie. She watched the two men in familiar camaraderie. Did helping Noah reach freedom erase all the years they had been master and slave?

Adam screeched when he saw his father. Noah stood. "I'm sorry." He raised his hands. "Let me take him."

"Oh, no," Cory protested. "Your wife wants you."

Noah looked puzzled. "Is something wrong?"

Cory smiled. "She misses you."

Noah bounded out the room.

"What's that all about?" Tyler asked. "We were talking."

"Something between a husband and wife." She turned away. "I'm going to take care of this little guy so they can rest."

He hurried after her. "What about me?"

"Maybe you should check on Clyde."

"Tyler followed her to the parlor. He peered out the window. "He's still down by the road standing guard."

Cory recalled Clyde's threat. "Do you think they'll bring a marshal?"

"It's easier for them to take Tess alone on the road and not involve any officials."

"Can't she make a fuss like Noah when he was arrested?"

"Edward has proof of ownership. If Tess is arrested, the marshals will escort her to the train for Edward."

"So he wins both ways."

"If they involve federal marshals it could attract a crowd," Tyler explained. "Abolitionists may try a rescue like they did in Wellington. That's why Edward hasn't contacted them, yet."

"I never realized how far the Fugitive Slave Law could reach. They can slap manacles on you no matter how long you've been free unless someone vouches for you." Cory recalled Tyler's words from their first meeting. "Noah is lucky to have you."

He frowned. "That's a funny thing to say to a slave owner."

"Now you're admitting you're a slave owner?"

Tyler didn't answer.

Chapter Twenty-Three

Cory placed Adam on the parlor rug. She made sure the front door and parlor windows were closed in case they made any noise. Then she took corn cob checker pieces out of the desk drawer and sat down on the parlor rug opposite the baby. She stacked the pieces. Cory worried how Tyler would react to the news she had guessed his secret and decided to ease into the revelation.

"It's not like you bought Noah." She added another checker to the pillar. "Did Miss Olivia leave him to you when she died?"

Tyler stretched out on the parlor rug. "She left me everything she owned."

Cory studied his face. It was the truth only because Miss Olivia didn't own Noah any more than her mother owned her. He was no more a master to a slave than a father is to a daughter or a husband to a wife. She concentrated on the baby instead of the confusing thoughts crisscrossing her mind.

"Knock them down," Cory urged Adam. She brushed the top piece off. Adam stared but didn't follow her example. Cory knocked all the pieces over. Adam's eyes widened, and he stuck out his bottom lip. "It's all right," Cory cooed when he appeared about to cry. She smiled at him and quickly stacked the checkers in a new pile. "Now it's your turn."

She took his hand and knocked off a checker. She clapped. "That's it. Knock them over." He waved his chubby arm in the air and collided with the pillar. The checkers crashed everywhere. Cory clapped and laughed. "Good boy."

She repeated the action, and this time Adam burst into a gurgling brook of baby noises when she praised his destructive task. Tyler took over. He stacked the pieces and encouraged Adam to knock them down. He reacted each time as if it was the first time.

A deep voice interrupted their laughter. "I hate to interrupt, but I'd like my son back." Noah stood in the doorway.

Cory looked out the window. It was dark. "I didn't realize it was so late."

"Watch this." Tyler stacked the checkers again, and Adam knocked them down in a fit of laughter. "He does that every time. Never gets tired of it."

"You always were easily amused," Noah remarked.

Cory's heart pounded in her chest. She watched as Tyler handed Adam to Noah. They stood side by side. Similar in height and build, but one dark and one fair.

She'd sensed something initially when they sat talking at the kitchen table, and Tyler's evasive answers had made her suspicious of the truth, but now she was sure. The two men were brothers. Half-brothers. What had confused her was thinking they shared the same father like Edward and Tess. The timeline didn't fit. Noah had been born after Miss Olivia ran away from home but before marrying Tyler's father.

"When will you be leaving?"

"As soon as Tess can rock Adam to sleep," Noah said.

Adam yawned and rested his head on his father's shoulder. Noah carried him to the back room.

"I love babies," Cory gushed.

"If you ask nicely, I might be convinced to give you one."

Cory stared at him through slits. "I have a feeling that is not a marriage proposal."

"I told you my family history." He put the checkers in a box. "Could any woman overlook that?"

Cory turned on him. "Don't use your parents as an excuse for not marrying me. Or any other woman," she hastily added. "Do you think I care that your mother ran a saloon or your father ran off in search of a fortune? It's your actions that count. If a man is serious about a woman, he courts her and declares his love. None of this sneaking around stealing kisses and making excuses for not marrying her."

"My mother did worse than run a saloon."

"The Dunking Witch was a whorehouse." She dismissed the fact with a wave of her hand. "I don't care."

"There's more."

Cory saw the pain in his expression. "You don't have to tell me. I already know."

Tyler shook his head. "You're wrong."

"You said your mother ran away from home when she was fifteen," Cory reminded him. "Was Noah born shortly after she left?"

"To Lydia." He ran his fingers through his hair.

"That's a nervous habit," she accused. "If Lydia was his mother, why not let your father sell Noah so he could stay with her?"

Tyler stammered. "Miss Olivia wanted to keep him

as a companion for me."

"She paid a high price to keep him." She gazed into his eyes. "You've said more than once he wasn't a slave."

Tyler didn't answer.

Cory jabbed her finger at him. "He wasn't a slave because he wasn't born a slave! If the mother is free, the child is free. Noah isn't your slave. He's your brother."

Tyler looked around. "Don't say that."

Cory stomped her foot. "You're no better than Edward."

He stepped back from her. "What?"

"He won't admit Tess is his half-sister, and you won't admit Noah is your half-brother. You're both hypocrites."

"It's not the same," Tyler defended. "Cyrus Vandal was applauded for his rapes and procreation, but a white woman can't allow a black man to look at her let alone touch her. Miss Olivia ran away because her father would have killed her rather than let Noah be born. He would have taken Noah's father and beaten him until no flesh was left on his body. Then he would have castrated him, cut off his hands and feet, and burned what was still breathing after he'd strung him up with a noose."

Cory felt sick. "Why? How can one be acceptable and the other not?"

"Because men are hypocrites." He smacked his fist into his palm. "They want no limits on their earthly pleasures, but they want women to maintain the purity of the white race. When Grayson found out Miss Olivia refused to sell Noah because he was her son, he nearly killed her. That's reality. We never talked about it. Miss Olivia told Cyrus about me, but she didn't say anything about Noah."

"Then I won't say anything," Cory promised.

"I don't like keeping it a secret, but in the South everyone knows, but nobody talks about it. One of the many unwritten laws we obey. I'm hoping for the day when I can admit the truth and claim Noah as my brother openly. But the secret doesn't stop us from taking care of each other." Tyler looked at her. "How did you figure it out?"

"It was the way you were at the table when I walked in," she explained. "Like two brothers talking about everything and nothing. The same as my sisters and me. Then I put everything you said about your parents and Noah together."

"Noah says I talk too much."

"Don't all lawyers?" she teased.

"This one does." Noah stood in the hallway outside the parlor.

Cory wondered how much he had heard. They joined him in the foyer.

"We're ready to go," Noah said. Tess stood near the sideboard with Adam asleep in a sling made from a scarf.

"I need a few things." Tyler dashed up the staircase.

"I can live with pretending to be a slave," Noah said to Cory. "I can live with never acknowledging Tyler as my brother. What I can't live with is him being so noble and honest, he throws away his chance at happiness. He's in love with you. Will this stop you from marrying him?"

Cory shook her head. "He hasn't asked me."

"Idiot."

She'd thought of him the same way once. "Younger siblings have to find their own way."

"Don't let him get lost," Noah warned.

Tyler bounded down the stairs with his valise and snatched his hat from the sideboard.

"I thought I told you not to come," Noah said.

"I'm not," Tyler said. "But if Clyde doesn't see me leave Glen Knolls, he'll tell Edward I'm sleeping under the same roof as two unmarried women. He won't hesitate to share his low opinion of me."

"He'd ruin my reputation along with yours," Cory realized.

"I'm going to convince Clyde to join me for a drink at the Red Pony Tavern. Maybe he'll tell me Edward's plans."

Cory looked at his bag. "So this is good-bye."

"Until tomorrow." He grinned. "I'm taking your father's advice and following social protocols. I already asked Miss Adelaide's permission to drive her to the picnic tomorrow. You're invited to join us unless Mr. Raymond is taking you."

Douglas. Cory had to decide what to do with him. If she accepted his proposal, she'd have a husband. Why had marriage been so important a few days ago? She looked at Tyler, but he was talking to Noah.

"If you run into any trouble, send word here. Miss Adelaide will know how to contact me." Tyler put on his hat. "Give me about ten minutes before you head for the woods." He put his hand on the door knob.

"Wait!" Cory called. "You may never see him again. Aren't you going to say good-bye?"

Noah grabbed Tyler into a bear hug. "He's sort of shy."

Cory hugged Tess, who was startled by the gesture. She looked down at Adam nestled on Tess' hip, unaware of the dangerous journey he was about to embark upon. She leaned down and planted a kiss on his forehead. "Be safe."

Tyler hesitated at the door.

"You better go," Cory urged him. "Get Clyde out of the way."

Cory listened at the open door as Tyler loudly greeted Clyde. Their voices carried across the yard and faded down the road. She led Tess and Noah to the kitchen and handed Noah a basket with food Adelaide had packed for their trip. She opened the back door and stepped outside. It was quiet. She looked around and then signaled them to come out. They headed across the yard to the woods. Cory watched as their shadows disappeared and listened for any noise of discovery. Silence.

****

Cory packed the baskets for the picnic. Noah, Tess, and Adam should have reached their next station and would be hid during the day, but her nerves were on edge. What if Edward and his chasers had found them?

Adelaide added some fried chicken to a basket. "Be careful you don't burn those biscuits."

Cory removed the biscuits from the oven and placed them on a napkin. "Are you sure you want to go to the picnic?"

"We want the chasers to search the house and barn while we're gone, don't we? They won't if I'm here. Besides, it's time I socialized. Hiram never believed in long mourning periods. He wouldn't want me to sit around waiting to join him."

Cory gave her a hug and looked around for any signs of their visitors. "I hope we didn't miss anything."

"Where's Tyler?"

"Hitching up Nell, I guess."

Adelaide studied her. "You two have a fight?"

"No," she answered quietly. "I have to think about my future."

"You're not the only one. He asked about the farm."

Cory was startled. "Why?"

"Maybe he wants to buy it."

"He's a lawyer not a farmer."

"Your pa is a doctor, but a farm feeds a family when business is slow."

First a job with Sam Morris and now talk of buying Glen Knolls. Tyler was putting down roots. Did his plans include her or any woman willing to take a chance on a young man with a good education and questionable bloodline? Beth was pretty, available, and had helped bring Tess to Glen Knolls. Maybe his plans included her. Could she see him in town, in church, or on the street knowing he belonged to another? Her heart felt like lead in her chest. And what about Douglas? What if he proposed? What would she say?

All thoughts of marrying Douglas vanished when Tyler entered the back door. Her breath caught in her throat. His hair was a mass of unruly curls that he raked his fingers through to brush back from his sky-colored eyes. He grinned as if they were intimate friends, and her gaze paused on his lips as fond memories of what a mere kiss from them could do to her resolve. It would take a lifetime to grow weary of looking at his handsome face.

"The buggy is ready when you are."

Adelaide handed him a basket. "Where did you sleep last night?"

"The Red Pony Tavern," Tyler and Cory echoed.

"I see you have your stories straight."

"I have the fleas to prove it," Tyler remarked. "If Edward wasn't staying at Darrow Falls Inn, I'd sleep there. The beds are cleaner."

Adelaide turned to Cory. "Is Mr. Raymond taking you to the picnic?"

"One of his students delivered a note." Cory glanced at Tyler. "He was needed at the college and will meet me later on the square." Cory finished loading her basket. "Any sign of Clyde or Buck?"

"No, and that's bad," Tyler remarked. "I hope Noah and Tess are all right."

"Can't help them by worrying," Adelaide said. "We can find out about Edward and his men from Paula. She'll know when they left the inn and what direction they took."

"Is Mrs. Stone part of the Underground Railroad?"

She frowned. "First rule of the Underground Railroad is not to ask."

****

The games were already under way when Cory, Tyler, and Adelaide arrived at the town square. Cory's family gathered around the buggy.

"How are you feeling, Addy?" Maureen asked.

"Show me to a shady tree with the other old people, and I'll be fine," Adelaide replied.

"The men are bringing out the benches from the

church."

"Miss Adelaide baked some pies for the contests," Cory told her mother. "Where do we put them?"

"The pies for the contest go in the church," Maureen said. "You can take mine."

Cory grabbed the two square pie baskets.

Tyler took one, and they crossed the square to the church. The white structure was three stories high not counting the steeple where a bell signaled Sunday services or hid runaway slaves from chasers.

Pies filled the table in the foyer. The kitchen door was open. Cory saw more pies arranged on the oak table where she had dined with the Davis family the day before. She removed the pies from the baskets and placed them with the others.

On their way out, they saw two men carrying a bench down the stairs. Tyler held open the church doors. "Need any help?"

"Check upstairs."

Chapter Twenty-Four

Cory and Tyler climbed the stairs to the meeting room on the second floor. Nearly all of the benches had been removed and the pews moved along the walls. Pillars supported a balcony on the third floor above them and along the sides. The dome ceiling had a huge brass chandelier, but it was only lit when the wall sconces and stained glass windows failed to provide enough light.

The pulpit had been removed from the raised dais at the far end of the room. The band would play there for the dance later in the evening.

"Do you attend church here?" Tyler asked. "I thought all Irish were Catholic."

"Grandma is German and Protestant, and Grandpa gave up religion a long time ago. Papa and Mama started coming here after I was born."

"Hello!" The Reverend Davis came out of a back room. "I'm afraid there's nothing left to remove." He lowered his voice. "I heard you had some visitors. Are they gone?"

"Yes," Cory answered. "Do you know where Beth is? I'd like to thank her."

"She's busy doing whatever needs done. No idle hands on that girl."

Cory wanted to talk to Beth before she met with Douglas, and she didn't want Tyler to be around for the conversation. If she wanted a husband, she could accept Douglas, but if she wanted love, she would have to gamble on whether Tyler loved her and wanted to build a future together. Her thoughts were interrupted by her three youngest sisters running into the room. Their voices echoed in the emptiness.

"I need your help, Cory!" Jules took her hand.

"What's wrong?"

"I want to win the sack race, and you need to help me."

Cory looked at Jess. "Why don't you help her?"

"I can't. I'm the competition."

"When is this race?"

"Now," Jules and Cass said in unison.

"I'm going to win it!" Jess didn't wait for her sisters. Her footsteps echoed down the stairs. The door slammed.

"Help us, Cory," Jules begged.

"Family crisis." Cory handed him the empty baskets. "Do you mind taking them back to Mama and Miss Adelaide?"

Cory and her sisters gathered in the center of the square where about a dozen girls were lining up for the sack race. The boys had already raced. Cory searched through several burlap sacks and handed them to her sisters.

"Help me get in the bag," Jules begged.

"Put it on the ground." Cory helped Jules and Cass step into the sacks and pull them over their skirts.

Cass started to hop toward the starting line but tripped over the bag and fell down. Tyler picked her up in the sack and set her down on the ground. "Keep your feet together when you hop."

"You came back?" Cory had expected him to join the men gathered around the beer wagon to talk about war and politics.

"I didn't want to miss the fun." He chewed on a chicken leg.

Most men had no interest in children, but she could easily see Tyler as a father who played games with his children the way he had amused Adam.

Tyler was studying her. "You want some of my chicken leg?"

"No."

"You look hungry."

Her hunger wasn't for food. She opened her fan and waved the painted screen in front of her face. Cory forced her attention toward her sisters. Cass fell down, struggled to stand, and joined the others at the starting line.

A gunshot signaled the start of the race. "You're ahead, Jess! Hold onto the sack, Cassie! Both feet together, Jules!" Cory jumped up and down like she was in a sack.

Cory grabbed Tyler's arm when Cass tumbled. "Get up, Cassie! Get up!"

Jess had gained the lead while Jules had fallen behind. She collided with another girl and fell after Jess crossed the finish line to win.

Jules remained on the ground. "Looks like Jules is hurt," Tyler said.

Cory was surprised he already knew her sisters' names.

"She's crying," he said.

"She's the dramatic one."

"Are you going to ignore her?" His frantic tone

made her smile. Other men thought her sisters were
pests. And they were most of the time, but they were
her sisters. She loved them. A good husband would
love them, too. Now she had to convince Tyler he'd
make a good husband.

"I'll take care of Jules," she said. "See if you can
untangle Cass from her bag."

Cory led Jules to the blanket near the bench where
Adelaide and Maureen were seated. "Our first
casualty."

"It hurts," Jules complained. "Where's Papa?"

"He's talking politics, and all this cut needs is a
little cleaning," Maureen said.

Cory took her lace edged handkerchief from her
purse.

"You'll ruin it," Maureen said. "Pa's bag is in the
wagon under the bench. Do you mind fetching it?"

"Where did you leave your wagon?"

"Near the Darrow Falls Inn. Pa put the horses in
their pasture."

"Might want to see if anyone is missing the
festivities," Adelaide said. "Paula said the two chasers
headed north before dawn, but Edward is still in town."

Cory headed toward the inn. She saw Edward
smoking a cigar while he watched the celebration from
a distance.

Tyler joined her. "What are we going to do for fun
now?"

"After I fetch Papa's bag, I'm going to invite
Edward to the picnic."

He frowned. "Why would you want to do that?"

"It'll be easier watching him on the square than
trying to track him down every hour to find out what he

and his chasers are doing."

They reached the Beecher wagon. "Clyde and Buck have had plenty of time to search Adelaide's place." Tyler boosted Cory up, and she searched behind the seat. "They should be back by now."

They were both worried. But the Cassell brothers wouldn't take Tess to Virginia without informing Edward. By watching him, they'd know if she'd been captured. Cory removed the doctor's bag and handed it to Tyler. "Here, take this to Mama."

Tyler hesitated. "Maybe I should ask Edward to join us."

"We want him to come," she argued. "Now go. And when he comes to the square, play nice."

"Should I invite him to a sack race? I think he'd look good tied up in one."

Cory shook her head. "There's virtue in everyone."

"I don't disagree. Even the most heinous murderer may love his mother, but life is a struggle between good and evil." He looked at Edward. "And sometimes evil wins."

Cory watched Tyler cross the street before calling to Edward. "Mr. Vandal, why don't you join us on the square? There's plenty to eat."

"I don't think so, Miss Beecher."

"Don't you celebrate Independence Day in Virginia?"

"Yes, we do, but don't you think Tyler Montgomery will object?"

"It's not Tyler's town."

"We don't like each other."

Cory wasn't ready to give up. Maybe if she understood Edward more, she'd understand Tyler's dislike of the man. "Why not?"

"I was Cyrus Vandal's son, and he was a poor bastard." Edward blew a puff of smoke. "He doesn't belong in the company of decent folk."

It was the same argument he'd shared before. She was glad Tyler had shared the information about his family, but it wasn't enough to explain Edward's hatred. Why did Edward want Tyler ostracized? She chose a topic he might want to brag about. "Tell me about Cyrus."

He struck a pose. "My father was rich and powerful. Men looked up to him. Women sought his attention."

"Like Miss Olivia?"

Edward tossed his cigar in the dirt and grinded it with his boot. "Miss Olivia thought she could seduce him into marriage."

"You didn't think Miss Olivia could make him happy?"

"Any whore can make a man forget who he is in bed. Tyler was the son of a whore," Edward said. "He pretended to belong, but he was a fraud."

"And you made sure everyone knew it."

He scowled. "So he told you. I didn't expect him to admit the truth."

"Like he did when he stood up for her?"

"I thought he'd run away in tears." Edward gave a short laugh. "Who defends a whore?"

"A son who loves her."

"She used her ill-gotten gains to pay for his education, but he's still a guttersnipe." Edward wiped his brow with a kerchief. "He'll never have my respect."

"Respect is important to you," Cory realized.

"No one laughs at a Vandal. My father demanded respect from everyone. I don't accept any less."

"What happened to your father?"

"He died. I was twenty-two when I became owner of the Silver Pheasant. Suddenly I was a young man of wealth and power. Those traits make you popular, especially with the ladies of town."

"Reggie, too?"

"I didn't even notice her at first," he admitted. "She worked in a little shop in town. She was quiet with the manners of a lady. When Tyler graduated from Harvard, Regina made him a vest. He strutted around town in it. They were a popular pair that summer. He didn't deserve it. He didn't deserve her. I started calling on her, and she married me."

"So you beat Tyler again."

"Did I? I bought Regina. She was a miner's daughter, and I made her the mistress of the Silver Pheasant. Her heart still belongs to Tyler."

Cory wondered. Tyler believed Reggie had showered him with attention to attract Edward. Reggie had to know Tyler could be wealthy someday, but she had refused his proposal on her wedding day. Yet Edward believed she had married him for his wealth. "Is your wife a smart woman, Mr. Vandal?"

"Why do you ask?"

"You admit you didn't notice Reggie until she made Tyler a vest. Her poverty and your wealth may have made her insecure. A smart woman would keep her husband close and attentive by creating an imaginary threat."

His brow furrowed. "Are you saying Regina lied to

me?"

"She doesn't need to lie. It seems to me, your imagination does most of the work."

Edward studied her. "You don't know how close they were growing up."

"They were friends. He was kind to a poor, frightened child, and she was grateful. Don't mistake loyalty for love. After all, she married you."

"Are you in love with Tyler?"

Cory hesitated to answer. It might give him ammunition to use against Tyler, but she didn't like to lie. "Yes. But more importantly, he's in love with me." At least she hoped so.

Edward put on his hat. "I think I'll join you, if you don't mind."

Cory introduced Edward to her mother and Adelaide, who kept him busy with a barrage of questions. Edward deflected the inquiries about the Cassell brothers by saying they were on an errand in Cleveland. Tyler had distanced himself from Edward by joining Sterling and some other men near the beer wagon. One of the men was Douglas.

The pie eating contest was announced, and Cory volunteered to help in the church kitchen. She found Beth standing at the table neatly slicing pies. Cory grabbed an apron and knife and joined her. The other ladies lifted the slices onto plates and loaded them on trays. Others carried the trays outside.

"That's it." Beth stacked a few empty pie tins and wiped her hands on her stained apron. She sighed and sat down. The other women headed outside with the remaining trays of pie slices.

Cory remained behind. "You look tired."

"Nobody realizes how much work a holiday activity can be for those making sure everyone else is having a good time," Beth said.

"Your work is important." Cory lowered her voice. "Thank you for all the help you gave our friends."

Beth glanced around. "We don't need to talk about it. My reward is in heaven not here on Earth."

Cory sat next to her at the table. "I want you to know how much I admire your courage."

"My knees were knocking the whole time I was in the woods. I don't know what I would have done if I ran into one of those awful chasers."

Chapter Twenty-Five

Beth's confession didn't deter Cory's admiration. She wanted to do something for her. She glanced around, saw no one, and voiced an idea she had considered since she found out about Beth's abolitionist support.

"Is your role helping others why you didn't accept Mr. Raymond's proposal? He made it clear he believes in colonization."

Beth looked started. "You know about his proposal?"

"Miss Adelaide said you turned him down." She watched Beth's expression closely. "She said he was looking for a wife."

Beth gasped. "Has he proposed to you?"

"No." Cory cleared her throat. "But I'm afraid he might."

Beth frowned. "Don't you want to marry him?"

Cory shook her head. "I don't love him. I wish I knew someone who did. It might help him with any disappointment he might have when I tell him how I feel."

Beth blushed. "Have I been so obvious?"

Cory took her hand and made up a slight fib. "He spoke highly of you. Was it politics that made you refuse him?"

She shook her head in denial. "His politics would

have been a perfect cover for my own."

Her confession surprised her. "You're a sly one, Beth. He insisted I change my views to match his. I know couples should have a few things in common, but not everything."

"Faith, morals, and how to raise the children," Beth said. "That's all I ask."

"Did Douglas meet those requirements?"

She nodded.

Cory hesitated but needed to ask. "Then you didn't love him?"

She shook her head, unable to answer as she choked on the words.

She had to be patient. Beth reminded her of Cass, who had to be gently coaxed to reveal her inner thoughts and feelings. She smiled kindly. "Why did you turn him down then?"

Beth looked up, tears brimming in her eyes. "I was a fool."

Cory couldn't imagine anyone as level-headed as Beth acting like a fool. "Because you said no?"

She nodded in agreement.

Cory guessed the reason. "Because you're still in love with him."

She nodded in the affirmative.

"If it wasn't politics or lack of love, why did you reject his offer?"

Beth removed a handkerchief from her shirt sleeve and wiped her tears. "I didn't think he loved me."

Cory didn't want to speculate. "Why not?"

"He was so analytical about marriage. You heard him the other night," she said. "When he proposed he didn't even say he loved me." Beth blew her nose. "I always wanted a proposal of marriage to be romantic like in a Jane Austen novel. I know it was foolish of me, but I dreamed he would declare his undying love and promise to cherish me forever. Instead he said how practical marrying a preacher's daughter would be. We could save money on the wedding ceremony." She burst into tears.

Cory bit her lip to keep from laughing as she patted Beth's shoulder. No wonder Beth had turned him down. "Maybe you're better off without him. After all, you'd have to play mother to his students."

"But that's what I like," Beth confessed. "I'd be part of his work like Mother is part of Father's work. They say a woman marries a man like her father. Douglas may not be as loud as the Reverend, but he certainly believes every word he speaks is the gospel truth like him."

Cory laughed. She looked to see if Beth was offended. She laughed with her. "Your mother seems happy enough."

"Douglas is like pie dough." Beth wiped up some pie crust crumbs. "He needs to be molded into a finished product. Someday he'll do great deeds. I'm sure of it. He just needs a little help achieving them."

"And you want to be the one to help him do it," Cory deduced. "So how do we convince Douglas he loves you?"

"He's above such base emotions. He thinks love is a mathematical equation. One plus one equals two." She held her thumb and index finger an inch apart. "All I'm asking for is a little romance."

"I don't think it's too much to ask for a man to declare his love before he marries you." Cory was still waiting for Tyler to say the words that would erase all the doubts about their future.

"That's why I said no. I love him now. What if he doesn't learn to love me after we're married? What if it's all one sided?" Beth shook her head. "I wonder who he'll court next?"

"Would you take him back if he courted you?"

"I had my chance."

"You can't give up so easily. Tyler said Southern girls make a man propose until they do it right."

"I doubt if Douglas will try again."

"Weren't you flirting with Tyler to make Douglas notice you?"

She reddened. "It didn't work."

"How do you know? Have you talked to Douglas?"

Beth looked around at the dirty kitchen. "I've been busy."

"Well if you're going to act like an old maid, you'll end up one. Go out, talk to people, and make Douglas notice you."

Beth looked at her dull work dress and dirty apron. "Maybe you're right. The dance starts soon, and I made a new dress. Why can't I have fun like everyone else?" She removed her apron. "Have you told him you're not interested?"

"I'll go find him." She pointed at Beth. "You better be ready to mend any cracks I put in his pride when I turn him down." She finished off a small slice of pie left in a tin and headed outside. She prayed Douglas took her rejection graciously.

She crossed Church Street and looked around the square. The beer wagon had a new crowd around it. Where was Douglas?

"You looking for me?" Tyler cleaned raspberry pie from his face with his kerchief. "I didn't win the pie eating contest, but my lips are all sweetened up for the kiss you owe me."

She ignored his comment as she searched the crowd. "Have you seen Douglas?"

Tyler made a sour face. "What do you want him for?"

"I want him to propose." She saw Douglas near a tree on the corner of Mill Street. "There he is!" She dashed past Tyler. "Wish me luck."

****

If Cory had a plan, it disappeared the minute she saw Douglas looking so vulnerable. Maybe it was the sunburn on his high forehead or the way he kept spinning his mangled hat around with his fingertips. She didn't like hurting others, but it was cruel to lead Douglas on with no hope of loving him. A quick severance was better than letting plans unravel over time.

"I haven't seen you all day." Cory tapped Douglas on the shoulder with her closed fan. "Where have you been?"

"I saw you with your family and Mr. Montgomery and hesitated to intrude."

I love him, and I don't love you. That might be too abrupt. Cory sat on a bench under one of the shade trees planted on the edge of the square. "You were honest and forthright about your plans for the future, and I wish to talk about mine."

Douglas sat next to her and took her hand. It was sweaty. Cory opened her fan and waved it with her free hand.

"Then you're not angry with me?" He lowered his voice. "About the kiss?"

Cory tried not to groan and moved her fan to block her face. "You were quite forward, Mr. Raymond."

"You make me bold." He knelt on one knee in front of her. "I will not jeopardize your reputation by hesitating to make my intentions clear. Miss Beecher, will you marry me?"

Cory had meant to gently coax his attention toward Beth, but a harsher voice would be necessary. She glanced around and saw only a few people nearby who might witness the scene she would create. She took a deep breath and launched her attack. "Is that it?" She snatched her hand from his.

Douglas fell back. "What do you mean? I asked you to marry me?"

"Without a declaration of love?" She stood. "Get up! You didn't even say I was pretty. When other men have proposed to me, they at least compliment me. You didn't even do that." She fanned herself with quick, agitated strokes.

Douglas looked stunned. "I'm sorry."

"Oh, don't apologize!" she snapped. Douglas cowered as if she'd struck him. He looked so scared that Cory had to fight the urge to soften her words. She closed her fan and smacked it against her palm. "It's too late. Why no self-respecting woman would say yes to such a proposal. A woman expects flowers, flattery, and a declaration of love from the man she marries. In fact, I don't think you love me at all. I believe you're still in love with someone else."

Douglas shook his head. "No, that isn't true."

Cory raised her voice not only in volume but to an

annoyingly high pitch. "Don't lie to me, Mr. Raymond. I won't be trifled with. I saw how you looked at Beth Davis when we were having supper the other night," Cory accused. "You couldn't take your eyes off of her. You still have feelings for her, don't you?"

"I have the highest regard for Miss Davis but…"

"Don't say another word." Cory emphasized the words with a slap of her closed fan on his shoulder. "I could never take second place in a man's heart."

"But she turned me down when I proposed."

"Proposed?" she gasped. "If you asked Beth to marry you the way you proposed to me, it's no wonder she turned you down." Cory lifted her chin. "No woman accepts a proposal of marriage with such callous calculation." She softened her voice. "You should tell Beth how you truly feel about her and demonstrate your affection with words and deeds if you want her to accept a second proposal."

Douglas looked confused. "Mr. Montgomery said something about Southern women not accepting the first time, but I thought Northern women were more practical."

"A woman has pride," she explained. "Not the same pride as a man. She has no career or is equal in education as a man, but she takes pride in little tasks. It could be the way she embroiders or the flaky crust on her pie. A woman cherishes these accomplishments. They make her life of hard work and drudgery bearable. Beth is an excellent cook, but did anyone compliment her on her pie crust but her father? Did you know she cut nearly all the pies for the contest on the square? She could easily handle the cooking and cleaning for a dozen men."

Cory paused to make sure he comprehended the implication of her last words. "Those are skills overlooked by most. Skills a husband should cherish. A romantic like Beth longs for words of affection and kindness, and she expects them from a man who proposes marriage."

"But to propose to the same woman twice doesn't seem to increase the probability of acceptance," Douglas said. "It's illogical mathematically. The answer is either right or wrong. It doesn't change the outcome by doing the problem over and over again."

"But Beth isn't a mathematical problem." How could one man be so obtuse? "She's a woman. She admitted she admires Jane Austen. She wants romance. Even Mr. Darcy had to ask Elizabeth to marry him a second time. I'm sure if you asked Beth, after a proper declaration of love, she would be tempted to accept your proposal."

"I don't think I could ask her again," Douglas said. "What about my pride?"

"Mr. Darcy swallowed his pride," Cory reminded him. "Any humbling on your part would be replaced by the proud announcement of your impending marriage."

Douglas thought on her words. Cory was growing impatient. What did she have to do to convince the man to court Beth?

"You said a woman wouldn't accept the first time. Is that why you turned me down?"

Good Lord. She was caught by her own words. She had given him hope instead of making it clear she had no interest in him. "I said no because I'm in love with another," she confessed honestly.

Douglas was shocked by her words. "Who?"

"Why, the man I've spent the entire day with, Tyler Montgomery." She raised her fan to mask her face. "I know we haven't known each other for long, but he has all the qualities I admire."

"But he spent the entire evening paying attention to Beth," Douglas recalled.

Cory lowered her voice to a whisper. "She was flirting with him to make you jealous."

"Why would she do that?"

"Because she still has feelings for you."

Douglas looked surprised. "I guess I should go and propose to Beth."

"You can't do that!" Cory shouted.

He cringed under her outburst. "Why not?"

Cory rolled her eyes. "Haven't you heard anything I've said about romance? You need to court her. Win her affection. Show how much you care. But first, you should ask permission to escort her to the dance."

"But wouldn't that be wasting time? I know the solution to the problem. I should act immediately."

"A woman doesn't like to be rushed."

"But I wish to be married before fall term begins," he said. "I don't want to waste any more time."

He was complaining about wasting time. Cory tried a new tactic. "But a dance accelerates your schedule," she reasoned. "It's the perfect opportunity to begin anew and show her how you feel, and it's a public declaration of your intentions." She put it in terms he would understand. "Dancing with Beth is equal to three Sunday visits."

"Three visits," he repeated. "Do you think she'll go to the dance with me?"

"All you have to do is ask," she prodded.

Douglas thought for what seemed like an eternity. "I'll do it."

Cory sighed when Douglas headed for the church. "Now he's your problem, Beth."

Chapter Twenty-Six

Cory crossed the square a safe distance from Douglas. She spied Beth coming out of the church in a pale pink ball gown and realized the dance would begin soon. Douglas wasted no time approaching Beth. She watched as they talked. He dropped his hat and picked it up. Beth nodded at his endless monologue. When he stopped talking, Beth smiled at him in the way women have smiled at men since Eve.

Cory looked for Tyler. Where was he? He hadn't requested permission to escort her to the dance, and now she wished she had paid more attention to her own love life. She headed for the family wagon to retrieve her dress. She met Jem and Cole carrying their dress boxes.

Cole glanced at the Town Hall and paced back and forth. "Do you want us to wait for you?"

It was Cole's first dance. Cory sympathized with her impatience. "Go ahead. I'll be along in a minute." Cory found her dress box jammed under one of the bench seats in the family wagon. She leaned over to retrieve it.

"Do you need some help?"

The box came loose suddenly, and Cory stumbled backwards. Edward jumped up on the wagon wheel hub to steady her. "Careful, Miss Beecher."

She regained her composure. "Thank you, Mr.

Vandal."

"May I?" He offered his hand to help her down.

She jumped with the box in her hands. "Have you seen Tyler?"

"Yes." He smiled. "I must compliment you, Miss Beecher."

He was happy about something. "Why?"

"I have tried for years to humble Tyler Montgomery, and your small, delicate hand has accomplished what my fist could not."

Cory shook her head. "I don't know what you're talking about."

"Women never admit the power they have over a man. Men certainly don't want to admit it. But take my wife, Regina. She's a delicate creature whose vulnerability makes me strive to protect her and solve all her problems."

Cory frowned. "Women don't want a man to solve their problems."

"But you seemed so distressed over them."

"We enjoy our emotions too much to have them dismissed with a solution." Cory smiled as she thought of Douglas and his logic. "All we want from a man is an understanding ear and comforting arms. We're not afraid of the hurt. We're afraid you don't care we're hurting."

Edward frowned. "Do you think Regina sent Tess away?"

"It probably hurt to see Adam with Tess," Cory said. "Taking her back won't solve the problem. But your return could. You've been gone a long time."

"I didn't mean to abandon her, but I didn't know how to deal with the grief. He was my son, too."

"Don't let it tear you apart." She paused. "Permanently."

"Well, Tyler looks like you've torn him apart."

Cory was baffled. "Me? I've done nothing."

"Come, Miss Beecher. The man is a train wreck. I've never seen him so despondent. I'm confident you're right. He doesn't love Regina. He has never been this broken."

Cory narrowed her eyes. "And you blame me?"

"He kept babbling about losing you to Douglas."

Cory digested this piece of news and laughed.

"You think marrying another man is funny?" He gloated. "I almost pity Tyler."

His cruel side was showing. "I'm not marrying Douglas. I turned him down so he could propose to Beth. Tyler must have misunderstood."

He frowned. "I suppose you'll have to set him straight."

"I would never hurt someone on purpose or lie about them."

"Do you think I lied about Tyler?"

"I meant Noah. You printed those fliers claiming he was your runaway slave."

"I only wanted to find him to find Tess," Edward defended.

"Your men beat him."

"He needed some persuasion."

"That's barbaric."

"Northerners don't understand the need for slavery."

"Maintaining your wealth at the expense of others' freedom and happiness is wrong," she said. "You must not be a good businessman if your fortune depends on the return of one woman and a little baby."

"It's not about money," he said. "It's about respect. She needs to be taught her place."

Tyler had warned her Edward would teach Tess a lesson and use it as an example to other slaves. Cory saw the hardness in his face and feared Tyler had been right about Edward all along. He could be cruel without conscience and had no regrets about hurting others whether it was Tyler by revealing his mother was the town whore or by whipping Tess for running away. She wanted to get away from him. "Do you know where I can find Tyler?"

Edward sneered. "He's drowning his sorrows at the beer wagon."

Cory heard the sound of musicians tuning their instruments through the open church doors as she headed to the square. Jess, Cass, and Jules played with a puppy on the blanket her family had occupied earlier. Adelaide watched them from her seat on the church bench. "The ladies are changing at the Town Hall."

Cory headed toward the beer wagon.

"Where are you going?" Adelaide asked.

She turned. "Tyler is at the beer wagon. He thinks I'm marrying Douglas."

"Douglas proposed?"

Cory was impatient to talk with Tyler. "Yes."

"You're marrying Douglas?"

"Who's Douglas?" Jess asked.

"I thought you liked Tyler," Cass said.

"I like Tyler," Jules said.

"I am not marrying Douglas." Cory announced to squelch all the remarks.

"Thank goodness," Adelaide said. "I didn't think

you'd ever realize he was all wrong for you."

"I wanted Douglas to propose so I could turn him down, but Tyler misunderstood. Now I don't have an escort to the dance."

Jess jumped up. "I'll fetch him!"

"We'll all go!" Cass grabbed Jules hand.

"Sometimes it's good to have little sisters," Adelaide said.

"It'll give me a chance to change into my gown." She turned to Jess. "Ask him to meet me outside the Town Hall."

"Are you going to yell at him?"

"I'm going to yell at you if he doesn't show." Cory watched her sisters run across the square followed by the puppy. She carried her dress box to the Town Hall.

The sandstone building faced the church on the opposite end of the town square. The double doors opened to a small foyer and the main room beyond. A narrow staircase led to the second floor where the offices were located.

Most of ladies were dressed and putting on the final touches to their hair or accessories when Cory joined them. She searched for her sisters and saw Beth helping them in a corner of the room. Her pink gown had a full ruffle across the bodice and was gathered in several tiers for the skirt.

"Beth, your dress is lovely." Cory put her box down on the floor next to her sisters' boxes and began untying the string.

"I want to look my best." She giggled. "Mr. Raymond is escorting me."

"That's wonderful!" Cory silenced any questions from Jem with a slight shake of her head. She had confided her hopes for a match with Douglas to her sister only last Sunday in church.

Beth stared at her reflection in a full length mirror someone had placed in the center of the room. "I wish my hair had some curl like yours. I can't do anything with it."

"There are some lovely ways to wear straight hair." Cory turned to Jem. "How should Beth wear her hair?"

Jem studied her face. "I think it needs to be up and draw attention to her eyes. You have lovely eyes, Beth."

"Let's pull it back and braid the length in loops near the back," Cory suggested. "We can pull some strands to frame her face."

"You better dress," Jem said. "I'll braid Beth's hair."

Cole helped Cory strip off her day dress and corset cover. She tightened the lacings on her corset.

"That's tight enough!" Cory gasped.

Cole tied off the ends. "Why do women have to wear all these silly clothes?"

"To attract a man," Cory explained.

"Seems to me a woman could attract a man more if she was naked."

Beth gasped.

Cory looked at Jem. "Remind Mama to have another talk with this one."

"It won't help." Jem frowned. "I plan to be securely married before she ruins the family name."

Cole helped Cory dress and loosely stitched the bodice to the skirt.

"A man likes a little mystery," Cory told Cole. She felt a bit hypocritical. Tyler had seen her in her nightgown already. She didn't leave him much mystery. Maybe that's why he hadn't proposed. She thought of the cow. "Don't give away free milk."

"Milk?"

"I'll explain later." Cory played her big sister role. "It's your first dance. Gloves worn at all times, arms' length distance between you and your partner, and don't leave the dance floor."

Cole slipped on her gloves. "All this so a boy can step on your toes."

Cory examined her gown in the mirror. "Grandma can perform miracles with a needle."

"I can't believe the little touches she adds. Did you notice the castle pattern on my skirt?" Jem pointed out an elaborate pattern in black braiding on the blue plaid gown that complemented her red hair and blue eyes. "She repeated the same pattern on the sleeves."

"She embroidered little roses on mine." Cole glanced at the door. "May I go now?"

"Who's escorting you?" Cory asked.

"The first boy to ask me!" Cole headed for the stairs.

"She isn't very particular," Beth remarked.

"She isn't worried about getting married," Cory explained.

"I want to look my best," Beth said. "This may be the most romantic night of my life."

Cory hoped it wouldn't be the only romantic night in her life and hurried to complete her ensemble. Beth deserved better.

Jem finished Beth's braids and pinned them at the crown of her head.

"Add a couple of ribbons," Cory suggested.

"How do I look?" Beth turned her head from side to side as she looked in the mirror.

"You'll be the most beautiful woman at the ball," Jem said.

"You look beautiful, too," Beth replied. "Who's escorting you?"

"Ben Collins," Jem confided. "I thought he was such a pest when we were in school together. Now I'm the pest mooning over him. How could someone so repugnant as a boy turn into such a dreamy man?"

Cory smiled. Jem was in love. She could tell by the excitement in her voice. Did she sound the same way when she talked about Tyler? She had declared her love to others, but maybe she should confess her feelings to Tyler. Edward said he was devastated when he thought she was marrying Douglas. That had to mean he loved her, too. Cory brushed back her hair and pinned it with gold combs. She arranged a cascade of curls down her back. She looked around. "Do we have everything?"

Jem took inventory. "Handkerchiefs, fans, and gloves."

"I'll take the boxes to the wagon." Cory tossed her day dress and everything she didn't need for the dance into her dress box, gathered the other two, and carried them downstairs.

Jess, Cass, and Jules were waiting outside on the steps. They stood up when they saw Cory. "We found him."

Cory looked around. Tyler was near the pump by the watering trough, bent over, and splashing water on his face. She handed the three dress boxes to each of her sisters. "Can you take these to the wagon, please?"

"Can't we watch?"

"What's going on?" Jem asked. She didn't wait for an answer. She waved to Ben when he approached. Douglas was with him and offered his arm to Beth.

Tyler watched the other couples head for the church. "You're not going with Douglas?"

Jess put the dress box on her head. "Would she need an escort if she was?"

"Why do you think we dragged you here?" Jules asked.

"Go!" Cory pointed toward the wagon. Her three youngest sisters, with dress boxes held aloft, walked along River Road toward the wagon. "Don't forget the puppy."

"Why is Beth with Douglas?" Tyler stared at the departing couples. "I thought he was going to marry you."

Cory heard the dance music and headed toward the church. "You were wrong."

He joined her. "You wanted him to propose."

"He did."

Tyler blocked her path. "On the Irish Rose you told me, '*we need to talk*.'" He studied her. "From my limited experience, that precedes '*I never want to see you again*.'"

"I wanted to know your future plans." She smelled beer on his breath. "How much did you drink?"

"One beer, but it seems to have affected my hearing. If Douglas proposed to you, why is he escorting Beth to the dance?"

"Because I turned him down."

Tyler put his hands to his head and rubbed. "You wanted Douglas to propose so you could turn him down. Why didn't you tell me that?"

"I didn't have time."

He grabbed her hands. "You're not in love with him!"

"I was never in love with him," Cory confessed. "I only wanted to get married."

"And now you don't?"

"Oh, I still want to marry if it's the right person and the right time."

He exhaled a long breath. "So I haven't lost you."

"Lost?" She showed him some of the shrewishness she'd shown Douglas. "When did you court me? Where are the flowers and candy? What about the poetry readings and romantic endearments?"

Tyler looked sheepish. "Southern gentlemen are known for their courtship manners, but I must have misplaced mine." He bowed. "Your gown is lovely but not nearly as lovely as the woman wearing it."

She scowled. "What is that?"

"A compliment."

"We have another term for it, and it's found in the barn." She headed for the church.

"What do you want?"

"If I have to tell you, then you're not paying attention."

"Hey, boys act stupid when they like a girl."

She hit him in the arm.

"What was that for?"

"Don't you remember? Jess beat up a boy for acting stupid."

"I'm sorry," he apologized. "What do I have to do?"

"Give me your arm."

He had his hand over the spot she had bruised.

"You're not going to hit me again, are you?"
"I'd like to go to the dance."

Chapter Twenty-Seven

Tyler tugged the white gloves Adelaide had loaned him from Hiram's wardrobe and offered his arm. "Miss, Beecher, will you give me the honor of escorting you to the dance?"

Cory took his arm. He was lucky no one else was available. She agreed with Beth. A woman deserved a little romance. Tyler's passion for her was evident in his kisses, but he had yet to declare his love or propose marriage. She was going to hold her ground until he did.

They joined the line of men and women outside the double doors of the church. The music filtered outside as couples climbed the steps for the promenade.

Once upstairs, Cory and Tyler joined the others and marched counterclockwise around the room. The holiday gave everyone an opportunity to wear their best, and social manners dictated gloves on both men and women to prevent any skin to skin contact. Women bared plenty of flesh with off-the-shoulder gowns, some cut daringly low. Couples danced gracefully around the room, the ladies' bell-shaped gowns tilting with the rhythm of the violins in a rainbow of colors. The lead couple joined with another couple and the four of them circled the room before joining up with the next four to form a line of eight.

The promenade was followed by a social mixer

where all the men were on the inside of a large circle and the women on the outside. Dancers completed a series of steps and changed partners. They repeated the steps with each new partner around the circle. The social dance was followed by a couple's dance. Tyler twirled Cory around to the waltz and nodded toward Beth and Douglas. "I'm confused. Didn't Beth turn Douglas down already?"

"You were the one who said a man sometimes had to propose more than once."

"So she didn't mean to turn him down?"

"She longed for romance, and he gave her logic and reason."

He frowned. "And now she doesn't want romance?"

"Every woman dreams of romance. You heard how Beth gushed about Jane Austen."

"And Douglas said it was nonsense."

"I don't think his opinion will keep Beth from reading it."

"Why not forsake Douglas instead?"

"She loves Douglas more."

He shook his head. "That's ridiculous."

"Is it?" Cory studied his face. "I thought you were a slave owner, and I fell in love with you against my better judgment."

Tyler stumbled. "You what?"

The words had come out in a natural defense to prove her point. It was too late to take them back. "You can't stop dancing in the middle of the floor." She apologized to the other dancers.

"But you said you loved me." Tyler grabbed her hand and glanced around. He pulled her toward the main doors.

"Where are you taking me? The dance isn't over." She stopped protesting when she saw Adelaide standing in the doorway. Something awful had happened. Adelaide's bonnet was askew, and her face was ashen.

They rushed to her side. "What is it?"

She spoke barely above a whisper. "The chasers have them."

Cory looked at Tyler to see if he had heard. He bolted down the stairs. She and Adelaide followed.

Buck rode into the center of the square. Tess was seated in front of him, her face set in stone. She clutched Adam in her arms. She wasn't nursing the baby, but her dress was open in the front. Buck withdrew his hand, and she clutched the opening tight.

Clyde rode in after him and yanked on a rope attached to his saddle. Noah stumbled onto the grass. Cory screamed. Noah was bound with a rope latched around his wrists. His clothes were torn and dirty. Blood streamed from the cuts and scrapes on his arms and legs. His face was bloodied and swollen. Noah collapsed when the rope slacked.

"Noah!" Tyler ran to him and knelt by his side. Cory followed.

Noah looked at them through swollen slits. "It's not as bad as it looks."

Tyler pulled his knife from his boot and cut the rope binding Noah.

"Papa!" Cory looked around the growing crowd.

"He's getting his bag." Jem had quietly appeared by her side. "I'll fetch some water."

"Tess." Noah struggled to sit.

Tess had a swollen eye and dried blood on a split

lip. Cory looked at Buck. "Let her go!"

Edward stepped out of the shadows.

"We found them," Buck bragged.

"This is how you treat a woman and baby? I bet Reggie would be proud." Cory reached for Adam in Tess' arms. He wailed as his mother handed him over.

"I think I'll keep this jezebel with me." Tess struggled to get down, but Buck held her tight against his chest.

Tyler left Noah's side and strode toward Buck. "What did you do to her?"

"I was guarding her 'til we return to Virginia, right, Mr. Vandal."

Tyler grabbed Edward by his coat. "You let him rape her?" His fist connected with Edward's face and blood spurted from his nose and down his white shirt.

Clyde jumped from his horse, tackled Tyler, and pinned his arms to his sides. "Go ahead and hit him, Mr. Vandal." Edward cracked Tyler across his jaw.

Tyler lifted his legs, braced himself against Clyde's thick body, and mule kicked Edward in the chest. He flew back and landed on the ground.

Tyler slipped free from Clyde and threw a punch that connected with his battered face. The blow opened a fresh cut above his eye. Buck dismounted and pulled Tess down with him. He shoved her toward Edward, who had staggered to his feet. Buck pulled a knife from his boot.

Tyler redrew his own knife as he braced for Buck's attack. Clyde wiped the blood from his eyes with a dirty kerchief and drew a gun from a holster on his hip.

"Put it back." Adelaide pressed the barrel of her pistol against his back.

Cory looked at Clyde. "She won't hesitate to blow a hole clear through you."

He shoved his gun into the holster.

People backed up as Tyler and Buck faced off and sidestepped into position. They jabbed their knives at each other and dodged in return.

Cory put her arm around Tess, who fumbled with what remained of the buttons on her dress. She bounced Adam on her hip to calm his cries. "We'll fix your gown."

Tess burst into tears. Cory embraced her to comfort her, but her arm trembled with rage. She stared at Edward, who pinched his nose to stop the flow of blood. She felt no sympathy. It was one thing for men to beat each other senseless, but how could Edward, who claimed he was a gentleman, allow such brutality against a woman?

Cory covered her mouth to stifle a scream when Buck lunged with his Bowie knife. Tyler dodged the blow. Buck stumbled into the crowd with his momentum, and a few women screamed when they were jostled by the crowd gathered to witness the fight. The men shoved Buck back at Tyler. Buck waved his knife at Tyler's midsection to gut him. He cut Tyler's coat, but Cory saw no blood. It didn't diminish her fear for his life.

Buck was older, a more experienced fighter, and Tyler was a big target. She gasped when Buck tripped Tyler, and he fell. Buck jumped on him, but Tyler's strength kept him from stabbing the blade into his flesh. He knocked him off and rolled to safety. They staggered to their feet to face off for the next round.

Sheriff Lane Carter broke through the crowd and

waved his rifle at the combatants. "Put the knives away. This is a holiday. I won't tolerate anyone disturbing the peace."

Tyler stepped back and turned toward Noah. Buck lunged, but Sheriff Carter knocked Buck on the side of the head with the barrel of his gun. Buck crumbled in a heap. He turned toward Clyde. "Are you going to give me any trouble?" Clyde shook his head.

With Tyler's safety no longer a concern, Cory joined her father. Sterling was examining Noah, and Jem washed dirt from his wounds.

Tess took the cloth from Jem's hands. "I'll tend him." She knelt on the ground and gently took Noah's arm and scrubbed at the rocks and dirt embedded in the torn flesh. He touched her swollen cheek.

"We lost our way in the woods," Noah whispered hoarsely to Tyler, who knelt by him. "I had to ask for directions. It must have been the wrong person. He led Clyde and Buck to our hiding spot."

"Noah fought them, but they threatened to kill the baby," Tess sobbed.

Cory turned to Edward who stood a few feet away. "You said they could kill the baby?" Her voice trembled. "No wonder you don't understand why Reggie made Tess leave."

"She can make more brats." Buck turned to Clyde. "She's got nice tits."

Noah struggled to rise, but Sterling held him down. "Wait," he whispered. "Let him impress his audience."

Cory looked around at the crowd. She knew some of them were abolitionists. Some of them were part of the Underground Railroad. They worked in secret, but members rallied publicly when necessary.

"Hey, we were doing our job," Clyde defended when the crowd advanced. He looked at Edward. "Old man Cyrus always let us have the women as part of our reward."

"And what happened to Noah?" Tyler demanded. "It looks like you beat him and dragged him down the street. I want these two men arrested for assault," he told the sheriff.

"You can't put us in jail!" Clyde argued. "He wouldn't give us the girl without a fight. If Buck hadn't grabbed the brat and held a knife to his throat, we'd still be fighting."

Lane pointed at Noah. "Is this man a runaway?"

"No."

"He aided this woman and her child," Clyde said. "He knew they were runaways."

"Did you know they were runaways?" the sheriff asked Noah.

Tyler spoke. "Don't answer."

He turned to Tyler. "Who are you?"

"I'm his lawyer."

Lane turned to Edward. "What's your part in this?"

"I own this woman and her child. My chasers helped me recover them."

"We don't mind a man peacefully recovering his property, but a fight means you'll all be in front of the mayor tomorrow morning."

Edward pointed at Noah. "I want charges brought against this man for helping a runaway."

Lane looked around. "Any other charges?"

Tyler looked at Tess. "Did Clyde or Buck force you?"

"He touched my breasts. Nothing more." She

wrapped her arms around her chest and looked away. Noah brushed a tear from her cheek.

"I have two cells," Lane said. "I can put the men in one and the woman in the other." He took Clyde's weapons and picked up Buck's knife from the ground before claiming his gun.

Buck pointed at Noah. "You put him in with us, and he'll kill us."

"I can't put him in with her," Lane argued.

Tess stood. "But he's my husband."

Lane surveyed his prisoners. "I guess you can share a cell. Never locked up a baby before."

Tess reached for Adam, and Cory handed him over.

Lane nodded toward Noah. "How is he doing, Doctor Beecher?"

"I'll need to do some more patching, but I can do it in the jail cell."

"Then let's head to the Town Hall," Lane said. "And everyone else can return to the dance."

Maureen placed a blanket around Tess' shoulders. "We'll gather some things for you."

"I'll help Papa." Cory picked up her father's medical bag and joined the group walking to the Town Hall.

****

Noah, Tess, and Adam were in one cell with Buck and Clyde in the opposite one. A single frame bed with rope supporting a straw-stuffed mattress was placed in each cell. A chamber pot and a stool were the only other furnishings. The municipal jail usually housed drunks and offenders of minor transgressions. The more serious crimes were tried at the county courthouse in

Akron. If a county judge found Noah guilty of aiding a runaway, he'd face federal charges.

"I hope this helps." Cory placed a cradle on the floor. "How is Adam doing?"

Tess put a clean diaper on him. "He's scared. He's old enough to know something isn't right."

"Poor little guy." Cory soothed him with a smile. "You should be thinking of nothing but a warm meal and a big hug."

Adam stopped fussing and stared at Cory's face.

Noah sat at the foot of the bed while Sterling finished stitching a gash in his head. His wounds had been cleaned, his bruises leeched, and cuts sewn up. "I must look a mess."

"I found you something to wear." Tyler tossed him a shirt.

Noah stood. He grimaced as he put on the shirt.

Cory noticed he had no lash marks on his back common on slaves. It supported Tyler's words about Noah never being treated like a slave.

"You men need me to take care of anything?" Sterling asked Clyde and Buck.

"You're not putting a leech on me," Clyde told him. "I'll live with my bruises."

Sheriff Carter allowed Maureen and Jess to enter the jail area and bring trays with plates loaded with chicken, cornbread, and pie for the prisoners.

"Looks good." Noah handed a plate to Tess and took one. "Thank you for feeding us."

"Plenty of extra food from the picnic," Maureen said. "Would you like coffee to drink?" She turned to Jess. "Bring a pot."

"Why are you treating them so nice?" Buck

demanded from his cell.

"You don't deserve to be treated any better than the animals you are," Cory argued.

"It's our job to capture runaway slaves." Buck scraped his spoon against his plate and shoved food into his mouth. "We do whatever we have to do."

"Assaulting a woman and threatening to kill her baby!" Cory turned away. She didn't want them to see the tears threatening to spill.

Her mother took her into her arms. "Let it go, Cory, or the hate will consume you."

"I want them to be punished for what they did."

"Let the law punish them, but you have to forgive them."

She was shocked. "Why?"

"Hate can eat a person up." Sterling packed his bag. "I've seen it become an obsession that festers and spreads like gangrene. Forgiveness cleanses the wound. That's one of the most important lessons we learn in life."

She looked from her mother to her father. "I know you're right, but knowing and doing is too difficult for me."

"Doing the right thing isn't meant to be easy." Maureen collected the dishes. "Are you coming outside for the fireworks?"

Her father closed his medical bag and put on his hat.

"I think I'll stay here." She shrugged. "They don't have much to celebrate. I don't think I could enjoy it."

"You can't spend the night," Maureen said. "Adelaide will be with us. Don't keep her waiting too long."

Cory hugged her parents. "Thank you."

"Come along, Jessie," Sterling told Jess. She filled Clyde's coffee cup and followed her parents. "Leave the coffee pot with Sheriff Carter. He may need it tonight."

After her parents left, Edward came in. He was wearing a clean shirt. His nose was swollen but his face was clean. He stopped and talked with the sheriff.

"I'm going to see what's going on." Tyler headed for Edward.

Chapter Twenty-Eight

The sheriff sat at a small table and guarded the door. He had a pot of coffee, a full plate of food, and two slices of pie arranged before him. A deck of cards was in the upper right corner beside a lantern. Edward argued with Lane about releasing his men.

"Are you still planning to bring charges against those two men?" Lane asked Tyler.

"They assaulted a free man."

"Noah? When did you free him?" Edward demanded.

Tyler had said the wrong thing to the wrong man. "It was my mother's wishes," he lied. "Even if he was a slave, your men had no right to assault him."

"They were defending themselves," Edward argued.

"They admit to attacking first."

"Only to seize Tess. If Noah hadn't fought back, no one would have been hurt."

"You don't know that," he argued. "Look at what they did to Noah once they had Tess."

"You have to prove the assault in a trial," Lane warned.

"It was two against one."

"The numbers won't matter when they see how strong he is," Lane said. "I can tell you the outcome."

"So they go free?"

"I can hold them overnight for disorderly conduct and disturbing the peace. The mayor will hold court in the morning. But the fines will only be a couple of dollars."

"Because disorderly conduct is a misdemeanor." Tyler knew he wouldn't be able to convict them of anything more serious.

"Helping runaways is a federal offense," Lane reminded him.

"Who decides that case?" Edward asked.

"The judge at the county court will hear the case. I'll transport Noah, Tess, and the baby to the jail in Akron after mayor's court," Lane said.

"Why Tess and the baby?" Edward demanded. "They belong to me."

"You'll have to prove they're runaways before the judge can charge anyone with helping them."

"Then what?" Edward asked.

"If the judge finds Noah helped your runaways, he'll be sent to Cleveland to stand trial on federal charges."

"How long will that take?"

"Depends on the docket. I'd plan on staying a few days in Akron, longer if the case goes to Cleveland. Your girl will be securely locked up in the jail."

Edward headed to Clyde and Buck's cell. Tyler followed him and overheard their conversation. "You'll admit to disorderly conduct tomorrow before the mayor then we'll head for Akron to take care of him." He nodded toward Noah. "I'm deducting your fines from your pay."

Edward turned to Tess. "You've caused me more trouble than you're worth. Don't cause any more."

Tyler stood behind Edward in the narrow hallway between the cells. "Don't you have a rock to sleep under?"

Edward put on his hat and left.

"There are some law books on the second floor," Lane said. "Might find something to help your case."

"Couldn't hurt," Tyler answered. "Thank you."

The sheriff jingled his keys. "Miss, Beecher, you'll have to leave the cell so I can lock the door."

Cory stepped outside.

"How good of a lawyer are you, Ty?" Noah asked quietly through the bars.

"I need to convince the local judge to dismiss the charges. If he sends you before the federal judge, it'll mean jail time and a fine."

"I can't let Edward have my wife and son." Noah glanced back at Tess as she placed a sleeping Adam in the cradle. "I might be able to rescue them from Vandalia, but if he sells them, I'll never see them again."

"If you go to jail, I'll stay close to Tess and Adam," he promised. "I'll save them. Whatever it takes."

Tyler knew what he was promising. He was willing to risk everything for Noah. He turned to Cory. "I'm staying. I might find something in the law books to help."

"I need to take Adelaide home, but I'll return in the morning. Is there anything you need?"

"My bag from the Red Pony Tavern," he said. "Looks like we'll be going to Akron after the mayor rules locally."

****

283

In the morning Cory found Tyler asleep in the mayor's office on the second floor. His head rested on an open law book, and a quill rested between his fingers. His notes were barely legible, smeared by his hand. The glass inkwell was nearly dry, and the candles had gone out, leaving frozen wax waterfalls over the pewter holders.

She hated to disturb him. He looked so peaceful, but peace would be fleeting. A judge would return Tess and Adam to Edward and throw Noah into prison if Tyler couldn't persuade him otherwise.

Cory had spent a restless night. She loved Tyler, but Noah and Tess needed him. She could never force him to choose her over his brother, especially in such a desperate situation. Marriage seemed selfish and silly compared to the struggle to escape slavery and reach freedom. She had her teaching to keep her busy, and her family to support her. She had to let him go.

Cory placed her hand on his shoulder and rubbed his back to wake him. He groaned in response, and she could feel his muscles ripple beneath the taut fabric of his cotton shirt. He had discarded his coat and tie in the middle of the night.

She leaned down and whispered his name. His eyes flickered and slowly opened. He was so handsome. Even the bristle on his face did not mar the perfection of his features. It only added to a masculine ruggedness.

"This is a nice way to wake in the morning." His voice was gravelly from sleepiness.

"How much rest did you get?"

Tyler stretched his arms overhead. "What time is it?"

"Eight. The mayor's court begins soon."

"I think it was about five when I fell asleep."

Cory looked around the room at the law books, some stacked, some open, and others discarded in his search for an answer. Cory placed a basket on the table and unloaded it. "I brought you something to eat."

He picked up a burnt biscuit. "How are Noah and Tess?"

"They're eating now. All the abolitionists are rallying for them. Then there's the other side, which supports Edward and his property rights."

"The only person who matters is the judge." Tyler stood. "A sympathetic one. The Fugitive Slave Law requires a slave be returned to his master, and anyone helping a slave escape is the criminal. I can't find an exception."

"We could help Tess and Adam escape like they did in Wellington," she proposed.

"That could result in a lot of innocent and well-meaning people being arrested," he said. "I'd like to keep the case from going to federal court, but I'd have to prove Noah wasn't helping Tess and Adam run away, which is exactly what he was doing."

"He didn't help them escape," Cory reminded him. "He only came to find them."

"It's a small point but one worth noting."

"What about Tess and Adam?" Cory asked. "What will happen to them?"

"Under the law, Edward can do whatever he wants with them. He owns them, and we can't do anything about it."

"I have some money I've saved. It might help buy Tess and Adam."

"I have some money, too, but knowing Edward, he

won't sell them. He'll want to punish them."

"As an example to the other slaves at the Silver Pheasant?"

"That's why I have to return to Virginia, especially if Noah has to serve jail time." He ran his fingers through his hair. "Edward would never sell Tess to me, but if he sells her at public auction, I have a few friends who can buy her for me."

"After her punishment?" Cory didn't want to say the word rape. "Did you see Buck pawing her? How can a man force himself upon a woman? How can he justify violence like that?"

"Not all men are like Edward and his men," he said.

"You were right about him," she admitted. "He wears fancy clothes and talks like a gentleman, but he only thinks about himself. Why can't he let them go?"

Tyler put his arms around her. "I'm supposed to be the vengeful one when it comes to Edward." He kissed her temple. "You're my rock of reason and tolerance. I need you to be level-headed so I don't lose mine and do something foolish."

"I'll do whatever is necessary," she vowed.

Tyler lifted his suitcase to an empty chair. "I better wear my good suit."

"What about Reggie's vest?"

"You want me to wear it?"

"Only if you want to make Edward angrier than he already is." She recalled her conversation with him. "He has to be the one others admire in Vandalia. It's his role. That vest made him notice Reggie and made him want to beat you by marrying her."

He removed the vest from his bag and examined it.

"I wonder what he'd do to keep me from wearing it?"

"Do you think he'd consider a trade?"

"I doubt he'd agree to it." Tyler put the vest back in the bag. "Tess is worth more than a vest even if Reggie made it."

"My mother says I have to forgive men like Buck and Clyde, but I don't blame Noah for wanting to defend his wife. Any husband would do the same."

Tyler stared at her with his signature lopsided grin.

"What did I say?"

"Husband," he repeated. "The law recognizes the sanctity of marriage." He grabbed a law book. "Noah has rights as a husband to protect his family."

"Does Edward recognize their marriage?"

"He had to approve it," Tyler recalled.

"Did he give her away?"

Tyler stopped turning pages. "What do you mean?"

"In a wedding the father gives the bride away. He hands her over to her husband, who vows to love, honor, and protect her." Cory frowned. "Haven't you ever seen a wedding?"

"I figured I'd wait until my own." He tapped the cover of a law book on the table. "The bride is a possession to be handed from father to husband."

"I wouldn't say a possession," Cory argued.

"Under the law she is." He grinned. "And Noah is Tess' husband."

Cory didn't hide her confusion. "So?"

"I need to argue my case." Tyler took off his shirt and tossed it aside. He withdrew a clean one from his bag. "You must be a good seamstress. I didn't break open the stitches." He showed his side to her before dressing.

Cory was more interested in the way his muscles rippled than his wound but nodded as she handed him a tie. "You were explaining something."

"The law recognizes the rights of a husband. Maybe more than those of a master."

"Do you have a case?"

Tyler tugged on the ends of his tie after tying it. "It's not much of a case, but worth arguing."

****

The mayor was not happy to see so many people in his courtroom early in the morning, especially since he had drank too much celebrating the Fourth. He fined Clyde and Buck for disorderly conduct and accepted the "not guilty" plea of Noah for aiding Tess and Adam. He ordered the sheriff to transfer Noah to the county court in Akron on the morning train.

Sheriff Carter escorted Noah, Tess, and Adam out of the Town Hall and headed for the train depot. Edward and the Cassell brothers trailed behind. Tyler stayed close to Noah. A crowd had gathered at the depot.

"Anybody tries anything, the baby will be the first to die!" Buck waved his knife in the air.

"Tess screamed when Buck grabbed for Adam.

"Put your knife away, or I'll take it away!" Lane looked around at the townsfolk. "No one is going to interfere with this trip. We're going to the county courthouse. If you plan to go, board the train."

"Stay close," Adelaide said. "The Irish Rose will be waiting at Mustill Store."

What did she mean? "Grandpa is in Cleveland."

"He turned back in case he was needed."

Cory looked around. "Who else is helping?"

"I can't tell you, but if there's trouble, we're prepared to take Noah, Tess, and Adam by force."

"Tyler doesn't want a lot of innocent people arrested."

"Then he better be a good lawyer." The whistle blew. "We better board."

Cory looked around. "I don't see my family."

"We only have one doctor in Darrow Falls, and with the Beecher name, we decided he should stay clear of the courthouse."

"Do I have to stay clear?"

"I don't think anyone could stop you from being with Tyler."

"I think I'll ride with Tess if they let me."

"Would you let them say no?"

No, she wouldn't. A few days ago all she thought about was marrying Douglas and living in a safe, secure world. Now, she was willing to risk everything for the freedom of a family and the love of a man. Cory watched Adelaide join the Reverend, his wife, and Beth. If the trial favored Edward, it wouldn't matter what Tyler wanted. The crowd would deliver its own justice.

Chapter Twenty-Nine

Cory and Tyler watched the sheriff place Noah, Tess, and Adam in a baggage car. Noah stacked some grain sacks to make a seat for Tess and sat next to her. Buck and Clyde sat opposite them on some crates. Edward and Tyler looked at each other.

"You riding with them?" Edward asked.

"If the sheriff doesn't mind."

"The more the merrier," Lane said. He took a position against the sliding door on the opposite side of the car.

Edward climbed aboard and sat near his men.

Tyler turned to Cory. "I'm going with Noah."

"I'd like to help Tess with the baby." It was a thin excuse to spend time together, maybe for the last time.

"It's not going to be comfortable," he warned.

"I've worked on a canal boat. I don't need comfort." He helped her into the car and made a seat from the sacks of grain.

The engineer blew several long blasts on the whistle, and the conductor closed the door to the baggage car. Everyone braced for the initial jolt of the train as it chugged out of the station before settling back for the short ride to Akron.

Noah played with his son while Tess leaned against him.

Cory didn't miss the lustful stares of Clyde and

Buck.

"The judge will lock you in jail for six months." Clyde sneered. "I'll make sure your woman doesn't get lonely."

"I've got first dibs," Buck said.

"We'll take turns," Clyde replied.

"You make me sick." Cory turned to Edward. "All of you."

"Women were made for a man's needs." Buck leered at her. "I could show you how."

Tyler bolted toward Buck, but Lane blocked him. "Sit." He turned to Buck and Clyde. "Not another word from anyone."

Only Adam broke the silence when he burst into a joyful laugh elicited by Noah. The baby lightened the mood, and Cory settled against Tyler's shoulder for the remainder of the ride.

When they reached Akron, the sheriff led his group down Broadway Street. The other passengers spread out through the town and took different routes that converged on the courthouse.

Edward looked around at the small crowd following them. "I know what your friends are planning," he told Cory. "I don't care what they do with Noah, but Tess and Adam belong to me." He nodded at Buck and Clyde. "They won't hesitate to stop anyone who interferes."

"We don't want anyone hurt," Tyler said. "There won't be any trouble."

Cory wasn't so sure.

Sheriff Carter wasted no time once they reached the courthouse. He filed the paperwork and took Noah, Tess, and Adam across Broadway Street to the jail.

Tyler joined Sam Morris in one of the empty rooms in the courtroom. Law books were stacked on one of the tables. She wasn't needed and turned to leave. Tyler grabbed her hand. "Thank you for everything."

A declaration of love would have been better, but she'd settle for gratitude. Cory found Adelaide on a bench on the first floor. She looked tired. "You don't have to stay if you don't want to. It may be awhile."

"I started this by letting Noah stay in my barn. I aim to finish it."

She realized the implication of her words. "What's our plan?"

****

The case was placed on the afternoon docket. The courtroom was full by the time the sheriff brought in Noah, Tess, and Adam. They were segregated off to the side. Tyler had argued against shackling them, but an armed deputy stood nearby.

Edward and the Cassell brothers sat behind the prosecuting attorney, Daniel Hossler. Tyler and Sam sat across from Daniel. Tyler looked behind him at Cory, the Reverend, and his family. The rest of the courtroom was full, but many familiar faces from Darrow Falls were missing. He didn't see Adelaide.

The bailiff announced Judge William Shoemaker, and everyone stood. He rapped his gavel on his desk, which was flanked by the flag of the United States. The bailiff called the court to order.

"Charges of aiding and abetting a runaway slave were filed this morning against Noah St. Paul," Shoemaker read. "What is your plea?"

Tyler stood with Noah. "Not guilty, your honor."

Murmurs passed through the crowd.

Judge Shoemaker rapped his gavel several times. "Let me make this clear to everyone seated in this courtroom. I will not have any disruption of the proceedings. We are all familiar with the Wellington stand-off. Federal marshals have not been involved in this case, and I would like to keep it that way. This is an informal hearing, but I see you are both represented by attorneys. I will not tolerate long-winded speeches. Let's focus on the facts. He turned to Daniel. "Call your first witness, Mr. Hossler."

"Edward Vandal."

Edward took the stand.

"Explain your relationship with this woman." Daniel pointed to Tess.

"She's my servant."

"You mean slave," Daniel clarified. "You own her."

"Yes."

"For how long?"

"All her life. She was born on the Silver Pheasant."

"The Silver Pheasant? Explain to the court what that is."

"My home in Virginia. Vandalia, Virginia. It's named for my family."

"Why is this slave in Ohio?"

"A month ago, without any provocation, she ran away and took this child with her. I had to hire men to find her."

"Who are these men?"

"Clyde and Buck Cassell."

"Did they find your runaway slaves?"

"Yes."

Daniel turned to the judge. "I will be calling these

men to testify."

The judge turned to the defense table. "Is there any argument that these slaves belong to Edward Vandal?"

"Yes, your honor," Tyler answered.

Edward stood. "You know I own them."

"Sit down!" the judge ordered. He turned to Tyler. "I've seen your credentials, and I approved your request to argue this case, but I hope you are heeding the guidance of Mr. Morris. I have no sense of humor when it comes to proceedings in my courtroom."

"I plead my case with all seriousness."

"What do you base your argument about ownership upon?"

"I admit he owned Tess at one time," Tyler explained. "But I plan to prove that he gave Tess away."

"Lies!" Edward shouted.

Judge Shoemaker pounded his gavel. "You are on the witness stand to answer questions by Mr. Montgomery." He turned to Tyler. "Proceed."

Tyler paced from the judge to Edward. "How do you keep slaves on the Silver Pheasant?"

Edward frowned. "What do you mean?"

"Are they shackled, locked up, or can a slave walk off the Silver Pheasant, walk down to the river, and board a boat?"

"A slave can't leave the farm without a pass."

Tyler turned to the audience. "So someone gave Tess a pass."

"I didn't give her one," Edward argued. "She must have stolen it."

"No!" Tess cried out. "Miss Regina gave it to me."

The judge hit his gavel and turned toward Tess.

"Do you have a pass, girl?"

Tess removed a medallion shaped like a bird on a leather strip from around her neck and handed it to Tyler. He showed it to the judge and then Edward. "Is this your farm's pass?"

He studied it. "Yes."

"Could anyone but Reggie give her the pass?"

"Regina," he corrected.

Tyler waited.

Edward had a stubborn look on his face.

The judge looked at him. "Mr. Vandal, you must answer the question."

"My wife could have given it to her. Or she could have stolen it."

Tyler decided to go straight to the heart of his argument. "Your wife, Regina Vandal, helped this slave run away, not my client. Noah didn't even know his wife was gone until three days later."

"Regina is ill." Edward looked at the judge. "She didn't know what she was doing."

Tyler didn't wait for any sympathy to build. "What happens to a runaway slave when caught?"

"They're punished."

"How?"

"Whipped."

"How many lashes?"

Edward looked smug. "The courts say thirty-nine is a fair number."

"Won't you have to make an example of her?" He pointed at Tess. "You don't want other slaves to run away from the Silver Pheasant. Won't you have to strip her naked and whip the flesh from her body? Leave her scarred and crippled?"

Tess sobbed.

"You're trying to make it sound like a bad thing," he argued. "It's necessary to maintain order."

Tyler took Adam from Tess' arms. "And this baby. What will happen to him?"

"A wet nurse will take care of him so she can work in the fields," Edward said. "Women work harder if they don't have children to tend. And she'll have to work hard for all the money she's cost me."

"Is that all? Hard work?"

Edward didn't answer.

"Is that all?" Tyler repeated. "Should I call Clyde and Buck Cassell to testify how women are punished at the Silver Pheasant?"

"She knew the risk she was taking when she ran away!" Edward argued.

"Precisely." Tyler smacked his hand on the table, startling everyone. He turned to Edward. "So why run away? Why risk being beaten and raped?"

Edward glanced toward Tess.

Tyler turned toward Noah. "Especially since her husband, Noah St. Paul, lived in Vandalia." Tyler looked from Noah to Edward. "How often did Noah see his wife?"

"He came by on Sundays. Mr. Yoder provided a pass."

"Did Mr. Yoder own him?"

"No, your mother did." Edward sneered. "But the whore was too busy entertaining men at the Dunking Witch saloon to bother with her slave or her son."

Tyler anticipated Edward's slander. He schooled his face and body to remain calm. "I once broke Mr. Vandal's nose for saying what he did, but I was a child then."

Edward frowned. He had black circles under his eyes and a swollen nose to prove more recent violence at Tyler's hands.

"My mother owned the Dunking Witch." Tyler's voice was loud and clear. "She was a good business woman and a good mother. She paid for my college education." He looked at Cory. He wasn't ashamed of his past any more. "Women have difficult choices to make in this world run by men, but Tess didn't have any choice!" Tyler pointed at Edward. "What happens if a slave refuses to obey an order?"

"They're beaten."

"When Regina drove Tess to the river, put her on a boat, and paid her fare, she ordered Tess to leave Vandalia. She had no choice but to obey."

Edward stared at Tess. "Regina wouldn't do that."

On the table was the packet Tyler had given Sam for safe keeping. He saw Noah's look of concern when he removed a document. "I have a letter written by Regina Vandal stating she ordered Tess to leave and even gave her money for her trip north."

"It's a forgery!" Edward shouted.

Tyler handed the letter to Judge Shoemaker, who handed it to Edward. "Is this your wife's handwriting?"

Edward stared at the letter. "Yes."

"Read it," the judge instructed. "Read it aloud."

Edward cleared his throat. "Dear Edward, if you are reading this letter, Tess did not reach freedom as I intended. I gave her a pass, money, and ordered her to go. I know what I did was wrong, but I couldn't bear seeing Tess with Adam every day while my arms were empty. I tried to stop you from going after her, but you were single-minded in your pursuit. Please don't hold anyone responsible but me. Regina."

The bailiff took the letter and handed it to the judge. "Your point is made, Mr. Montgomery, but this woman and baby still belong to Mr. Vandal, and he has a right to claim them."

"But he doesn't have the right to assault and kidnap Noah St. Paul, not once but twice." Tyler took a flier from the packet and handed it to Edward. "Did you have this flier printed?"

Edward refused to answer.

"Wasn't this man, Noah St. Paul, beaten and arrested because of this flier? Wasn't he placed in the jail across from this very courthouse not today but nearly a week ago?"

"I don't recall."

"Is Noah St. Paul your slave?"

"No."

"But by printing this flier, don't you claim to be the owner? Didn't you leave your name with the sheriff if anyone had information?"

"I only wanted to find my own slaves."

Tyler waved the flier toward Noah. "Then why beat him over the head and drag him through the streets after you had Tess in custody?"

Edward pointed at Clyde and Buck. "That was them."

"You pay them," Tyler reminded him.

"I pay them to recover my property. How they do it is none of my business."

"And that washes your hands clean?" Tyler turned his back on him. "I have no more questions for this," he paused, "gentleman."

Chapter Thirty

Buck and then Clyde testified they found Tess and Adam with Noah trying to escape. Tyler exposed how they threatened to kill the baby and used brutal force against Noah even after Tess was in custody. Neither man showed any remorse.

Daniel summarized his case by pointing at Noah. "She was in the company of this man, Noah, who helped her escape." He looked at Judge Shoemaker. "The law states you must return a runaway slave to its master. And anyone aiding a runaway must be punished. I only ask that you uphold the law."

"Your turn, Mr. Montgomery," Judge Shoemaker said. "Call your defense witnesses."

"I call Noah St. Paul."

"He can't testify against a white man!" Daniel reminded him.

"He won't," Tyler assured them.

Tyler removed something from his packet of legal papers. "I would like to provide a marriage certificate between Noah St. Paul and Tess." Tyler handed the document to the judge for examination.

"Slaves can't marry," Edward spoke.

The judge silenced him.

"Mr. Vandal has a valid point, your honor," Tyler said. "The law doesn't allow slaves to marry in the South. Sometimes they'll perform a ceremony called jumping the broom. Slaves recognize it as a marriage contract between two people, but it's not recognized by the law." He turned to Noah. "Is that how you and Tess were married?"

"No, we were married in a church. A Quaker church."

"Note the name of the church on the certificate of marriage."

"I don't see how that makes any difference if the law doesn't recognize marriages between slaves," Daniel argued.

"But God does," Tyler stated. "Perhaps not under the law of the Commonwealth of Virginia, but in the eyes of God they can become husband and wife, and the child is proof of the union between Tess and Noah. The Quaker religion does not recognize slavery and married Noah and Tess in their church before God and witnesses."

"So they're married," Daniel stated. "Your point?"

"Does the court concede they are man and wife?"

Daniel looked at Edward, who nodded. "We do."

"Then Noah is not guilty of aiding a runaway. He was protecting his family, a God-given and legal right in this country."

The judge removed his glasses. "What do you mean, Mr. Montgomery?"

Tyler pointed at Edward. "When a woman marries, she leaves the protection and authority of her father or a brother and is placed under the protection of her husband."

Edward jumped to his feet. "She's not my sister! And you have no evidence that Cyrus Vandal was her father."

"I was speaking generally," Tyler explained calmly.

The judge rapped his gavel. "Sit down, Mr. Vandal." He looked at Tyler. "Get to your point."

"As master, Mr. Vandal doesn't need to have a fraternal relationship with Tess to be her protector," he clarified.

Tyler pointed at Noah. "The law clearly recognizes the transfer of protection and possession to a husband on the wedding day."

"Go on," the judge conceded.

"When he consummates the marriage, he also claims any wealth or property of hers and makes all future decisions for her," Tyler expanded. "A wife and her children belong to the husband in legal matters. He must provide and care for them."

Tyler lifted Adam in his arms. "A master like Edward Vandal can tear a child from his mother's arms and sell him to the highest bidder. Edward claims this little boy belongs to him because he owns his mother. But what about his father's rights?"

"There's no proof the child was fathered by him," Edward shouted.

"Look at the date on the marriage certificate." Tyler pointed at the document. "Under the law any child born to a woman after the wedding day is the responsibility of her husband and considered his legal child."

"How old is the baby?"

"Eight months."

"They've been married for nearly two years by this date." The judge looked at Noah. "He's legally responsible for this child, whether he fathered him or not."

"But I own him," Edward said.

"There are cases where an indentured servant was owned by one man but married to another. The rights of the husband were upheld." Tyler retrieved a law book from the table. He opened it to a marked page and handed it to the judge.

Judge Shoemaker read down the page. "I'm familiar with this case. How far do you consider this protection?"

"You heard Mr. Vandal testify that Tess would be whipped and raped," he reminded him. "A husband not only has a right but a responsibility to stop violence toward his wife."

"I was speaking as a master!" Edward interrupted. "I still own her."

"But you gave her away in marriage." Tyler showed the wedding certificate to Edward. "Who witnessed the mark made by Tess? Isn't that your signature, Mr. Vandal?"

"The preacher told me to sign. I didn't read it."

The judge examined the document. "It's a binding agreement requiring your permission, which you gave by signing it."

"I still own her, and she ran away."

"But my client, Noah St. Paul, was not helping a runaway. He was aiding his wife and son. Buck Cassell testified he took liberties with this young woman. Would any husband stand by and allow another man to molest his wife?"

Judge Shoemaker rapped his gavel to silence the murmurings of the crowd. He turned to Tyler. "You've introduced an interesting argument, young man. I will have to think on this matter." The judge stood, took the book Tyler had given him, and headed for his chambers.

"Court is recessed," the bailiff announced as the judge disappeared through the door to his office.

"What does it mean?" Cory leaned over the railing. "Is he coming back?"

"It means he's going to render a verdict after he considers our arguments."

"But he was impressed by you."

Tyler wondered. "I had more arguments. He didn't even wait for my summation."

"It wouldn't have made any difference," Sam said. "Something you said triggered a decision. He needs to reason it out."

"What you said was enough," Noah said. "You're a good lawyer. Miss Olivia would have been proud."

Tyler turned to Sam. "My mother is dead, but I'd understand if you don't want me to practice law for you."

"Folks like a colorful yarn and a little scandal," Sam answered. "Especially in court. That story probably won some clients for us."

Tyler grinned. "I think I'm going to like working for you."

"I'm already thinking of a partnership."

****

Cory had joined the Reverend and others in prayer. Only twenty minutes had passed when the door to the judge's chamber opened, and Judge Shoemaker entered. He took his seat and the bailiff told everyone to be seated.

"You made an eloquent argument, Mr.

Montgomery, and although the father retains his parental rights when a child becomes indentured, the master decides the punishment and training of the child. Noah may be the husband and father, but Mr. Vandal is the master. The law is clear on this subject. A runaway slave, whether married or not, must be returned to its master. This woman and her baby belong to Edward Vandal, and the court will return them." He took a deep breath. "On the other matter of Noah St. Paul aiding a runaway, I find your argument has merit."

Judge Shoemaker nodded at the defense table, and they stood. "I find through the evidence of the pass, the letter, and ease of the slave's escape, Mrs. Vandal was key in urging Tess to run away."

Edward stood to protest, but Daniel shoved him back into his seat.

"I also believe this man, Noah, was acting as a husband and father in his behavior to protect his wife and child. These men, Clyde and Buck Cassell, have testified they made no attempt to ask the woman to return with them peacefully but instead took her by force. Therefore, I find Noah St. Paul was protecting his family from these men and is not guilty of aiding runaways."

A spontaneous cheer erupted from the citizens seated in the courtroom. Judge Shoemaker pounded his gavel to silence them.

"Therefore, I do not find enough evidence to make any federal charges against this man. However, Noah St. Paul is guilty of obstructing the law, and I sentence him to one day in jail, already served, and a two-dollar fine."

Edward stood. "That's ridiculous!"

"Are you calling this court ridiculous, Mr. Vandal? I could have you fined and jailed for contempt."

Edward sat in silence.

Daniel Hossler stood. "I ask your honor to detain the defendant, his lawyers, and those in the courtroom until the train leaves with the girl and her baby. I wouldn't want to see any more violence or a futile attempt to rescue the runaways."

"I agree." Judge Shoemaker looked around the courtroom. "Sheriff Carter will escort Mr. Vandal and his property to the depot."

The judge turned to the court deputy. "You will escort Noah and his attorneys to the clerk's office to pay his fine and guard them until the train is gone. Everyone else will remain in the courtroom until I dismiss you."

Cory needed to leave the courtroom. Adelaide had given her the task of protecting Adam in case Buck and Clyde tried to use the baby against Tess or Noah again. She watched the deputy lead Sam, Tyler, and Noah out the door first. Cory saw Tyler's bag on the floor and grabbed it. She rushed past Sheriff Carter with Tess, Edward, and the Cassell brothers and handed Tyler his valise.

They gathered in the hallway at the top of the staircase, each waiting for the other group to go downstairs first.

Noah stroked tears away from Tess' cheek. "I'll come for you. I promise."

She shook her head. "Don't."

"I'll buy their freedom." Tyler put the valise on the floor and removed a wallet from his coat pocket. "How much will it take?"

"I wouldn't take a dollar from you," Edward said.

"What about me?" Cory opened her purse and removed the money she had saved from teaching. "I have a hundred ninety-six dollars here."

"That's barely enough for the babe."

"Sold!" Tyler took the money from Cory and waved it at Edward. "The baby is hers."

Edward looked at Tess. "You'd give away your baby?"

"You're going to take him away from me anyway." She shoved Adam into Cory's arms. "Take him."

Edward refused to take the money. "No deal." He grabbed Adam, who wailed at being passed around. "He should grow to be a big strapping boy by the looks of him."

Edward tried to hand Adam back to Tess, but she refused to take him. She turned her face away.

"No one is going to buy him for what he'll be some day," Cory warned Edward. "Babies die when we least expect it." His face paled, and she knew her words had hit a mark. "It's an awful big gamble with talk of emancipation. This money is guaranteed today, right now." She waved the bills and shook the coins in her purse.

"You seem to forget no one can buy a slave in Ohio," Sam said.

Cory closed her purse. Now what? She saw Tyler's valise on the floor. "Can we barter a trade?"

"What are you willing to trade?" Buck asked.

Cory ignored Buck's lewd stares and opened Tyler's bag. She grabbed the vest Regina had made and waved it like a flag. "Will you trade this vest for the baby?"

Edward stared at the vest but made no offer.

"No deal!" Tyler yanked the vest from Cory and stroked the embroidery. "I plan to wear it at every trial I'm in. Reggie's fine needlework ought to impress the judges."

Cory frowned at Tyler. Why was he making a fuss about keeping the vest? He turned away from the others to put the vest back in his valise and winked at her. He was fueling the fires of competition with Edward.

She could help. "I thought that vest didn't mean anything to you!" Cory shouted at him. "You still love Reggie!"

"I knew it!" Edward pointed his finger at Tyler.

"No man ever forgets his first love, especially when he has such a special token of her affection." Tyler removed his jacket. "Let's see how it looks on me."

"Do you want the baby or not?" Edward demanded.

"An even trade of property," Tyler argued. "The vest for the baby." He put on the vest and buttoned it.

Edward stared at the vest. "Deal."

"Give Adam to Noah." He removed the vest and held it out.

Edward made the exchange and handed the vest to Buck. "Cut it up."

Buck and Clyde flashed their knives and reduced the beautiful needlework to a pile of shredded fabric and frayed threads.

Cory gasped. "Why?"

"He didn't care about the vest," Tyler explained. "But he wanted to make sure I never wore it."

"Regina is my wife. No man has a claim on her

affections but me."

"You can't buy affection," Cory argued.

"You can buy anything." He looked at Tyler. "You bought a slave."

"You heard Sam. I can't buy a slave in Ohio, but Adam is free." Tyler looked at Noah. "Like I promised."

"He'll be free?" Tess glanced at her baby. She kissed him several times and looked at Noah. "Tell him I gave him away because I loved him." She swiped away the tears on her cheeks and turned to Tyler and Cory. "Thank you."

"What about Tess?" Tyler removed his wallet and dropped it on the floor. "There's two thousand dollars in it. You could pick it up and leave Tess behind. The baby will need his mother to feed him."

Edward picked up the wallet and handed it to Tyler. "Nice try. I don't mind giving away the baby. He's useless to me, but I plan to recover all my money and more from this gal."

"But why?" Cory demanded.

"She ran away."

"You read Reggie's letter. Tess had no choice."

"Regina had no right to give away my property. I own the Silver Pheasant and everything on it. I decide what to keep and what to discard. Regina will learn that soon enough."

Cory thought of the little girl lost in the dark coal mine and worried about Reggie's future.

Chapter Thirty-One

A train whistle sounded in the distance.

"The train will be leaving soon," Lane said. "You want to board or stay here and barter some more?"

"Let's go." Edward signaled his chasers. "You and Noah stay here until we're gone," he warned Tyler. "That's part of the deal."

"I don't want to go!" Tess cried as she clung to Noah. "I'll die first."

"I'll come for you," Noah swore.

She glanced at Buck and Clyde and shuddered. "There won't be anything worth coming for."

"Get her," Edward ordered the two men.

Tess screamed.

Cory stepped in front of the two men. She nodded toward the closed courtroom door. "You don't want to create a scene. If you let me walk with Tess, I can convince her to come peacefully."

"She'd keep her calm," Lane said. "You don't want a hysterical woman in the middle of a town this size. Might create trouble."

"You can come," Edward agreed.

Tess ran to Noah, and they kissed. Adam reached for her, and she took him in her arms. "I love you."

"If she changes her mind and takes the brat, he belongs to me," Edward said.

Tess handed Adam back to Noah. "I won't change

my mind."

Cory put a protective arm around Tess, and they headed down the stairs. They exited the courthouse and walked along Broadway Street to the depot.

"You won't be able to protect her on the train," Buck reminded Cory.

"I won't think about it," Tess whispered to Cory.

"It's against the law to rape a woman," Cory said. "If you allow it, you're no better than them."

"He's Cyrus Vandal's son!" Clyde announced. "He took any woman, any age, any color. He slapped Edward on the back. "It's about time you followed in his footsteps."

"All the time you were on the Silver Pheasant I never touched you. I never let any man touch you," Edward said. "No more."

"It's a long ride back to Vandalia," Clyde remarked. "I bet you'll be worn out before we reach the Ohio River."

Cory could feel Tess shudder. She prayed Adelaide's plan worked.

When they reached the station, Cory saw a familiar face with red hair and blue eyes standing in the depot.

Her cousin Jake was taller and stronger than his siblings, Ethan and Paddy. He had several friends of equal size with him. He nodded and lowered the brim of his hat to cast a shadow over his face. She watched him and his friends move out of sight on the far side of the locomotive engine.

"I brought you to the station without incident," Lane said. "That ends my role in this drama. I'm going to eat and then catch the northbound train to Darrow Falls. Good bye, Mr. Vandal." He shook his hand.

"Seems like an awful little girl to cause so much trouble. Might be better next time to let her go."

"I won't tell you how to do your job, Sheriff, if you don't tell me how to do mine."

"Fair enough." Lane tipped his hat to Cory and Tess and headed for downtown.

Edward bought tickets while Clyde claimed their bags from the storage room. He watched the porter load them on a cart and take them to the baggage car.

"She can't ride in the passenger car," a conductor informed them when they attempted to board with Tess.

Edward frowned. "Can she ride in the baggage car?"

"It's full." He pointed to a closed car near the caboose. "There's room in the livestock car." He led the way. He put a step in place and opened the door. A couple of horses were tethered inside. "Better board," the conductor said.

Tess turned to Cory. "Tell Noah I loved him."

Cory didn't miss the meaning of her words. She didn't plan on seeing him again.

Cory couldn't offer any words of comfort. She didn't want to tip off the Cassell brothers by hinting of a rescue. Tess would have to believe the worst.

"I'm dead once I board this train," Tess said. "It's best if he forgets me."

Her words frightened Cory. What if the plan failed? "Don't give up."

Clyde stepped into the livestock car. "It smells like manure and piss in here."

"You're smellin' yourself." Buck lifted Tess into the car. His hand groped her in the process. "Why don't you ride in the passenger car, Mr. Vandal? We'll keep a close eye on her."

Edward looked at the dirty car. "I'll be up front."

The conductor turned to Edward. "Time to close the door. You better hurry to your car." He slammed the door and shouted, "All aboard!"

Cory heard Tess scream. She chased after Edward. "You'd leave Tess alone with those monsters knowing what they're planning to do?" she shouted. "How can you let them violate your own sister?"

He turned on her. "She's no kin of mine. She's nothing but a whore. She'll welcome Buck and Clyde to feast on her body, and they'll give her a whelp to replace the one she gave up."

Cory was aghast. His words shook her faith in any remnant of decency he may have possessed. Tyler had fought to protect Noah, but Edward had no concept of honor with Tess. Tyler hadn't acknowledged Noah publicly, but his actions spoke the truth. He loved Noah. Edward, on the other hand, didn't love Tess. She recalled the violent way he had destroyed Reggie's vest and shook with fear.

Edward boarded the train.

"Tyler was right!" she shouted above the noise of the locomotive.

Edward paused on the top step and faced her. "When was he ever right?"

"He said Reggie was making a mistake when she married you," she shouted. "I think she did."

Edward's face was etched in granite. "Regina knows the consequences of disobeying me. She won't make the same mistake twice."

****

The train whistle echoed beyond the courthouse as

the locomotive headed south. "The train is gone!" Noah held Adam against him and wept.

"We'll get horses and head off the train at the next stop."

Noah shook his head. "It'll be too late for Tess."

Tyler knew what he meant. Buck and Clyde had made their intentions clear. "She'll need you more than ever then."

"She gave away Adam." Noah looked at his son. "I failed to protect her. She doesn't want me to come for her."

"If she can survive, you have a duty to rescue her."

Noah's voice was cold. "She's too gentle and sweet to survive those animals."

The deputy looked at his watch. "You're free to go."

"Go where?" Noah remained seated.

Tyler didn't want to forsake hope. He looked at Sam. "There's still time to catch the train, right?"

"There's a livery near the depot," Sam said. "Go after her."

"Come on," Tyler urged Noah to his feet. They turned toward the east door.

"Wait." Beth Davis hurried down the stairs. The rest of the courtroom spectators followed at a slower rate behind her. She pointed at the west entrance. "You're heading the wrong way."

"We're going to ride after her."

"If our plan has worked, Tess won't be on the train," Beth whispered. "She'll be on the Irish Rose. Do you know how to reach Mustill Store?"

"I remember."

Noah stood. "What plan?"

"I only know my part," Beth confessed. "I'm to make sure you go to Mustill Store to board the Irish Rose."

"What's the Irish Rose?" Noah asked.

"A canal boat," Tyler said. "That's where we'll find Tess." He led the way out the door and downhill along the route he had taken previously with Cory.

Noah hurried with each step.

When they reached the Irish Rose, only Captain Donovan, Ethan, and Paddy were on board.

Tyler looked around. "Is she below in a cabin?"

Captain Donovan shook his head. "No sign of her or news from the others."

"The train left ten minutes ago." Noah sat down on a crate, his shoulders slouched. "Something must have gone wrong." Adam fussed and chewed on his fists.

Tyler wasn't ready to give up. "We need to get horses and go after the train. Every minute leaves Tess in their hands."

"I know where you can borrow two fast horses," Captain Donovan said. "What are you going to do with the baby?"

"Give him to Cory." Tyler reached for Adam.

"Wait!" Paddy shouted from the deck of the boat. He pointed to the road.

Captain Donovan raised his hand to his brow to shield his eyes. "There's the Mustill wagon."

Tyler saw the box wagon coming down the hill at a fast clip. It stopped in front of the store.

Paddy pointed at the driver and the young man next to him. "It's Jake and Tom Mustill!"

Jake jumped down and opened the back. Out came Adelaide, Cory, and Tess.

****

Tess ran to Noah and Adam. Her dress was torn, but she was smiling. Noah engulfed her in his arms, and Adam squealed. She covered them with kisses. "Let's get aboard," Captain Donovan ordered. "It's a long trip to Canada."

"Maybe if Lincoln is elected, the Republicans will repeal the Fugitive Slave Law," Adelaide said. "You can come back to Darrow Falls."

Cory thought of poor Lou. "We need a blacksmith."

"How much time do you think we have before the Cassell brothers follow?" Tyler asked.

"Are those the two big hairy fellows?" Jake tossed a pair of knives and guns into the hold of the boat along with a large club.

"What did you do with Buck and Clyde?"

"Gagged and trussed like vermin," Jake announced. "Appropriate since they were in the livestock car. It won't be a comfortable ride back to Virginia for them."

"And Edward?" Tyler demanded.

"He rode in the passenger car," Adelaide said. "He won't discover what's happened to his companions until Noah and Tess are out of his reach."

Tyler looked at Adelaide. "This was your plan. How did you do it?"

"We paid the conductor to put Tess and the men in a livestock car," she explained. "Then Jake and his friends opened the door on the other side, overpowered the men, and rescued Tess."

"Two old men against me and my friends," Jake bragged. "They never stood a chance."

"One lesson we learned from Wellington," Adelaide said. "Don't attack head on. Sneak in the back door for a quiet rescue."

"But we beat you here to the boat," Tyler said. "What took you so long?"

Cory wondered if he would be angry with her. "I sent a telegram." She stepped toward Tyler. "I wanted to warn Reggie."

"Warn her about what?"

"You were right about Edward. He didn't like Reggie helping Tess, and he won't be happy when he finds out Tess escaped."

"You think he'd hurt her?"

"I didn't want to take any chances," she confessed. "The telegram said Tess free. Edward angry. Be careful. I signed your name."

"I forgot all about her." He stroked a stray curl back from her face. "I didn't think I could love you more, and you give me a whole new reason to marvel at how lucky I am to have met you."

He loved her.

Paddy tossed the towline to Ethan, who secured it to the Irish Rose. Noah, Tess, and Adam had already gone below and out of sight. Tyler tossed his bag to Ethan.

Cory grabbed his coat sleeve. "Are you going, too?"

"I want to guarantee they reach Canada safely. I couldn't sleep otherwise. But I'll be back." He grinned. "I have a job working with Sam."

He had said he loved her. How could he be so cavalier? Tears sprang to her eyes. "Is that the only reason you're coming back?"

Tyler embraced her. She resisted, but he wouldn't release her. "Don't look so worried, my love. I'll see you on Sunday."

"Why Sunday?"

He chuckled as he tightened his arms around her. "It's called courting, Miss Beecher. I dress in my finest clothes and bring you flowers and sweets and try to make a good impression."

She shook her head. "I didn't think you believed in all that tea-sipping nonsense."

He rested his forehead against hers, their eyes locked. His mouth was so close she could taste his words. "Depends on whether all that nonsense is worth the reward."

"Is it?"

"You tell me." His lips brushed against hers, sending a wave of pleasure through her body. He kissed her, and Cory made sure he had no doubt about the answer.

Epilogue

Cory tossed the quilt off her warm body and slid out of bed. Where was her husband? She poked at the fire. It had burned down to embers. She added a log and stirred up the flames. She looked around Adelaide's former bedroom. Tyler had bought Glen Knolls, most of the furnishings, and livestock.

Adelaide had taken the bedroom furniture, her rocking chair, and her personal items when she had moved in with her daughter in August.

Cory and her sisters helped Tyler clean the house, polish the woodwork, and stock the pantry. Tyler had taken her shopping for new bedroom furniture the day after he proposed.

He was impatient to marry, but they had set an October wedding date to give the local school board time to find a new teacher to replace Cory. The board had hired a graduate from the normal school in Cleveland. Cory missed the children but was too busy to miss teaching.

Tyler traveled to Akron at least three times a week to work with Sam in their law office, and he helped Cory with the chores on the farm the remainder of the time. They made love often, each experience adding to their desire to pleasure each other.

So, where was her lover? She looked out the window. Lulu had given birth to a calf yesterday. Tyler had helped deliver Bessie. Frost partially blocked her view of the barn, but she saw no light. He wasn't in the barn.

Cory donned a lacy dressing gown. She left the matching nightgown on top of a cedar chest at the end of the four-poster bed. She had been naked, waiting in bed for her husband. She glanced at the mantel clock. An hour had passed since he had promised to join her.

She hurried down the stairs, wishing she had remembered slippers. The crisp fall air penetrated the cracks in the house. She locked the front door.

On the sideboard was today's newspaper. The voters had elected Abraham Lincoln as President. Douglas would be upset, but Beth would calm her husband. She knew how to gently persuade him to change his mind.

Beside the paper were several letters. One was from Noah. Tyler had helped them reach Ontario safely after leaving her at the Mustill Store. Noah and Tess had settled with other former slaves in a small town, and Noah had opened a blacksmith shop. Tess enjoyed running her own home, and Adam had taken his first steps.

Another letter was from the Yoders. Reggie had received Cory's warning, and she had stored a traveling bag with her belongings with them, ready to flee if Edward turned violent. But fate had provided an alternative. The state representative from their district had died, and the Southern Democratic Party needed to appoint a replacement.

When Edward arrived home, he was greeted by two state representatives with an offer to fill the vacant seat. Regina encouraged him to campaign. No word yet on whether he had won, but politics had erased any threat to punish Reggie for her role in Tess' escape.

Cory heard the scratching of a quill and stood in the doorway to Tyler's office. She silently watched her husband work. In order to spend more time with her at Glen Knolls, he brought home endless legal paperwork. His head was bent over a long document as he wrote in small cursive strokes.

Cory glided into the room outside the glow of the lamp illuminating his work space. She admired the law books on the shelves and examined the neat stack of papers on a side table. He was nearly done with his work. She ran her hand along the smooth surface of the large desk she had bought as a wedding gift with her dowry money and sat on the edge. Her robe fell away to expose a bare leg.

The scratching of the pen stopped. "What time is it?"

"An hour since you promised to join me in bed."

He leaned back in the leather chair and raked his fingers through his hair. "I'm sorry. I didn't realize it was so late."

"You work hard." She sat on his lap and put her arms around his neck, nestling close to steal a bit of his body warmth. "You need to relax."

He peeked beneath the lace robe. "Where's your nightie?"

"Upstairs." He had discarded his coat and tie. Cory stroked the intricate embroidery on his vest and unbuttoned it. "Nice vest."

"A beautiful woman made it for me." He leaned forward so she could remove it. "She's skilled with her hands."

She tugged his shirt from his trousers. "That's how I recognized Reggie's skill."

"What other talents do you want to show me, my love?"

She kissed his neck and worked her way to his lips. "I'm good at games. What would you like to play?"

Tyler stood and grabbed the lamp. "Hold on."

Cory clutched his neck and wrapped her legs around his waist as he carried her out of his office. "I was comfortable on your lap."

He hurried down the hall. "You said you're in a playful mood, and I've had a fantasy since the night we met." He turned into the parlor.

She pointed toward the staircase. "The bed is upstairs."

"We first met on the parlor rug."

"I don't want to lie on the hard floor."

"I'll be on the floor." He gazed into her eyes. "As much as I enjoy your position, you need to unwrap yourself."

Cory unhooked her legs and stood. "Now what?"

Tyler placed the lantern on the floor. "I want to recreate that night."

"Should I put on my blue and green plaid dress?"

He stretched out on the braided rug and tugged on the hem of her robe. "Your attire is perfect for my purposes."

She straddled his body. "Do I get to shoot you?"

He pulled her down on top of him. "No, but you can play with my gun."

A word about the author...

Laura Freeman has been a reporter for the past nine years and covers the historic town of Hudson, Ohio. She has won the Press Club of Cleveland's Ohio Excellence in Journalism award in 2013 and 2014 and the Ohio Newspaper Association awards in 2011, 2013, and 2014.

Her novel, *Impending Love and War*, takes place in the fictional town of Darrow Falls but is based on the historical traits of the small towns in Northeast Ohio, where she lives. She is working on her next book, *Impending Love and Death.*

Visit her on:

      Facebook.com/laurafreeman.5648

and Twitter:

      @LauraFreeman_RP

or her blog:

      Authorfreeman.wordpress.com

Thank you for purchasing
this publication of The Wild Rose Press, Inc.

If you enjoyed the story, we would appreciate
your letting others know by leaving a review.

For other wonderful stories,
please visit our on-line bookstore at
www.thewildrosepress.com.

For questions or more information
contact us at
info@thewildrosepress.com.

The Wild Rose Press, Inc.
www.thewildrosepress.com

Stay current with The Wild Rose Press, Inc.

Like us on Facebook
https://www.facebook.com/TheWildRosePress

And Follow us on Twitter

https://twitter.com/WildRosePress

www.ingramcontent.com/pod-product-compliance
Lightning Source LLC
Chambersburg PA
CBHW071528260626
47170CB00002B/550